ALL IN HER HEAD

BY PAULA JOHNSTON

ALL IN HER HEAD

A CIP catalogue record for this book is available from the British Library.

ISBN: 979-8324616526

BOOKS BY PAULA JOHNSTON

There are three sides to every story.

His.

Hers.

The truth.

The Lies She Told

The twisted psychological thriller that proves there's a price to pay for infatuation…

'Twisty, clever, pacy and fun!' – Best-Selling Author of *Little White Lies*, Philippa East

PRAISE FOR PAULA JOHNSTON

'An extremely brave voice.' – Best-Selling Author of *Little White Lies*, Philippa East

'A toxic and twisty thriller.' – Best-Selling Author of *The Shallows*, Holly Craig

'Along comes Paula Johnston's incredible second novel. A masterclass of how to write a twisty, dark thriller that leaves you right on the edge of your seat.'

'She's only gone and done it again…but even better.'

'Paula is a literary genius. Read this book, become obsessed, and you'll love *All in Her Head* as much as I did.'

'I read this book front to back in one go.'

'Gut punching twists that will leave you completely breathless.'

Dedication

To Grumpy,
As promised, this one is just for you.

Part One

I shut my eyes, and all the world drops dead.
I lift my lids, and all is born again.
I think I made you up inside my head.
– Sylvia Plath

The Unknown

She stares at the ghost reflected in the bathroom mirror.

Searching for a glimmer of who she once was, she sees nothing familiar. Her past life is now entirely overshadowed by the stranger looking back at her.

Her skin is deathly pale, dotted with imperfections, and deep frown lines have embedded themselves into her forehead far before their time. Angry red snakes have started to invade the whites of her eyes, teasing their prey before inevitably launching an attack, consuming her whole.

Her throat is raw, but she must still try to eat whatever he cooks. The recipes have stayed the same, but her taste buds' reaction to them has drastically changed. No longer are his handmade meals an innocent romantic gesture, bathed in the warm glow of candlelight. It's hard to believe they ever were. Everything he serves now fizzles painfully on her tightly held tongue like it's been dipped in poison and seasoned with deceit. She gags on every forkful, forces down the taste of disingenuous memories. Her ability to hold anything in long enough to benefit from essential nutrients is rapidly dwindling. A once strong stomach now convulses in disobedience with every bite.

Trapped, suffocating, there doesn't seem to be a way out – at least not one that she knows of. All she can do now is keep trying to get by – one agonisingly slow day at a time.

The power of his love once made her feel dizzy. Euphoric. Invincible. It ignited a wildfire deep in her belly. A parade of dancing flames that refused to be tamed because the heat of your first love is intense and untouchable.

But life is very different now, and she has so many rules to follow that didn't exist in the beginning. The alarm that woke her this morning, set for six o'clock, seven days a week, is just one example of far too many.

She looks down at the journal resting on her lap: fragile, damaged, and barely holding itself together. She understands how that feels, unable to feel the strength of her own spine.

As her frail right hand grips the red plastic biro she found in the kitchen drawer, she hovers over the blank page staring up at her. There's so much that she wants to say – needs to say – but doesn't know where to start.

The unmistakable sharp click of the key turning in the lock reminds her that time is no longer hers.

She quickly jumps from her perch on the edge of the bath and wraps the journal back up in the ragged checked tea towel. Despite danger fast approaching, she somehow manages to return it safely to its hiding place.

Just in time and no more.

Before she makes herself visible, she takes a deep breath with one last glance in the mirror, pinching the slightest bit of colour into her hollowing cheeks. She can feel her puppet master getting closer and his strings begin to tug the corners of her lips until a pretty smile is stretched from ear to ear.

She's met at the door with an angelic smile and her stomach twists with fear. She knows that grin and knows all too well by now how easy it is for someone to disguise the most devilish of thoughts with such dashing good looks.

One

Cassie

An unexpected rattle on the front door makes me jump. My heavy eyes fall to the watch wrapped tightly around my right wrist: a yellow-gold digital Casio that I treated myself to during one of my impulsive retail-therapy sessions. Spotting the flicker of a changing minute, I realise that it's only ten thirty-one. My guest isn't due for another fourteen, to be precise, and his seemingly eager need for punctuality has summoned a surge of panic in my chest.

I don't feel ready to do this yet.

My pupils ache as they dart wildly around the room. Left to right, left to right, straining in vain. Searching for a glimmer of guidance. It's stupid really, just a waste of precious time, because what I really need more than anything is a big-fat-miracle.

Reaching to the side, I flick the stylus on my record player to the sky and reluctantly cut the dulcet tones of Stevie Nicks and her greatest hits. I can't help acknowledging that bowing out on Landslide is ironically meaningful to my life right now, because I'm also a whole lot of debris, momentously crashing to the pits.

I lift the remote for the television, bring it to life, and push the YouTube button, quickly scrolling through the playlist I've created in preparation for days like this. Despite there being plenty "high vibrational" options to choose from, I settle on the same melody as always – because consistency is supposed to be good for you. And I guess it doesn't really matter that I haven't strayed from the one with the most plays, because all it needs to do is float through like a calming lullaby while I carry out our session.

I drop the remote back down on the table with a low groan because not only do I know it's totally unacceptable for someone my age to throw a tantrum and scream. I'm also fearful that he might hear me. I consciously unclench my jaw and persuade my shoulders to drop from my ears, but of course, they disobey me and ping right back up.

If only there was some place I could politely ask him to wait until the clock reaches the time I originally allocated, but I've made absolutely zero attempt at forging any kind of professionalism in here. I know I should have some sort of pretty reception area to accommodate early arrivals, because I suspect there'll be more early birds, eager to catch the worm, if I do decide to carry on with all of this – but there's not. There's no swanky Chesterfield couch positioned nicely in front of a glass table offering a box of tissues, no high-tech coffee pod machine offering a variety of flavoured lattes. And there's definitely no water dispenser with those dainty plastic cups that remind me of the dentist. It's just me, this room, and a grubby glass jug sitting on the table, still waiting for me to fill it.

A familiar but still hugely unwelcome voice whispers in my ear, reminding me that I really don't have a clue what I'm doing. Even in the comfort of my own home, I'm nothing but an imposter. A fraud. And what's worse is that there's nowhere in this bloody flat for me to run and hide.

Rubbing my temples, I apply as much pressure as I can, trying to clear the fog that's refusing to budge. Suddenly I wonder how hard I would have to push my thumb or index finger into my skull before it finally does me a favour and just explodes. Then I wouldn't have to deal with this haze of self-loathing that's been following me around like another unwanted house guest for some time now.

Chap. Chap. Chap.

'OK, OK, OK,' I affirm, bringing my thoughts back into focus. I can't leave him standing outside in the cold any longer. I have no choice but to welcome him inside. Even if he is far too early, somewhat rudely causing me to abandon my umpteenth attempt at structure.

Clambering to my feet, I straighten my top, tuck a few rogue strands of my wishy-washy auburn hair behind my ears and take one last gulp of my chamomile tea. I wince as the last of the floral notes catch in the back of throat and feel my nose scrunch. It's definitely an acquired taste, but it's supposed to be relaxing, so I've been trying my best to stick with it. God knows I need all the help I can get. I had hoped it would eventually become enjoyable, less like a punishment, but I'm yet to see the results. In fact, I don't think it would be that huge of a loss if I called it quits now and stopped bothering with it all together. If anything, it makes me incredibly nauseous, and that's the last thing I need. to be throwing up on a client.

Or is it a customer? I'm still not too sure what to call people, but I do know that I don't want to look stupid, so I make a mental note: *Brush-Up-On-Lingo*.

Somehow, I've managed to find my feet, but I feel a bit light-headed. Steadying myself by gripping each side of the wooden doorframe, I reluctantly force one foot out and into the long, narrow hallway.

The slippery floorboards in this flat always remind me of the rink that a bunch of us would frequent on a Saturday night many years ago. It was always a much-anticipated night out for any fifteen-year-old, after what we believed to be a gruelling week at school. Especially for the girls I hung around with. But just like today, I always felt like an outcast because they were always so much more confident than me. They had no qualms about smuggling quarter bottles of vodka in their backpacks, stashing them at the bottom underneath their skating boots. Even though I was welcomed along – although grudgingly, I suspect – I didn't fit in. Of course, it didn't help that I was a terrible skater and had to watch from the sidelines as they whizzed around in circles to 'Heaven' by DJ Sammy.

Pushing the memory of rejection aside, with both fists clenched, my left foot shuffles forward. 'One more step. Just one more step,' I whisper to the ceiling. My nerves are skyrocketing. Gold stars scatter above me, and I wish on any one of them that one day I'll be able to find some sort of magic potion to fix whatever it is that's wrong with me. Why I always feel so bad no matter how hard I try to turn things around? The same wish has trumped any other for many of my thirty years.

Every birthday candle blown out, it's always been the same, but it's getting exhausting now.

How long must I have to wait for my very own genie to produce the goods? I don't know if I have much willpower left in me.

I spot Finlay Munro's silhouette pacing back and forth on the other side of the stained-glass window, to the right-hand side of the door. My chin falls to my chest, my eyelids aren't far behind, and the godawful drum inside of my chest is reaching a painful crescendo.

I should try those affirmation things again. 'Keep pushing forward. You've got this. *I've* got this,' I mutter under my breath.

My neck cracks as I glance behind me, down the hallway.

I could just turn back.

Bang. Bang. Bang.

Vibrations from the force on the door penetrate my aura from the ground up, causing me to flinch. My bottom lip wobbles, and I bite down hard to prevent a full-blown meltdown.

'Two seconds. I'm just coming,' I call out.

I must quickly remind myself why I'm doing this. Why it was necessary. Because it really was. For me, it was a matter of life or death. I no longer wanted to go to sleep at night, wishing I'd never open my eyes again. Something needed to change. I was shuffling closer to the edge, finally ready to give up the fight.

'I can do this. I have to do this. It's now or never,' I whisper to myself.

My hand trembles as it reaches for the brass handle. I twist the knob and the door swings open. The wind lashes my face like a solid leather belt. But it's not the wild nip of the air that almost sends me flying, it's the sight of *him*.

Two

Blair

He reaches an arm across the gear stick and gently squeezes my thigh. It's reassuring, comforting, and evokes a totally different feeling to the rush of adrenaline his palm cupping my knee under the table in a fancy restaurant usually gives me. Less lustful, yes, but on this occasion, that's not a bad thing at all. In fact, it feels almost momentous, as if we're unlocking a new level in our relationship and I'm stepping through a door I didn't even know I wanted to see behind until I met *him*.

I imagine meeting your boyfriend's parents for the first time is a daunting experience for anyone, so I should be thanking my lucky stars that it's just his mum we're on our way to see, but even though there's one less person to impress, it's no secret that this meeting is the most important. This is the one that could change everything, potentially ruining what we have. I already hate her for it.

Perhaps after I gain her trust, she'll allow me to set her up with an online dating profile. If she has someone else to worry about and pander over, then she'll be less involved with her son's life than she is right now.

'You excited, babe? She's going to love you,' George says, beaming at me with such childlike hope. His beautiful green eyes, wide with anticipation always make me melt.

It has to be done, and I know this. He's made no secret of how close the two of them are. They're always doing something together, whether it's running marathons, visiting new cities, or just browsing the shops for food or clothes. They even FaceTime each other. Every fucking day.

I have to admit, I don't quite understand it, think it's quite creepy actually, because off the top of my head I probably couldn't pinpoint the last time I spoke to my mum. A month ago? Maybe two? *When are you going to get a proper job? You're not as young as you think anymore, you know. You just need a nice, strong man to take care of you. When are you going to settle down?* It doesn't really matter to me. Our periodic catch-ups suit me just fine because the less nagging I hear, the better. She's like a bloody record player from the sixties stuck on loop and as hard as I try to block her out, I'm always left with a whopping migraine after listening to her.

Of course, I understand that everyone's relationship with their parents is different. There are children of non-neurotic mothers out there who aren't weighed down by old-fashioned expectations. A lot of people have normal, healthy relationships with their families, so I try to tell myself that this bond I've heard so much about is sort of cute I suppose. They're the best of friends. A doting mother and her only son.

But he has *me* now. *I* should be the priority, and what is it they say? Three is most definitely a crowd.

'Yup.' I smile back at him briefly before returning my attention to the road in front of us.

Personally, I couldn't give less of a shit about her opinion. It's her own to make and if she doesn't think I'm suitable for her darling son, then stuff her. I know I'm more than good enough, so it's water off a duck's back to me. But unfortunately, if I want that ring on my finger anytime soon – the pink morganite with a white-gold band, the one I saw on his iPad because he forgot to close the browsing tab – I will at least try to be on my absolute best behaviour today. I'll make sure mummy dearest gives me a glowing five-star review.

I'm struggling to concentrate as we make our way over the Erskine Bridge on our way to Balloch. I hate heights, and I also hate deep water, so the fact that there's a huge drop at either side, every glance out the corner of my eye reminding me that I could potentially plunge to my death, isn't helping. I was so stressed about reaching this point that I even missed the last cut-off and almost sent us back in the direction of Glasgow Airport.

Not that it would have been such a terrible thing – heading back home to our little sanctuary. Once his, but now mine, too. It's no longer a bachelor pad of dreams in the heart of the bustling South Side, it's the love bubble of all bubbles. The décor could still do with a bit of feminine flair but at the speed we're moving, it's only a matter of time before he caves and lets me zoosh it up a little. Put my stamp on things. Mark my territory properly.

He removes his hand from my thigh and returns his attention to his phone, leaving my leg feeling abandoned. I always want his hands on me at all times. I can't get enough of him.

Safely across the bridge and turning left, the road is telling me to keep two 'chevrons' distance from the car in front of us, but I'm not really following the rules. For a start, I don't even know what the hell a chevron is but I'm guessing it's the pointy arrow things on the road, and second, I'm definitely pushing the speed limit so we can get this whole thing over and done with.

My mates and even the punters at the bar I used to work at told me I was off my head for moving in with someone so quickly. Someone I hardly even know. But how fast is too fast? Especially when you finally meet the one person who says and does everything right. Gives you everything you didn't even know you needed, never mind wanted. As if they were made from dough with specific ingredients picked just for you. It's extremely rare to find something like that. I tried telling them that they were the crazy ones, that he's the best thing since sliced bread – and not just an ordinary Warburtons, a fucking delicious tiger loaf – they looked perplexed.

'Bullshit,' they'd say. 'That guy is at it. He's after something. I'm tellin' ye, no guy wants to give up his freedom that fast. Have you got money stashed away somewhere? An elderly uncle with a heart condition and a castle in the Highlands?'

I feel my top lip twitch with satisfaction, thinking about how wrong they were – even with the 0.5ml recently injected that shouldn't budge at all. Three months in and I'm continuing to smash pivotal milestones like a game of whack a' mole and giving up my independence and walking away from a cushty flat share in the city centre of Glasgow was the best decision I've ever made. And after today, it's only going to get even better. We're already the perfect couple, compatibility wise in the bedroom and aesthetically. Couple goals.

After exiting the outskirts of Dumbarton, we finally reach the huge roundabout that takes you straight on towards Loch Lomond or you can take the second exit and head into Balloch. I can hear my heart thud, beginning to pick up pace as I reluctantly slow the car, yes still fast approaching *his* desired destination.

Pushing the stick into park, I swiftly push my seat back, unclip my belt, flip down the visor, and swipe open the little mirror. I want to check that my make-up hasn't creased or smudged from sweating buckets crossing that bloody bridge. Although for almost forty quid a bottle, it really shouldn't have.

'Are you sure I look OK?' I ask, turning to face him, swiping my tongue over my front teeth and then grinning widely for him to inspect. 'Any lippy?'

'Babe, you look amazing. Honestly, you'll be fine,' he says with that drop-dead gorgeous smile I love so much.

'Hmmm,' I murmur, checking myself once again. I trust him, but today has me acting like a magpie, highly alert, searching for shiny things that might go wrong. Because that absolutely cannot happen today. I won't let anything jeopardise what we have. Especially not a monster-in-law.

I reach behind, grab the bunch of pastel pink coloured roses from the backseat and quickly peel off the Marks & Spencer's price sticker that's still making me want to vomit. I didn't even notice it when I picked them up. I'm not exactly the flushest right now, what with being jobless, so when the girl at the checkout presented me the amount and told me to tap my card to the machine, my arse almost collapsed. I've been penny-pinching for as long as possible to avoid having to ask him for help since leaving the bar. Not that I think he would deny me anything I needed, but it's a dent in your pride isn't it, having to rely on someone else to pay your way? But they're a gift for his darling mother, aren't they, so how could I refuse his suggestion that they're her favourite? I couldn't. Still, I've got the strongest urge to water them for her by spitting on the silky petals that he dishes out to his mother like some kind of weekly wage slip.

As we step out of the car, slamming the doors behind us in perfect unison, I take in the sight of the red-bricked bungalow in front of me. It looks posh but there're darker patches shadowing the windows that tell me it's weathered many a storm and the fact that it's lost its pizazz a little puts me at ease a little.

Not so perfect after all, mother dearest.

I pull my newly blonde highlighted hair to the front of my shoulders and take a deep breath and puff out my chest. It still irks me a little, smelling the peroxide. You'd think George was Vidal Sassoon the way he twisted a strand around his index finger and said it just needed a few more lifts with some bleach and then I'd look even more incredible.

It's not that I feel I have to change myself to please him, but what's the harm in a new hairdo, really? I can always dye it dark again if I want.

Come on, B. You've got this, I tell myself as I reluctantly follow him up the driveway towards a white

PVC door, that I realise is already swinging open before we've even had a chance to stand on the wicker doormat and ring the bell.

Here we go.

THREE

CASSIE

Standing there, dressed in a simple grey hoodie, slim pale-blue jeans, and a clean pair of white trainers, I can't stop my eyes from shamefully flickering over every part of him. He must be a good three inches over six-foot, and he towers over my 5ft2 stature like a guardian angel.

No, more like a god. A magnificently handsome god.

He clears his throat but doesn't formally greet me, and I worry that he's annoyed with me for taking so long. And I suppose, who could blame him? It's just opening a door, for god's sake.

Even the most basic tasks are proving too problematic for me now. I used to be able to do so much more.

Taking a deep breath, I try to do one of those techniques that I've read about and hold my breath until my flaring nostrils feel ready to burst. I can't even reach five seconds. Pathetic.

Avoiding his penetrating glare, instead of breaking this uncomfortable silence, I find myself dissecting every inch of my body. Searching for inevitable flaws and berating myself for not wearing something more stereotypical.

Maybe I *should* have kitted myself out properly with some sort of floor-sweeping lacy gown and purple smoky shadow painted across my eyelids. I could have blended the colour into a sharp, winged liner too. And if that didn't work, I could have tried something simple…like a silky headscarf adorned with gold coins. I actually might have one already, stashed somewhere from a previous trip to a charity shop. It might even be quite handy on days where I haven't managed to wash my hair, which I admit – shamefully – is most of them now.

Yet despite being more than aware of all the ways I *should* be doing better, of course, I haven't made a single improvement to my uniform since I decided to give this new venture a go. It's so frustratingly typical of me, constantly obsessing about a problem rather than taking any healthy action to solve it seems to be my thing. Probably a habit of many lifetimes.

The best I managed to pull from my wardrobe today: a grey cotton V-neck T-shirt that I spotted in the sales for a fiver sometime last year and a pair of black high-waisted leggings that have seen better days. There's even a tiny hole below my left bum cheek, threatening to expose me at any minute, and all morning I've caught myself reaching behind, tugging at the hem of my top and patting my backside to check that it's hidden. I cringe. If anyone saw me, they'd swear I'm auditioning for a role at Asda.

'Eh, hi. You all right?' He finally speaks, blinding me with a perfectly straight set of pearly whites. The freakishly hot mannequin has come to life, and for one short moment, it feels like I'm levitating.

Is this what heaven feels like?

Or perhaps I'm dead? Part of me really hopes so. Maybe then I wouldn't have to fight so hard with all these intrusive thoughts racing through my head.

Is he struggling to digest my disgraceful outfit? Is he shrivelling up at the sight of five days' worth of dry shampoo that's helping the disastrous messy bun cling to the top of my head?

'Hi. Hello,' I practically squeal. The embarrassment brewing underneath my skin is red hot, and I fear I might burst into flames.

Without any hesitation, Finlay Munro confidently steps through my doorway, and I quickly slam the door behind him, before he can change his mind.

An intoxicating woody scent fills my nostrils and although I don't have a clue what brand of aftershave he's wearing, he smells like sheer royalty from the heavens above. Unlike me. feeling more like a peasant. Not worthy enough to be in his presence.

My palms are gross and clammy, so I wipe them against my bum as blasé as I possibly can, but when I look down, I want the ground to swallow me whole as I spot the ankles of my leggings: still firmly tucked into fluffy white pyjama socks. *Urghhhh.*

The unexpected movement causes my head to whip back up.

Leaving me gawking awkwardly behind him, I watch as Finlay strides down the hallway. When he reaches the end – of what feels like his catwalk runway – he turns, almost flooring me with another flash of that charming grin. It's wicked, but seductive, and no doubt casts a spell over every woman who meets him. I've not felt anything like this for so long, but now he's here, I'm sure that I'm about to be his next victim.

Not that he would look at someone like me twice in that way. And still, even knowing this, all the excuses I've made to justify giving up on my new project start to fade into the distance. It looks like this gig might have some benefits after all.

Besides, what right do I have to feel so hopeless when there are a lot more people far worse off than me? And anyway, haven't I been experiencing an influx of signs? The ones that suggest I might *actually* be gifted. For example, the screech I'm hearing now in my right ear. It's much louder than I've heard before, as if someone got too excited and cranked up the volume in celebration of this man's arrival.

Get it together, Cassie, I tell myself. All you need to do is recite the information you've studied, present it with a pinch of pizazz, and hope it resonates with the receiver. It's no different from any other session. Not a big deal.

I thud my forehead with the back of my wrist. Who am I kidding? Someone who looks as hot as him is a very big deal indeed.

Why is it so difficult for me to just be happy? Like *normal* people are. Why do I have to work so hard for it? It feels so unfair. I'm not a terrible personal. a murderer or a thief. This isn't where I saw myself in my thirties. I believed things would improve. But they didn't, and the dream of a happy marriage, a few kids, and a flourishing career feels more out of reach than ever before.

'In here?' he asks, gesturing to the correct room. A lucky guess, I think. almost losing myself in his husky, familiar Glaswegian accent. Completely unable to take my eyes off his thick, dark hair, styled to perfection.

Why would someone like him need *anything* from someone like me? Especially seeing as he looks like the type of person I imagine would judge me – like so many probably do. The thought of so many harsh critics has me tossing and turning in my bed every night. Flopping around like a stupid salmon that's found itself trapped in a cold river of fear. One that I willingly chose to swim up. I hate that what other people think bothers me so much, but I've always been this way.

It's Alanis Morissette, 'Ironic', really. That even knowing how I react to unkindness I was the one who created an open invitation for it by posting my advert online. I can't even bring myself to allow the option of receiving reviews. I'm sure folk ridicule me enough as it is without allowing the world to see.

I slowly begin to make my way down the hallway. This is the closest I'll probably get to feeling like I'm walking down an aisle, so I want to savour it. Strangely, my guts are churning, warning me to be cautious – but my heart is much more powerful, dominating.

With a tilt of my own head, unintentionally mirroring his body language, I confirm, and allow him to lead us into the room. It seems the right thing to do, because today, it feels like it belongs to him and not me.

'Um, so just take a wee seat,' I say, pointing to the empty chair closest to us. There are only two: one nearest to the door, and the other at the top, in front of the beautiful bay window with a solid ledge underneath that I wish was comfier to sit on. When setting up my spooky cave, I thought it might be a good idea to create a strict seating plan. One where people felt they had an easy exit route if they felt at all uncomfortable.

'Do you mind?' he asks, completely disregarding my instruction as he bounds toward the window.

All four legs scrape against the unpolished wood like sharp claws being dragged down a chalkboard, and all I can do is watch in horror as yet another attempt at routine goes up in flames.

He sits down and scoots in. Clasping his hands, his signal is crystal clear. He's ready to do business.

Four

Blair

The witch I'm about to be introduced to bounds towards her son like an excitable Labrador. With an impressively athletic figure, she's dressed to show it too, in skintight sports leggings, and a matching red vest top exposing some seriously toned biceps. She tucks her waist-length jet-black hair behind each of her ears and grabs his strong arms, pulling him into a cosy embrace. There's no denying she looks good for her fifties. A bit of Botox here and there wouldn't go a miss, but I'll give her credit where it's due: she definitely looks after herself.

Still, that doesn't take away anything from the fact she's coming across a little eager beaver. Has she been sat in her kitchen, staring out the window since the crack of dawn? It seems excessive, but I'll cut her some slack because maybe she's just nervous and wants to get our first exchange over with.

Not as much as I do.

Straightening the sleeves of the crisp white blazer he so generously bought me. I curse under my breath as I spot a tiny speck of red on the cuff. At first, I panic that it's the fancy cherry nail polish he picked out to match, but I realise that I've somehow pricked my thumb clutching the thorns on these stupid roses. I give it a suck to stop the flow from trickling down my hand and I can't help thinking that this sort of shit only happens in fairy tales, when things are about to turn sinister.

'My boy. My baby boy. Gosh, I've missed you so much, son,' she wails, planting kiss after kiss on his perfectly chiselled jaw.

It takes all the willpower I have to keep my eyeballs from rolling back and getting lost inside my skull. You'd think he just popped out the womb for god's sake. She literally saw him less than a week ago. Talk about clingy.

He ever so gently manoeuvres his mother to arm's length and grins.

'It's good to see you too, Mum. Although, I almost didn't – with this one's driving skills,' he says, tilting his head in my direction, acknowledging my awkward, almost gooseberry-like presence.

'Oh behave. I was absolutely fine,' I quip back, joining him at his side and taking his hand in mine to show that despite his little – and very out of character dig – we're a strong team. Solid as a rock. Nothing is going to crack us. Not even her. Or a rare, silly remark from him. I know it was just a joke, and I'm all for a laugh with a few playful jibes, but what a way to set the tone for a first impression by highlighting one of my flaws with a big yellow marker. What he failed to mention it was my first time driving his car, and before he insisted today that I take a shot, my ass hadn't sat in a driver's seat since passing my test all those years ago. I never needed to. Living in the city centre of Glasgow meant everything was so accessible and I could hope on a train or bus at my whim.

I wasn't exactly jumping for joy that he chose today to insist I drive while he sat back as if he were going on a school trip, leaving me to figure things out for myself. And on the one day I could have done without the extra pressure. But anyway, not to worry, I think, as I tuck the roses under my arm without releasing his grip and reach out my free right hand with my bold and unchipped nails. I still prefer black, but they're not so bad. 'Hello, it's so lovely to finally meet you. I'm Blair.'

Maria's face gargoyles instantaneously, twisting and hardening further with every second my hand remains on offer. Her eyes disapprovingly fly over my black leather leggings and nowhere near quickly enough to be considered discreet. Rude, I think, but maybe that was her intention. If so, she nailed it.

Finally, she extends an arm, and reluctantly takes my hand – very firmly – in hers. 'Oh. Yes. Hello,' she forces through tightly pursed, creamy nude painted lips.

'These are for you.' I thrust the flowers into her arms, hoping to sweeten the sour that's ripping out of her. Like she's got a lemon wedged between her gums and isn't allowed to spit it out.

Her slender and I now notice, also blood-red polished fingertips, grip the initiation gift I've offered so tightly that I think they might explode into dust, so I decide against saying anything else for the time being until I can suss her out a bit better.

My jaw drops as she tears her sharp eyes away from mine, whipping her son into her arms for another hug, forcing our clasped hands to part. Furious, I fold my arms across my chest and wait patiently to be included in their gang – like I'm supposed to be. But instead, with one arm still slung around his shoulders, she turns back to face me. 'He brings me these exact ones every week. They're my favourite. He's such a sweetheart. And so thoughtful,' she squeals.

I bite my tongue as hard as I can and force a falsely oblivious smile across my face. I know what she's doing. Making a point of telling me something that she hopes will stir up some jealousy inside of me. She wants me to know just how important she is, that she is number one in her son's life. That I should be mindful of that fact so not to overstep.

Wow, I think. I knew she was going to be hard work, but I might have underestimated her bitchometer level.

She smugly marches us inside the house like toy soldiers, and I close the door behind me, turning around to see my handsome man removing his trainers and pointing at my feet. I unzip each black, thigh high stiletto heeled boot, shimmy them down my shins, and then yank them off and pair them together next to his. A subtle but pointed statement of my own.

I'm not sure if she even notices, but either way, ignoring everything and anything to do with me, she darts inside a room to the right, which I assume is the kitchen. 'Just head into the living room, son. I'll be with you in a minute.'

Taking my hand in his, he spritely leads the way and I almost give myself an injury straining my neck, trying to take in each photograph lining the wall of the hallway. There are so many, and all of them are of her precious boy at various stages in his life: first day at school and graduation with floppy tassel included. There's even one that looks as if it has been cropped. A hint of a female arm resting on the table beside Mother Maria and saintly son, gleefully smiling for the camera.

I wonder who that was…and what they might have done to warrant their entire presence being erased from the memory, leaving nothing behind but the glimmer of a ghost. I can picture her now: rocking back and forth menacingly with a pair of scissors.

As we enter the living room, I marvel at the beautiful beige and white décor, sprinkled with touches of black. It's a bright and airy space with grand glass doors that, on a sunny day like this, allow beautiful, natural light to fill every corner of the room. The room screams class. More specifically, I'm gawking at the brand-new 60-inch telly that I know he recently bought for her birthday, hanging proudly in the centre of the widest wall. It pisses me off a little that he seems to spoil her better than me, but then again, if that's the kind of gifts he's buying for birthdays, then I'm surely in for a treat when mine comes around.

And going by the wooden sideboard underneath, decorated with an excessive number of unlit Jo Malone candles, I might also strike it lucky at Christmas time going by Maria's taste.

I wonder if she would even notice if one somehow fell into the car today and mysteriously ended up on our coffee table back at the flat. I'm sure I could make one disappear subtly if I really wanted to.

He plops himself down on one of the two brown leather Chesterfields and yawns, both arms stretching high, and I pause for a moment before joining him. I can't help but smile at the view, because it's so nice to see. You can tell he likes coming here, back to his childhood home. There's a contentment about him that's making my heart swell to the brim with love. Just him, existing, and enjoying the moment. Not worrying about the future or what he might do next. Because he's always planning *something*. He can't resist doing things to make sure I'm happy: treating me to the most delicious meals, surprising me with soppy love notes written in my best lipstick on the bathroom mirror. That morning, I saw the words 'I love you' in Ruby Woo Red. I didn't even care that he'd foolishly used a brand-new Mac. That's when you know you've got it bad.

It must be exhausting, being so bloody lovely to both of us at the same time. I guess that's just who he is though: selfless and genuinely wholehearted. Surely, he needs a break, though. A change in the dynamic. A wedge – even in the form of me – might offer him some respite, so it might not be a bad thing if she hates me after all. I'm sure he'd choose me if push really came to shove, despite any of my previous concerns.

I plop my backside down next to him on the couch and plant a kiss on his cheek. There's no way I'm going to let anything, or anyone jeopardise my turn at true happiness.

FIVE

CASSIE

Even though I could speak up for myself and ask Finlay to move, for some strange reason, I'm now engrossed in the shape of his hands resting on the table. They look strong, protective, and incredibly inviting. A fluttering of dainty wings takes flight in my stomach. It's been so long since I've felt anyone's fingers entwined with mine.

The thought occurs to me that if I weren't such a fraud, I'd be able to cast my own spell to freeze time. Allowing me to tiptoe over to him and clasp my own hand with his. Instead, with no such luck, I find myself – once again – just staring at him, blinking rapidly like a total idiot.

'*Sit down,*' a voice scalds me.

My fingers, polish chipped and tatty, find the back of the chair. I pull it out grudgingly and lower myself into unfamiliar territory. The grooves of the wood don't recognise the weight and shape of my body. However, like me, they have no option but to submit to the surprising turn of events.

Now that we're both in position – albeit the wrong one – I suppose it's time to begin.

What was once a living room, I converted into an appropriate space for my work. One that meant I could stay home and avoid the daily commute on a dingy bus into the city centre. In the middle of the large oak table, the bundle of white sage – still tightly wrapped in green string – is smoking thick and black, removing any stagnant energy from our surroundings. At least, I think that's what it's doing. I've only recently discovered sage, and there are so many different types: clary, woodland, juniper, lavender. And many more that I can't remember right now. I'm not clued up on the ins and outs of what they're all for yet, but the type I own smell nice and look the part.

I make another mental note: *learn the blooming meanings*.

'Hello, again.' I try to sound as pleasant and as confident as I can, a bid to salvage some sort of normality before things get out of hand. 'Thanks for coming today to see me. It's Finlay, isn't it?' I feel my tongue swipe my lips, savouring the sweet taste of his name as it's spoken out loud for the very first time.

Instead of engaging in small talk, he gives me another one of his firm – but still friendly enough – nods in agreement. I almost fall off my chair as his morphs into the Cheshire cat.

It's that smile. It puts me in some kind of trance.

Could he be a hypnotist?

I feel dizzy. Warm. The gold sparks of light are back, only this time they look like shooting stars. I can't breathe. Am I having an out-of-body experience? I feel like an avatar that's just been smacked by a hammer. I swear bubbles will appear above his head any second, shaped like love hearts.

Attempting to pull myself from whatever this delirium is, I give my head a sharp shake and try again. 'OK, cool. Well, I'm—'

His eyes lock onto mine, refusing to release me an intense clutch. 'I know who you are. And it's very nice to meet you, Cassie.'

My jaw drops. The hairs on my arms become as spiky as a cactus as they stand to attention. I frantically wrack my brain. How does he know my name?

My *real* name.

The ringing in my ears strikes again, and I gasp, realising I've been holding my breath. But instead of calming down, the sound of a symbol clashing is still vivid.

Oh…it's coming from his pocket.

He breaks the invisible chain between us as he whips out his iPhone, rolling his eyes as he accepts the call. Rising to his feet, he mouths an apology and exits the room.

Plunging my face into my hands, I try to think, and quick. It's impossible for him to know that my name is Cassie. We *definitely* haven't met before. I would remember that. Probably wouldn't ever be able to forget. So how does he know me? I don't understand. Especially because when meeting or chatting with customers, I always present myself as *Nova*, not Cassie.

I envision my ad now in my mind's eye: *Natters with Nova, Meet Nova, your very own Glaswegian Goddess. If you're seeking a little guidance, she's the gal for you. With absolutely zero judgement, paired with infinite understanding, Nova will do whatever she can to help. Simply DM today to book your reading,*

Absolutely zero mention of Cassie Torrance. Which there wouldn't be, because I deleted all my personal social media accounts. And in this room, I don't just wear that identity like a jacket or slide it over my face like a mask. I completely become her, never giving the game away. I'm almost possessed to a point. Like a demon, but a useful one. In astrology, they say your rising sign represents the person people perceive you as. Nova is that for me, my bad-ass Scorpio. She's confident but still mysterious, oozing with sass. Everything Cassie and her stupid sun sign lack. I reasoned that if some people say I'm being deceitful, I'd remind them that lots of celebrities use stage names: Rhianna, Elton John, Lady GaGa. All very successful people in their field. Surely, they're all channelling their ascending personality, too. And nobody calls them out, because it's harmless, just a game of make-believe.

My ears prick as I catch what sounds like the ending of a conversation. 'Aye. Aye, that'll be fine. I'll call you tomorrow. I have to go. I'm dealing with something.'

My time for piecing the puzzle together is up, but I try just one more thing. Bringing my hands together, I point to the ceiling and beg the universe for help. '*Universe, please, I am literally begging you. Give me the answer: how does he know my name?*'

Aha. I think, hitching a ride on the first explanation that comes to mind. I *must* have introduced myself as Cassie when I opened the front door. It probably just slipped out in a fluster.

'Of course,' I mutter, slapping my forehead with my hand. 'Of course, I did.'

'Cassie.' He practically purrs as he renters the room. 'Sorry about that, won't happen again. And thanks for seeing me at such short notice, by the way. I promise I won't waste any more of your time. You've got my full attention. Word on the street is you're a busy woman.'

With a quick squeeze to my shoulder, imprinting his touch on my skin like a painless tattoo I'll never want to remove, he casually takes his place again at the other end of the table.

'Not at all. No, don't be daft. I wasn't busy. You're all good.'

Frustration rushes over me instantly. Why on earth would I say that? Why would anyone in their right mind tell a paying customer that their diary isn't jam-packed, filled to the brim, bursting at the bloody seams?

He smirks, and my stomach churns, wondering if he can tell that I'm lying to him. I've probably only seen about ten people, if that. Not even a varied lot, as most were women in my age bracket. Some believers and some sceptics. But he is my very first male, and for some reason, my most challenging encounter yet.

'Not quite,' the voice whispers to me again, reminding me of a session that happened just two days ago. This totally rude chick who'd visibly injected so much Botox into her forehead she could barely muster a frown despite being so mardy. And her session was completely free, too. On impulse, I made a half-ass attempt at running a competition, but in the end, I just selected the first person to apply as the winner. Until Finlay appeared, I've not been able to get her out of my head. She's haunting me and she's not even in the ground. I know it's not very "love and light" of me…but good riddance to bad manners. She needs an exorcism from my memory.

'Stop now,' the voice commands. As always, it sounds nothing like me, but I don't know who's it is. It sometimes feels like there is an army of people living inside my brain. Perhaps they're creepy entities, sneaking through to this world from the other side without being given permission. Or maybe I am truly mad after all. Either way, I refuse to obey this one.

'So, Finlay, let's get started, shall we?'

Six

Blair

I was instantly attracted to George. Not quite love at first sight like he proclaims it was for him, but there was definitely a lot of lust sloshing around my veins. Still is. And I wasn't the only one feeling the heat before we'd even started cycling. The eyeballs of almost everyone in that spin class bulged at the sight of his toned torso, threatening to tear through the fabric of his navy-blue sports top. And his sparkling smile illuminated every single person who walked through the door, as if they were all important to him.

However, as much as I so obviously fancied him, he looked very…vanilla. You know, the type who doesn't stray from what's expected of him and abides by the straight and narrow. He really should have been a complete write-off when I think about it, because I lived for the pain of being swept away by red flags. When his eyes lingered on my face – completely bare of any war paint or false lashes – far longer than anyone else's as I attempted to straddle the bike as seductively as I could, I thought, *don't bother, you'll eat that guy alive.*

Still, here we are, because curiosity got the better of me, like it always does – except it never kills this kitty cat. And surprisingly, there's something else…an edge of rocky road to him that tickles my taste buds quite perfectly. He actually makes me feel understood, in a way I never thought falling for the nice guy ever could. He swept me off my feet and now here I am, obsessively in love with the most incredible, thoughtful man on the fucking planet. Who'd have thought it? Me: Blair Cameron – with the good guy. It's not what I was originally playing life for, but I've hit the jackpot, and now I'll take the lot.

'Son. Could you give me a hand, please?' Maria's voice pierces the air, interrupting my private trip down memory lane.

'I'll be back in a minute,' he says, getting to his feet and leaning down to kiss my forehead.

I slap his bum as he passes by. 'You're such a good boy. So obedient,' I joke, but he ignores my cheeky quip. Something he'd normally find quite funny.

Never mind. He's just a little on edge.

With both of them out of the room, I use the opportunity to tiptoe my way around, explore before lunch is served. I'm trying to get a better feel for the monster-in-law and what makes her tick.

My hand caresses a crystal Rennie Mackintosh ornament, but just as I'm about to pick it up, the kitchen door is slammed shut. An almighty eruption of raised voices spring to life but they're detached and therefore not clear enough for me to be able to grasp the full story of what the hell is going on in there.

I creep forward, towards the living room door and crane my neck as my ears try hard to merge some of the words together.

'I told you not to bring another...'

'It's different now...'

'I know what I'm doing.'

There's a crashing of what sounds like pots or pans being dumped in the sink.

'*She won't ever be…*'

Oh, for fuck's sake, I think. I've had enough of this. I want to know what's going on, so I don't think twice as I fly down the hallway and press my ear against the kitchen door, hoping to understand what's happening in there and why. But despite the initial slam, it wasn't fully closed, and as it flies open, I find myself tumbling into the middle of Maria and her son's domestic.

The first thing I notice when I get to my feet and swipe any dirt from my knees are the roses. Dumped in the sink next to dirty utensils. The second is his that his fingers are now wrapped around my wrist so tightly that my hand is turning pale.

'Eh, ouch. I'm fine,' I say, pulling away from him, baffled as to why I'm being restrained like a naughty child. It's not like I can run away and leave him here. 'I'm sorry to intrude. I just wanted to check if you needed any help setting up lunch. I hope I'm not interrupting anything?'

Maria's neck twists round to face me like an angry ostrich. 'Take your seat, *Becky*. I'll grab an extra plate and cutlery, shall I, George?'

I'll allow it. Just this once.

The two of them exchange a stern look before she turns her back to me. Busying herself, she pulls open a drawer with so much force I'm surprised the handle didn't fall off.

'Yes, good idea,' he says, morphing back into his usual cool and collected demeanour, dropping my arm, and chivalrously pulling out my chair at the glass dining table.

'What's going on?' I mouth quietly to him as he takes his seat across from me.

The frown lines on my forehead are creasing deeper by the second with confusion and I cannot afford a top-up of Botox right now.

Either he didn't hear me or has chosen not to tell me, but he bursts into song about his favourite footy team playing later on tonight, how many points they have, and who they have to beat. All the time he's speaking, his eyes, darker than usual, are pinned to his mother's back as she continues to plate the Sunday roast.

Of course, Maria serves her son first, then she delivers her own plate to the table, even though she isn't ready to sit down to eat yet – leaving mine till last. I know what she's doing: just another way for her to hammer home her position in the hierarchy of his love, but I've got bigger things on my mind right now. Like the fact she's already poured gravy over my entire plate.

I feel a droplet of sweat run down my neck and tickle my spine. 'Oh, erm…this is awkward – but is this gravy gluten-free?' I say, waving my hand over the plate like I'm casting a spell.

She stops instantly, Ugg slippers frozen to the tile below her. And if looks could kill, I'd be as dead as the chicken that's been slaughtered and sliced thinly on our plates.

'Absolutely not.' She practically spits venom.

I'm lost for words, can't for the life of me work out why she finds the idea so preposterous. She knew I'm unable to eat anything containing gluten, didn't she? It causes my stomach to inflate like a hot-air balloon and

George told her beforehand about my intolerance. I remember it well, because when he said he'd already made her privy I thought it was really sweet of him. That he cared enough about me to go that extra mile to ensure I'd be able to eat whatever Maria had in mind for lunch and not be left out. I offered to take something of my own to ding in the microwave if it was going to be any trouble, but he wouldn't hear a word of it.

'It's all right, Mum,' he says, finally stepping off his fence. 'Blair can just eat a wee bit of it. She's a bit of a drama queen, but she'll be fine.'

I whip my head to face him, alarmed, horrified, utterly bewildered that the words just left his mouth.

SEVEN

CASSIE

'Have you ever received a guidance reading before?' Erupting into a hearty laugh that fills every corner of the room, making even the cobwebs quiver, he holds his hands up in confession.

'You caught me. First time doing anything like this. A total virgin.'

I practically choke. *Virgin,* hah. I find *that* hard to believe. I guess I'm not the only fibber in this room. Little white lies sit comfortably with both of us.

'To be honest, Cassie, I'm a bit nervous, if you don't mind me saying. I've...well, I guess you could say I've always been a bit of a sceptic – until recently.'

I feel slightly triumphant. Nerves are good. Not for him, obviously, but they benefit me. And as for scepticism, that's cool. I've been dealing with that my whole life. No matter how hard I tried as a child to tell those closest to me that something was fundamentally wrong with me, that I needed their help, nobody has ever taken me seriously. Not family. Not friends. Definitely not past boyfriends. And all because I don't *look* like I'm suffering.

In the end, I gave up voicing my concerns, which was the catalyst in me deciding it best to cut everyone out of my life. I may not have any visible wounds for them to kiss better, still for many years, I've felt like I'm slowly bleeding out. But not so much in here, in this flat. I may have willingly cooped myself up like a pigeon, but at least I don't have to pretend anymore. Long gone are the days that I wished to break my arm or leg, because then everyone would gather round me. They'd sign my stookie, send me huge bunches of flowers, feed me grapes.

As for the bouts of loneliness, I try my best to combat those with a new hobby of mine: sticking my nose deep in a book. Often using sticky yellow Post-it Notes to mark a page that contains a paragraph or quote written by some guru or another that I find sort of relatable. There are so many different self-help titles out there for people to take their pick from, an abundance of help at our fingertips. And I do enjoy them, but secretly I feel that such a high demand for these aids is quite a depressing thought. If so many other people experience these difficulties, then why do I still feel so misunderstood?

Sometimes I think the authors of these books only view life from one perspective. They don't look at the bigger picture, accounting for a total failure like me. Someone who no longer has anyone of importance to rely on.

Only the universe knows what percentage I'm running on right now. How close I am to fizzling out for good and being left to rot.

My right eye twitches, threatening to produce a tear.

Stop this, I command silently. *You can't go there now. You're Nova, remember? Nova doesn't cry.*

Trying my best to keep my voice steady, dodging any cracks, I get back to work. 'Please don't be. You're not alone in feeling that way. Loads of people are nervous before we get started.'

He scoffs, begins to laugh at my pitiful attempt to soothe him, and I find myself trying to capture the pinballs of paranoia in my mind's net. *What must he be thinking? Does he know there haven't been many before him? What will he tell his mates about me after today?*

Although my chest feels like it's being crushed by a slithering boa, I have to keep ploughing on. 'Right, so…I'm going to give you a quick rundown of what we're going to do today, and if you feel like you might not be comfortable with anything – or even just change your mind – you can let me know. Does that all sound good?'

'Sounds great, Cassie,' he replies, and my heart swells at how my name spills off his tongue once again.

I start to explain that I'm legally obligated to inform him that I am not, in any way, shape, or form, a doctor or a therapist. I hate delivering this spiel because it's fussy. Still, I have to say this stuff to everyone in case someone decides to sue me or something. A meaningless disclaimer really, because I suppose there is always a risk that people might take my guidance as gospel and end up doing something that completely ruins their life. Thankfully, despite not yet being supernaturally equipped for the role, I haven't had anyone hunt me down so far.

'I also can't promise to connect to a spirit or a loved one, so if that's what you're looking for today……I might not be the right person for you and would completely understand if you wanted to leave.' A lie, of course. That's the last thing I want.

I bite down hard on my bottom lip, praying that he still wants to stay.

'All good, Cassie, I trust you. You're the expert, right?' he responds.

A thick fog of guilt rises from the pit of my belly, weaving its fingers around my throat. 'Right. Yes. I suppose I am.'

'Maybe you should come clean?' a voice suggests.

Or not, I retort silently. Because people don't always do what they should, do they? And Finlay Munro could end up being more than a paying customer.

The deck of cards I laid out for today is still sitting at my usual side of the table, so I politely ask him to pass them across, fully expecting him to stand up and hand them over to me with a stretch. But my tri-coloured eyes – green, grey, and blue – bulge, almost popping out, and splattering onto the floor. With one swift movement, he rises, lifts his chair with a strong and clearly muscular arm. Now next to me, he places down the seat that looks like it belongs in a dollhouse. Our knees are almost touching, and everything suddenly feels more intimate. More intense. I can smell the minty freshness of the gum inside his mouth as his jaw clenches and releases with leisurely chews, and I'm desperate to pinch it and taste for myself.

'Run!' a voice hollers.

Woah. I flinch, clasping my ear. So, they're shouting at me now? That's an interesting development. I can't physically see anyone, but I swear I can *feel* a third person in the room. Of course, I refuse to listen, because even engaging in a confrontation with a voice in my head makes me want to shrivel up and die with embarrassment.

Closing my eyes, I drop my hand, and quickly start to shuffle the Tarot cards.

Although…I consider. If there *is* someone else here with us: a messenger or helper – that suggests I am in fact not losing my mind. And Finlay Munro has been the one to finally awaken something truly powerful within me. Suppose he was always destined to come into my life? He's the one I've been waiting for. The reason I've never connected with anyone else.

A light bulb illuminates above my head. He's not just here for a reading, the true purpose of his visit is a sign from the universe. Someone *can* understand me. *Is* able to love me. If I pass this test, I'll never need anyone else.

What is it fellow spiritualists say? Everything happens for a reason.

With both eyes wide open again, more alert than ever, I notice the rose quartz crystal sitting next to the bundle of sage in the middle of the table. A great whopping rock that you need both hands to lift. It can't be just a coincidence that I recently bought the crystal of love.

Everything *does* happen for a reason.

The edges of the cards fly through my fingers. I know whatever three cards he picks today are entirely out of my control and we're fast approaching the grand reveal. But all it will take is one contradictory explanation for my hopes to be squished to a pulp. I plan on avoiding that at all costs.

Eight

Blair

I bloody will not just have a *wee* bit of it. Has he lost the fucking plot? What the hell has gotten into him?

Whatever he and his mother were arguing about had clearly got to him or he wouldn't be saying something so bloody ridiculous. He's allergic to onions – or so he says. Personally, I think he just doesn't like them and is being a tad dramatic, but either way I wouldn't force any of them down his neck now, would I?

I don't know what to do for the best, seeing as it seems I'm on my own here, so I'm forced to step in and take the brunt of looking like the bad guy. I mean, what choice do I have? I'm not fucking eating it, I know that.

'Actually, I'll just give you guys my meat if that's OK? I'll just have some of the mash and veg that's not got any gravy on it yet, if that's all right? Sorry, I don't mean to offend you, Maria. I'm sure you've gone to a lot of effort.'

I swear to God this woman is hard of hearing because the number of times she ignores me is incredible, but instead of stressing too much about it I stab a carrot with my fork and shove it in my mouth. It's hardly going to fill me up, especially since I didn't eat any breakfast to avoid spoiling this stupid lunch, but it seems to pacify her enough that she takes her seat at the table.

As I watch them slicing away at their succulent breast meat, I try as hard as I can to pretend that I'm enjoying the fluffy cloud on my plate. I even munch a few sprouts – which I absolutely hate – but they taste nowhere near as awful as how uncomfortable sitting next to Maria feels. The red-hot tension is radiating from her, torching me like a marshmallow.

'So, Blair,' she suddenly starts. 'What is it you do?'

'Oh,' I say, wiping my mouth with the napkin, staining the cloth with my red lipstick – another thing she'll have something to say about, I'm sure. 'Well, right now I'm just figuring a few things out since leaving the bar.'

'The bar?' she scoffs.

'Yeah. I worked in a funky cocktail bar in Glasgow. It was so much fun, and I loved everyone there, but it was time for a change. Actually, it was your son's genius idea.' I point my fork in his direction. 'He said I'm destined for greater things.'

I smile adoringly at my handsome man, his dark hair matching his black hoody perfectly.

She puts down the cutlery and wipes the disgust off her lips with her own napkin. 'So, you're unemployed?'

Ouch. The shot has been fired, and it's blasted my confidence to smithereens. I mean, yes, technically I am, but I've been writing loads with my free time. When he goes to work, I pull out good old-fashioned pen and paper. I've always loved the idea of writing a book of some kind, but never truly believed in myself until I met him. He told me I could do anything I put my mind to, because he believed in me. He saw potential in a part of me I couldn't identify in myself until I had free rein to explore it. George gave me that freedom by taking care of all the bills, telling me there was absolutely no need for me to be working all those late nights anymore. I must admit, I was conflicted about leaving, but the night I handed my notice to my manager, I felt strangely liberated. My life was changing at high speed and yet I wasn't scared. It all felt so right.

'Self-employed, I like to call it.' And smile at her. Because that's what he told me to say if anyone ever asked me. 'I'm thinking of writing a book or something like that.'

She just about chokes on her slice of gravy-soaked breast meat.

'That all sounds wonderfully optimistic, Becca. But how do you live? Where does your money come from?'

'Blair,' I instantly correct her.

'Excuse me?' She glares.

'Sorry, it's Blair. My name is Blair.'

'Yes. Right. Well, *Blair*, the question still stands. How do you contribute to that beautiful flat my boy saved so hard for when you aren't currently making any money?'

I gag on my tongue, searching his face for a sign that he's about to step in and squash this bullshit interrogation – but he's giving me nothing. He has well and truly thrown me to the big bad wolf and doesn't seem to notice that I'm being eaten alive.

She makes me sound like some sort of gold digger, but little does she know that from the week I turned sixteen, I've worked my backside off. I've done every job imaginable to make sure I could support myself.

Didn't matter how grim or seedy. I have never had to rely on anyone, and I never wanted to because I learnt from an early age in a dysfunctional household that even the people closest to you might offer you help and then snatch it back, demanding interest. Anything my mum ever did for me or gave me, she sure as shit made sure she told all her friends all about the hassle of it.

I made a promise to myself that I'd never ask anyone for anything when I was able to earn a wage for myself. And I still haven't. I still don't ask George for a penny. It was his idea to pack in the bar job. He said that he made more than enough money to support us and that he wouldn't feel comfortable with me being wolf-whistled at by drunken men if we were to be together. He wouldn't take no for an answer and in the end, I couldn't bear seeing him sat upright in bed, red-eyed and worried for my safety when I finally did return to the flat after a 1 a.m. finish.

My situation right now is temporary. I deserve the break to kick back, relax, and let someone else take care of me – but it won't be forever. Just until I figure out what to do next with my writing. I don't know if it's a pipe dream – creating your own novel – or if I should just stick to a journal or blog, but either way it's definitely none of snooty Maria's business.

'Well, fortunately, I've found someone who supports my dream enough to look after me until I can repay him.' I put down the fork for good now, too sickened with anger to eat another bite despite my stomach still grumbling. 'Which I will, by the way, in abundance. He'll get what he deserves and I'm very grateful because whatever you might think about me, I do love your son very much.'

'Yes. I'm sure you do,' Maria replies with a smirk and rises from her chair. 'Now, who wants pudding?'

'I am burst – but definitely. Sticky toffee pudding, is it? You know it's my favourite,' George answers. As if he's only just found the key to his zipped mouth as he bared witness to the whole horrid interaction.

'Of course, my boy.' She delights. 'Just you and me. I doubt the fussy eater in the corner would be able to bare such delight.'

As she pops two slices of cake into the microwave, sets the timer, and stands tapping her nails against the kitchen worktop, I say nothing out loud. I won't give her a reaction or another reason to dislike me. But inside my head, I'm imagining shoving Maria's head into the microwave and preparing her for George's next plate.

NINE

CASSIE

I hand the cards back over to him.

'Give them a shuffle like I just did, OK? Do it as often as you like, and I want you to think of why you've come here today. When you feel ready to receive the message, split the deck into three piles on the table.'

He shuffles with ease, like a highly esteemed magician. Still, I do spot the tiniest glimmer of hesitation as his hand momentarily hovers before producing a row of three.

From what I know about Tarot, the cards you instinctively select offer guidance from a higher place. I'm not sure exactly what the higher place is, but I've been calling it the universe and that feels right because I've never been big on religion. Originally, they were just a party trick originating from the seventeenth century, enjoyed among friends during a good old bevvy session. But nowadays, reading Tarot, collecting different coloured crystals, and waving around some smoky incense sticks have grown to become extremely popular. An array of weird but wonderful tools to assist with life's many conundrums.

However, what I don't know about Tarot, is how to use them properly. Sure, I've read a few books...OK, mostly looked at the pictures, but I've just been winging it and hoping for the best. There're far too many decks to study: angels, divine feminine, black magic, and even hilarious animal cards. I decided just to opt for a traditional Tarot deck that includes the most well-known cards: cups, swords, hermits. And you don't really need to be a medium or psychic to be able to perform a reading. It's not an *essential* requirement. To keep yourself right, you just have to familiarise yourself with the images and a snippet of what they mean and let them speak for themselves.

I instruct him to place his hand on a deck of his choice. Reaching over, I collected the other two that were no longer needed.

'Now, if you just spread all your cards out – sort of like a fan – and slide out three of your choice. But don't turn them over yet. Just leave them face down, OK?'

I wait for him, study his face as it contemplates which cards to pick, taking notice of a slight crease between his perfectly groomed eyebrows. It could be a scar from an injury or simply the beginnings of a wrinkle forming, but I don't care either way because it's unbelievably sexy.

My brain buzzes as it downloads a new thought. I wonder how old he is. My prediction would be his early to mid-thirties. Someone older than me could be a good thing. They're more experienced, have more to teach me.

His index finger slides each card out towards the edge of the table.

'You can go ahead and flip the first one over now.' I urge him.

His hand moves forward, finds the lip of the first card, and turns it over to reveal our first message.

'So, what this card represents is your past. As you can see, you've pulled the Five of Cups, which indicates you might have experienced some sort of grief. You might even be feeling some guilt, remorse, or—'

'Are you asking me or telling me?' he interrupts.

I clench my jaw, stopping it from falling. 'Telling you.' My tone is sharper than intended, and it surprises us both, but I can't let his question derail me. 'If you look closely, you can see that the figure on the card is dressed in a black cloak. He's mourning over the three cups in front of him. Those cups mean loss.'

He backs down, nods in agreement. An awkward silence fills the room like a bad smell.

'There are two other cups behind the man in the card that he seems unaware of.' Pointing to the gold chalices on the ground with a chipped red nail, I feel him edge closer but try my best to stay in character. 'You see? New opportunities and stuff are waiting for him.'

His top lip twitches. Picking up the card, he caresses its face with his thumb.

Is he thinking the same as me? Shiny new opportunities and all that.

Could I really be one of them?

I instruct him to flip over his second card that will tell me more about his present situation. My throat is dry, desperate and thirsty for more information. Sometimes folk spill their guts immediately and tell me everything that's been weighing heavily on their shoulders. I've even had a few sessions where before I've had a chance to ask them to start shuffling the cards, they've served me their entire life story on a plate. Of course, they're not supposed to. This defeats the purpose of fortune telling, but it does make the whole card reading process go a lot smoother when I know exactly what they want to hear.

But not Finlay. who's keeping his own cards very close to his chest. A heart throbbing silent assassin.

I prise my eyes from his face and witness the Ten of Swords. This card can represent betrayal, bitterness, and I'm quickly digging deep into the box of facts to find the right words to recite to him. But even with all my knowledge, I struggle to say anything because he's staring at my lips. Somehow caressing them without moving a single muscle.

I wish I could genuinely read his mind right now. Would it tell the same story as mine?

I lick my lips in preparation. I think…I think he's going to kiss me.

'You seem very passionate about what you do,' he says, leaning back in his chair. My stomach churns as I realise my mistake. God, I'm so stupid. Ridiculous. Pathetic. I feel the heat creep up my neck, embarrassment clutching my throat.

Deflated, I sigh, 'Yeah, I guess I like helping people.'

'That's cool. I like that. But what about you?'

I don't understand the question and begin to stutter a reply, but he stops me by placing a hand on mine. I freeze at the close contact, blinking until I inevitably realise that I'm hallucinating.

But I'm not. My skin is tingling under the warmth of his.

'Who takes care of you, Cassie? Is there a man – or a woman?' he says, holding his palms in the air. 'Or…is that position still open?'

Ho-ly shit. Is he flirting with me? *Please*, I beg silently. *Angels, guides, ancestors, anyone. Tell me that he's flirting with me. I'm begging you. Show me a sign. Please.*

Nothing comes. Nothing moves. Nobody appears. Even the voices in my head are eerily quiet.

'Sorry,' he says, holding his hands up. 'I didn't mean to pry.'

I don't know what to tell him. That there's nobody? That everyone I've ever dated has said I'm too emotional, too sensitive, too doom and gloom for reasons neither of us can understand? That all my attempts at holding down a relationship of any kind have always been destroyed by my erratic mood swings? That it's just me, boring, lonely, un-showered, and clinging on to a belief that could see me sectioned.

'It's just me,' I finally reply. 'But anyway, let's get back to business, shall we?' The surface of my thumb stings as I press my nail hard into my forefinger. 'Turn over your third card, please.'

Seemingly unbothered by my hesitation to share any more, he clears his throat, slides out his final card, and then flips it over. We both stare at the image that's captured both of our attention. And for good reason.

Chin wobbling, I straighten my shoulders and lift my head.

'Death,' I blurt far too loudly. I gulp, swallow the lump in my throat. 'You've pulled the death card.'

Ten

Blair

The drive back home was eerily silent. A complete turnaround to how we arrived. I didn't even want to speak to him let alone glance across at him after the lack of backbone I witnessed earlier today, but every time I had no choice but to ask for directions, he'd huff a little bit more, pretend to focus on something outside, and leave me to figure it out myself.

I can't understand why he's so annoyed at me. If he should be angry at anyone, it should be that battleaxe of a thing he calls a mother.

I've come to the conclusion that she hated me before I even stepped foot in her front door and really there was nothing I could have done differently that would have changed her mind. She thinks I'm a leech. Among many other things, it seems. And the fact he didn't stand up for me once was a real eye opener.

Maybe he's not the man I thought he was…I dunno.

Finally, back at the house, I scrub my face clean in the bathroom, quickly change into my pyjamas and I'm more than ready to get lost in the duvet and watch something trashy on the television. As I pull back the cover, about to jump into bed, he groans, and kicks the pile of clothes I'd stripped off and left by the door.

'You know, leather leggings...wasn't one of your best choices, was it? Neither were the boots. What were you thinking?'

'Huh?' I ask, because surely, I cannot be hearing him right.

'And that top, too. When you unbuttoned your blazer, you were too exposed. Your tits were practically falling onto the table while we ate lunch.'

I glare at him, confused, but also, strangely, feeling a bit embarrassed, so I pull my dressing gown tighter across my chest. He told me I looked great. He watched me get ready. Why didn't he say something?

'She went to a lot of effort for you today, by the way,' he continues.

'Yes, I know she did. And I'm very thankful for her having me round. I told her that before we left. What the fuck has gotten into you?'

He storms out of the room, leaving me completely bewildered. I barely recognise him right now. I've struggled to find him all day, no matter how hard I searched. Where is my softly spoken, respectful, and compassionate man? It's like he entered his mother's house Dr Jekyll and came out Mr Hyde.

I'm far too exhausted to get into a fight with him, so I'll let him have his little tantrum this once. Whatever went down in that kitchen has clearly rocked the dynamics of our relationship but I'm too angry and too hungry to think clearly.

Which reminds me, the Chinese should have been here about half an hour ago.

'Babe,' I call through the wall. 'Has my food arrived yet?'

I hear a faint chuckle.

'No. And it's not going to. I cancelled your order. Figured since you wasted your lunch you wouldn't be up to eating anything else.'

The volume on the telly fires up before I have a chance to respond. He wouldn't hear me even if I shouted at him as loud as I want to. I could stamp right in there and give him a piece of my mind because who the hell does he actually think he is? He can't just decide when I can or cannot eat. This is a relationship, not a bloody dictatorship.

I'm ready to launch myself out of bed like a rocket, but I hesitate at the last minute. Something about the way his eyes emerald eyes stopped sparkling and darkened like a polluted sea has unnerved me and I don't know why.

For the first time in my entire life, I decide to back down from a fight, but that doesn't mean I'm prepared to sit in this bed like a scalded child who's just been put on the naughty step.

Quietly, I get out of bed and find the clothes I wore today from the bedroom floor. I push my legs back into the leather leggings he suddenly took a dislike to and wiggle them up and over my bum. Pulling my top back over my head, I decide to ditch a bra because at this point, I don't even care if my nipples are poking people in the eyes. Not where I'm going. Instead of shrugging the white blazer back over my shoulders, I grab my black leather jacket hanging on the door handle and quickly put it on. I don't bother re-applying a full face of make-up and instead I chuck my red lippy in my handbag to apply on the way.

With my boots under my arm to shove on once I'm outside to avoid them clicking on the wooden floor, I slowly open the bedroom door. The television is still up loud in the living room, but the door isn't fully shut, so I have to be careful or else he'll hear me. With each footstep, I wince, fearful of being caught, but I make it to the front door and turn the key. It clicks loudly, the way it always does, but I'm praying it's gone unnoticed because I've managed to open the front door and he's still not at my heels.

The soles of my feet sting on the cold concrete because I forgot to put socks back on, but I continue to pad my way down the close the way someone would if they were participating in a hot coal ceremony.

The main door to the block of flats is already wide open, and I quickly hop out and jog around the corner, out of sight. I press my palm flat against the wall and pull each of my boots on, and then I start walking towards the main street.

Hah. I think as I book an Uber to collect me from the restaurant he first took me to – The Battlefield Rest. I'm heading straight to the bar I used to work at to have some fun of my own. That'll teach him. He has no right speaking to me to like that, and if he thinks I'm just a silent trophy girlfriend, he can think again. I'll go and have a few drinks with some of my old colleagues and leave him wondering where I've got to and by the time I come home, I'm sure he'll be ready to apologise for his behaviour.

Waiting for my driver, I scroll through Facebook. Lisa, my mate from secondary school – who I haven't spoken to in years but still quite enjoy having a little nosy into her life – has posted yet another picture of one of her kids. Boring. Ashleigh, who still works at the bar I used to, has proudly shared her latest Slimming World achievement. Yawn. And then there's Adam, a guy I used to date, who has started competing for body building titles and really thinks people care about the spray tan he's just had to try to accentuate his muscles. Couldn't care less.

I'm much more interested in seeing what freebies I could win by putting my name forward in a prize draw. So far this month I've tried to bag a romantic two-night trip in Paris, a hot-tub getaway in a fancy lodge up by Loch Lomond, and a skincare bundle worth over one-hundred pounds. Sadly, I've heard nada, and even though it's starting to feel like a waste of time, I can't resist entering just one more. This one is a bit out of my comfort zone and to be honest, not really my cup of tea, but what the hell? I'll try anything once I suppose. The wind blows my hair across my face as I hit the like button on the post, type out my name in the comment section and hope for the best.

As I'm about to put my phone back in my bag, it pings, notifying me of my carriage to take me to the ball. I spot a silver Skoda parked on double yellows across the road and roll my eyes at the thought of having to find a gap in traffic to run across. I suppose it's close enough to where I asked to be collected from, but his tip depends on the rest of the journey.

I dart between the cars lined up at the traffic lights and as I reach for the door handle on the car, a hand grips my shoulder.

'It's all right, mate. Just cancel this one,' George says, leaning down, instructing the driver through his open window.

'What are you doing? How did you know where I was?' I ask shocked, pulling away from him.

The driver hesitates, looking over his shoulder to check for confirmation from me.

'Sorry, can you just wait a minute?' I ask him. 'Just give me one minute, please.'

George puts one hand on the roof of the car and turns to face me. The man behind the wheel seems annoyed by someone touching his car but chooses not to say anything.

'I'm sorry, Blair. I shouldn't have snapped at you like that. Please, just come back to the flat and I'll order in some food.'

My eyes dart between him and the driver, not quite knowing which man to leave with.

Was he following me? And for how long? I'm so tired from the rollercoaster that was today that I can't think straight.

'Look at you, you must be freezing. Let me run you a warm bath. This is stupid, Blair. Please?'

'Fine,' I huff, and push my icy hands into my pockets.

'Cheers, mate,' George says, tapping the roof, sending the car on its way and as it pulls away from us, he wraps his arm around my shoulder, kisses my forehead, and begins to lead us back to the flat.

'You're crazy. You know that, right?' he asks as we continue to walk home.

'If you say so,' I reply, refusing to look at him. Still too annoyed about earlier today. Although his fingers digging deeper into my upper arm, clutching on to me in case I begin to sprint in the opposite direction, tell me that it was more of a rhetorical question.

Neither of us exchange another word as we continue down the path and for some strange reason – whether it be my overactive imagination or simply the silence between us – the heels of my boots clicking off the pavement sound terrifying. Almost like gunshots. And the closer to home we get, I can't help but feel that something dangerous is waiting to snare me in its trap. The craziest thing about the notion is there's one thing in particular niggling at me the most: that it almost seems possible the predator could turn out to be my other half.

Eleven

Cassie

'What do you mean death?'

Something about the sharp edge to his tone scares me a little, but I know his reaction is perfectly understandable. It might look bad, but it's not always something to stress about. It doesn't necessarily mean someone is about to pop their clogs or that he's about to become a serial killer. The Death card can also represent a chance for new beginnings, a shot at a fresh start, or a transformation.

'Listen, I know this card looks scary, but I promise it's not. Honestly, it's fine.' I hear myself floundering, but I can't stop as I continue to ramble. 'It means that some things might need to come to an end for you to be able to move forward. And that's sort of like a death, isn't it? Does that make sense?'

He licks his teeth with his tongue, unconvinced. 'Does it ever actually mean death, though? Say…the death of a loved one?'

I have no idea what to say. I'm sure it must have at some point, but I'd only be able to know that if I was able to connect with spirits, right? Which I obviously – despite multiple attempts – I cannot do.

His head suddenly falls into the palms of his hands. He rubs his eyes vigorously and the room suddenly feels stuffy, and I'm struggling to breathe. I don't know what to do, but the urge to grab the sage from the middle of the table, pull out my lighter, and set the whole thing alight like a big fat joint is overwhelming. It's supposed to heal, right? It might be able to help.

'Cassie,' he says, whipping his head back up. 'I don't know if I'm supposed to tell you this or not, but I'm here because of my girlfriend.'

The word stings as it plays on repeat in my ears. *Girlfriend. Girlfriend. Girlfriend.* I have once again made a ridiculously foolish mistake. I want to curl up into a ball and tumble out of the room like a bowling ball.

My lips wobble as I open my mouth. 'OK. Um, well, would you like to tell me a bit more about that? You don't have to, though. Totally up to you…'

He bites the inside of his right cheek and rubs his hands on the top of his thick thighs. 'Well, I lost her about a year ago now. And it's all been a bit fuckin' strange to be honest.'

I nod. He takes my silence as an invitation to carry on.

'Right, so it was just a normal day. Nothing out of the ordinary happened, but she wasn't at home when I got back from work. All her clothes were still there, and everything looked exactly the same as when I left her sleeping in bed that morning. I don't know what happened. Honestly, I don't. And I haven't heard a thing from her since.'

I swallow every single word carefully, digesting what it means.

I should feel guilty. I *should* be professionally concerned about the obvious. There are probably a lot of other things I should be thinking about right now, but my heart is clinging to the realisation that the girlfriend he previously mentioned is now technically an ex. As in no longer *ex-ists*.

Golden opportunities…The card was right.

Catching me off-guard, he laughs – but I'm not sure what's so funny. I don't think I'd be quite as blasé about being ghosted. But then again, a year is quite a long time. Perhaps he's well and truly past the snot and the tears stage. Ready to heal and move on.

My gut instinct is yodelling that this is fantastic, but still, I can't ignore the niggling question: *what exactly does he want me to do about it?* I'm a trick or treat card reader, not a private investigator. This isn't Netflix. We're in the Southside of Glasgow, not a thriller set in New York City.

'Umm, so obviously I'm really sorry to hear that. It's just I don't know what you think I can help you with. I'm sure I mentioned earlier that I can't make any promises to talk to spirits. Is that why you're here?' I pause momentarily, but not enough time for him to get a word in. 'To ask your ancestors or guides why she left you?'

'No. That's not why I'm here,' he says firmly. Sharply. 'What I'm trying to say is, I think there's more to it. I don't think she just left me. I went to the police and reported her missing – like you're supposed to do, right? But they said people run off from their relationships all the time. The bloke said there was nothing they could do.'

The police? I gulp. My excitement has taken a nosedive at how serious this situation has become.

He claps his hands together and then rubs them vigorously. 'Right. So, this will sound absolutely mental, but I have this feeling in the pit of my stomach that something bad has happened to her. Do you know what I mean? What would you call that? Intuition?'

My heart can't resist humming in awe at the use of the spiritual lingo, but so many other thoughts are taking over, bulldozing any joy.

What do you mean there was nothing they could do? What do you think has happened to her? Why do you think something has happened to her?

He must have valid reasons for thinking the way he does, especially if he's taken it as far as going to the police. I suppose it's quite possible that she may have been harmed in some way, because the news these days speaks for itself as it continues to report yet another case of an innocent woman being attacked in broad daylight. It's terrifying to read or watch as members of authority such as bloody police officers are being charged for such terrible crimes. My heart aches to know that these ladies have all been doing something so simple when it happens: out on their daily jog, or just walking the short journey to the shop for a pint of milk. We don't expect our protectors to view us as prey. We shouldn't have to take one ear pod out because two would block out the footsteps of others. Our keys shouldn't be wedged in between our fingers with the sharp edge ready to attack should someone feel they were entitled to do so.

Finlay must be so frustrated. He's probably losing his mind trying to find the answers and nobody is willing to help. I don't know what I can do to be of any use, but I suppose, at the very least, I can try. I could help him find some peace so that he can move on, right? Whatever that involves…

Suddenly, the music in the background stops and we're plunged into a haunting silence. We both look at each other for an answer as tension hanging in the air replaces the gentle sounds that tried to create a sense of calm in a morning of chaos. A sharp screech almost pierces my right eardrum. It's growing louder and more urgent. Suddenly, a shot of pain is injected into my forehead. My fingers fly to my temples, and I squeeze my eyes shut.

Silence. It's gone.

His face is fixated on mine, full of concern.

My mind scrambles, trying to piece all the facts together, but the pain is distracting. I wonder if I have any paracetamol in the kitchen cupboard.

Not that there's time to grab some now, though. Because what's more important is that as of twelve months ago, Finlay Munro – regardless of how it happened – became single, and his ex, or whatever you want to call her, hasn't been in touch since. I totally understand his frustration and why he finds it impossible to believe that she'd just walk out on him. I mean look at him – I know I wouldn't – but there is still a possibility that she did. She could quite easily be living her best life in the Maldives, happy to be rid of him for all I know. There's no evidence to support that she's actually been harmed.

I refocus my attention on the Death card still gawking up at me from the table and consider my next sentence that's waiting impatiently on the tip of my tongue.

I'll probably never know what happened to her, but death, or no death, the message that the card has to offer remains the same: he must move on with his life. And suppose someone could confirm what he already believes to be true…would that help him? If he once and for all had a definite answer?

Gripping the arms of my chair until my knuckles turn pale, I brace myself for impact. The urge to say it's burning the back of my throat as I struggle to hold it inside. I breathe in through my nose, exhale through my mouth, and my eyes ping open. Turning my head slowly, I lick my chapped lips and absorb his beauty once more. Such a glorious face, with a perfectly sculpted, and trimmed beard decorating a jaw that's been chiselled by angels. My eyes flicker to the ground and back up again. Noticing that his elbows are balancing on jutted knees.

I can fix this. Fix him. Fix me.

'Did you see something? You did, didn't you? What did you see, Cassie? Please, tell me. I need to know.'

Don't do this, a voice in my head commands.

But I have to. It feels right. I must step up – no, not step, leap. This is my one shot at happiness. It's my time now, I know it.

'Cassie, tell me what you know. Is she – is she…'

My mouth fires open, my tongue cocked and ready to pull the trigger. He's thinking it anyway, isn't he? It's almost like he wants me to say it for him. To put him out of his misery.

I gulp, place both hands on the table.

'She's…' I pause, unsure of the gentlest way to say this, but I guess there isn't one. 'Dead.'

I cup my open mouth with the palm of my hand, attempting to shovel the words back in, but I can't. It's too late. I've said it now, so I may as well continue. 'I'm sorry, Finlay, but I'm afraid you're right. Your girlfriend is gone.'

The walls begin to close in on me. The furniture becomes fuzzy. Finlay's face melts in horror.

Oh my god, what have I done?

Twelve

Blair

His newfound foul mood is really starting to grate on me.

After living up to his promise and running me a nice warm bubble bath, I scoffed the pizza he ordered and then we both fell into bed together. Neither of us spoke about my plan to creep out to the bar without telling him and instead our make-up sex was passionate, frenzied, but also fuelled by something new that I couldn't quite work out. It did feel good though, so I didn't dare complain. It was unusual for him to be so dominant, but it felt good, so I ran with it.

'Why are you soooo grumpy? You're doing my head in.' I moan, pushing myself away from his solid chest with the palm of my hand.

I notice small yellow circles dotted across my arm from where his hands pinned me to the bed, rendering me submissive.

I thought everything would be fine between us today – that we might even go at it again, like the seemingly wild animals we were last night – but my attempts to seduce even just a sliver of affection from him this morning have gone down like a lead balloon and I'm both confused and mentally wounded by his rejection.

Groaning, he pulls the covers up to his eyebrows and then flips over, turning his back to me and offering nothing but the silent treatment. Is this how it's going to be between us now? Fleeting between overwhelming me with affection to dismissing me altogether with no warning or explanation? It wasn't like this before.

He wasn't like this before.

Fuck him, I think, and swing my bare legs out of bed, stretching my arms high with an exaggerated yawn, just to piss him off that tiny bit more.

'Fuck's sake,' I hear him mutter under his breath.

Perhaps he's growing tired of my…theatrics. Which is silly really, because my personality is what he claimed to love most about me in the first place. He said I had an edge about me that made me different from anyone he'd ever met. He knew exactly what he was signing up for and yet since we went for lunch with his mum, it's almost like he can't stand me.

It was he who offered to walk me to the bar that night after spin class and insisted that he bought me a drink to start my shift. I don't usually drink while working but I found it hilarious that my fitness instructor was encouraging me to get wasted, so I humoured him and said "yes, of course you can – but only if you join me".

I didn't think he'd agree, but he proved me wrong, and that one drink turned into many as he propped up the bar the whole night, still in his work uniform, not giving a shit who saw him. I thought that was actually pretty edgy of him, that he looked like a walking contradiction and didn't give two shits about it either. That's when I first thought there's more to this handsome guy than just bright white teeth and delicious muscles.

Goosebumps pimple my thighs as I open the bedroom door and step out into the cold hallway.

Just like that first night at the bar – the first time I went home with him – I'm wearing one of his football T-shirts and nothing else. He usually loves when I wear one of his favourite team's tops, instead of skimpy pyjamas or a silk nightie to bed, and it actually gives me a thrill that he finds me so attractive in just a simple baggy top. Even first thing in the morning with no make-up on. I'm not short of confidence, but the way he adored me without any fuss required definitely boosted my self-esteem. Not to mention that it saved me a fortune on forking out for expensive sets just to win some male attention. As an added bonus, I also no longer had to worry about sneaking out of the room in the morning to apply a full face of make-up before the guy beside me woke up and thought he'd been catfished.

George is different. He says he loves me just as I am. Right now, though, I'd rather be wearing a bin bag – or literally anything else – because the netted fabric feels like a dead weight pressing down on my chest and I have the strongest urge to tear it from my body in case his stinking mood is contagious.

But first, before anything: coffee. Always coffee in the morning. It's a rule in this flat, and despite being a complete arsehole, I'll still make him one. Just how he likes it. 'Because I guess that's just the kind of gal I am,' I say, giggling quietly to myself, dropping a spoonful of sugar into his mug.

The old me would have let a man die of thirst for treating me the way he is this morning, but I decide there's no point in making a big deal out of it. It won't last and is probably just a blip, so it'll be easier just to get on with it than to rock the boat any further. Today is feeling far too choppy already.

Plus, I can't behave the way I would have in the past, because I don't live there anymore. And he's not like anyone I've dated before. He's a good man. The right man. What's a real relationship without a bit of bickering, anyway?

As I go through the ritual of preparing our morning beverages, the soles of my feet begin to ache on the cold kitchen tiles, forcing me to tiptoe my way around like a ballerina. I've kicked off my socks in the middle of the night and haven't retrieved them from the bottom of the bed – something he'll no doubt kick off about when his foot finds one under the covers.

On my return to the bedroom, he mumbles something under his breath as I pop his mug down on his bedside table. I ignore him and make my way over to the window, sitting my favourite mug of coffee down on the wide window ledge. I watch in slow motion as the liquid sloshes over the lip and dribbles down the white porcelain and onto the freshly painted wood.

SHIT. SHIT. SHIT.

It forms a milky ring stain underneath, and my eyes stretch as far to the corners as possible, straining to see his reaction. He hates mess. More than anyone I've ever known. It practically makes his skin crawl to pick up a pair of my knickers from the bathroom floor. Which doesn't make much sense to me either when he's usually the one to remove them in the first place.

I wait with bated breath for the childlike tantrum to erupt, but it doesn't come, so assuming I'm safe to continue, I swiftly collect the cup without a peep and wipe the mess clean with my forearm. At any minute, I'm expecting him to yell at me to get a cloth instead.

Personally, I would have just left it and cleaned it up later. It's hardly the end of the bloody world, but he'd have had a fit simply at the idea of that being an option. We're just a bit different that way. But hey, they do say opposites attract, don't they? So, I guess we're perfect for each other.

I head into the cupboard at the bottom left-hand side of the bedroom and sit my mug down on the carpet. Considering what to wear, I start pulling at a few different tops and dresses, but nothing stands out the way it used to. In fact, I'm not sure everything that I once owned is even in here. I swear he threw out a bunch of my low-cut tops and replaced them with high-neck polos and long-sleeved dresses, but I didn't want to sound ungrateful. What woman would say no to a man buying her clothes? So, although at first, I was furious at the fact he had no right to touch any of my belongings I realised he just wanted to do something nice for me and I was acting like a spoilt brat. However, I did subtly suggest that perhaps next time he wishes to treat me, we go shopping together. Not that we ever have, though.

I pull at the collar of his football top, desperate for air. It's all so cramped and depressing in this little cupboard. Nothing gets a bloody chance to breathe in here. Including me. I still don't understand why my existence is acceptable in here but not anywhere else. The oak wardrobe in the corner of our bedroom is enormous. His hoodies and jeans barely reach the halfway split on the pole, leaving ample space for new additions. The same goes for the wide set of matching drawers that sit underneath his obscenely large television mounted onto the wall. Six deep spaces are sprinkled with more of his clothing: still nowhere near total capacity. There's so much room for my stuff to co-exist with his: plenty space for my bras, undies and socks at least.

Yet it seems that all those places are out of bounds. This is my domain in here. Everything I own lives here and has done since day one. I suppose I should be lucky that I have something resembling a walk-in wardrobe, I think as I look around. But the cupboard: damp, dark, cold, and only about a metre and a half in length is a far cry from Carrie Bradshaw's.

My knees click as I crouch down and tug at a plastic box filled with umpteen pairs of leggings. Tossing the lid to the side, I snatch the first pair of black cycling shorts I see, and then go on a scavenger hunt for a clean set of white socks in the pile of fresh washing that I'd previously pushed to the back, out of sight. A few days ago, George had asked me to put some clean washing away instead of leaving it sitting on the edge of the couch, but I really couldn't be bothered, so I made it disappear another way. As long as it was out of his sight, then it would be out of his mind, I reasoned.

I grab the first pair of undies I see and stand up to pull them and my shorts on. Finally, I tug at an oversized varsity sweatshirt I haven't worn in ages from a plastic hanger and pull it over my head and pull my hair free from the neck.

'What were you doing in there?' he asks as I reappear from my cave, fully dressed.

My god, it finally speaks. *It's a miracle*, I want to shout, but I don't. I can't be bothered with him this morning.

'I was getting clothes – obviously. What do you think I was doing?'

'Yeah, I guessed that much, but why? I've not made plans for us today. Why don't you come back to bed, and I'll make it up to you?'

My hand finds my hip immediately. 'OK, first of all, I don't need to do everything with you. I'm perfectly capable of spending time alone. And second, I told you last night that I was going to see that woman today.'

He sits up straight, back pressed firmly against the headboard. 'Eh? You said you don't believe in any of that shit. You've not changed your mind, have you?'

I shake my head in frustration.

He does remember. He's bloody at it again, and I'm not in the mood to pander to whatever game this is today. In fact, the whole reason I'm going to see her in the first place is because of him and his sudden personality change. I'm in dire need of sort some guidance, for god's sake. That's why I took a chance on the competition in the first place: I want help in getting him over whatever's bothering him so we can carry on with the life he promised me. The life that looked so different only just last week. I can't believe I've finally won something. It's not the fancy hotel in Paris, but I'll take what I'm given at this point. Besides, it's not like George is in the mood to be wining and dining me in a different city.

I avoid his gaze as I pull on my high-top trainers and tie the laces.

'You're leaving now?' he whimpers. 'Why don't you just sack it off and I'll take you for breakfast instead?'

I can't believe what I'm hearing. His moods are flying and down faster than a fucking see-saw. 'Yep, I sure am,' I reply, stuffing a scrunchie into my mouth as I scoop my hair up into a bun on the top of my head. I tut the fabric from my tongue and then secure it in place. 'And it's fine. Thank you. I'm going to grab a coffee and a croissant on the way.'

'Don't be ridiculous, you've not even looked at the one over there,' he says, tilting his head towards the window ledge.

I watch his face twist as he realises that my mug isn't there. It's still sitting on the carpet in the cupboard – also a huge no-no.

'If there's any left that isn't already on the window ledge,' he snarls.

Of course, he noticed my clumsy spillage. He seems to know everything these days. My eyes squint, trying to study his face, hoping for a glimmer of humour – but there is none, and as much as I wanted to climb him like a tree earlier, I can't believe how much I want to get away from him now.

Ignoring him, I grab my phone from the floor at my side of the bed and unhook it from the charger.

'It looks like a nice day, and I fancy an iced coffee,' I say, trying to keep a light-hearted and happy voice.

I can't help myself though, the sight of his face is making me want to scream but I can't do that, or I'll get called crazy again, won't I?

Instead, I resort to petty sarcasm. 'Anyway, I might meet some nice lamp posts with better conversation than you've given me all morning.'

He opens his mouth, but I don't hang around to hear what he has to say and march out of the bedroom. I'm not even going to apologise. He deserves a taste of his own medicine if this is how he's going to be.

'Blair,' he hollers, 'Get back here. I was speaking to you.'

I pull the front door shut behind me and speed out of the dimly lit close. I begin to run; I have no idea why. Maybe I'm worried he'll come after me again like he did last night and convince me to stay. It's so hard to resist his charm when he has it switched on.

Panting like a thirsty dog – and cursing George for stopping me going to his spin classes anymore – I come to a halt a couple of streets down to take a deep breath. I thought good sex was supposed to be great cardio, but maybe that's just a myth.

Staring up at the sky, watching the grey clouds darken, I pray that the woman I'm booked in to see will be able to help me fix whatever is wrong with my perfect man.

I don't really believe in all the freaky sort of stuff she probably does, but I'm willing to give her the benefit of the doubt. At the very least, I'll get some time to myself to regroup.

Although something deep inside is telling me that the way it worked out – how quickly I applied and received a response – maybe I won that competition for a reason.

THIRTEEN

CASSIE

Hands clutching his throat, Adam's apple visibly bobbing up and down, he jumps to his feet and begins to pace the length of the room. 'Can I…Could you…' He gasps. 'I need a glass of water.'

'Of course.' I yelp, immediately jumping to my feet. 'I'll get you one. No problem at all. I'll get it right now.'

I launch myself out of the room, flying across the hallway into my kitchen as fast as my short legs will allow. My body is rattling like a maraca from head to toe, but I manage to stumble towards the sink and grab the pint glass that I'd left sitting upside down on the draining board. I twist the cold tap and let the water flow down the plug hole for a couple of seconds before filling the glass to the brim. Gripping it with all my might in both hands, I bring it to my lips and gulp the water down quickly.

And now I'm coughing, spluttering. Choking. I can't breathe. My eyes are starting to feel too big for my head, bulging out of their sockets. I'm terrified that they'll pop out and roll onto the floor. My chest is heaving, and I feel like I'm being stabbed. What if I'm having a heart attack? The glass falls from my hands and lands in the sink with such a clatter, I'm surprised it hasn't smashed.

Suddenly, my intuition tells me to try something I've never done before. I don't know if I've read the idea somewhere previously or I'm just grasping at straws. Plunging both my wrists under the icy water that's still running, I hold them there, despite the sting. I focus on the liquid as it pounds against blue, pulsing veins.

After a few moments, I feel my heart rate begin to slow back down. Exhaling a wave of relief, I cup my hands and scoop a few handfuls of water onto my face. The droplets pour off my forehead as I hang over the basin of dirty plates and sticky cutlery. My fingertips find the edge of the worktop. 'I'm OK. I'm fine. Everything's fine,' I mutter.

Remembering why I entered the kitchen in the first place.

Finlay.

I lied to him. Why did I do that? And what the hell am I going to do now?

Two voices in my head are fighting to take charge. One wants me to march myself straight back into the room and confess. It knows I've just blown my morals to smithereens, but it's offering me a chance at redemption if I take heed. But surely that comes with great risk? I don't know how he'll react when I tell him that I made it all up. I don't know him well enough to gauge how short his temper is. Which makes me more inclined to listen to the second voice, suggesting an alternative solution. It wants me to stick with my decision, trust that I've made it for the right reason, and see it through 'til the end.

But who do I listen to?

Collecting the glass with trembling fingers, I refill it with fresh water, twist the tap to stop the flow, and then turn on my heels and head back to the room. To do the right thing.

Thankfully, the first thing I notice before even stepping a foot back in the room is that he's sitting down again, patiently waiting for my return as if I'd just nipped to the loo and nothing more. As if he hadn't just entered a stranger's home to be told his missing girlfriend had popped her clogs.

Turning his head to face me, he smiles, seeming much calmer now. OK, this is good. Strange, because I definitely didn't expect this reaction from him, but nevertheless, I'm grateful for it. My rigid shoulders drop a little.

I tiptoe over to him and silently hand him the glass of water.

'Cheers,' he says, holding it in the air before tilting his head back and downing the lot.

'Are you…like, are you OK?' I ask cautiously.

He offers me a thumbs up.

I can do this. I can do this. I can do this.

'Finlay, what I'm about to tell you might upset you and need you to know, I'm so, so sorry.'

He clenches his jaw in preparation for long-awaited closure, staring at my mouth as my lips refuse to part.

'What's happening, Cassie? Please, I need to know.'

I want to explain as best as I can, but I'm terrified I'll say something wrong and the roof will cave in, trapping me under the rubble of all my lies.

'Finlay…I know that this will probably leave you with a million more questions than you came with, but I can only tell you what I know to be true and I'm sorry if I've made things so much worse, but I swear I only want to help you.'

That's the most important thing to remember right now, that Finlay needs my help to move on and live a happier life. I can ease his suffering. I can give him closure of some sorts. Even if it's not what he wants to hear.

'You came to see me today because you wanted answers on your girlfriend. You wanted to find peace, and I want to help you do that, so I hope you can forgive me when I tell you the truth.'

His brow creases. He looks as confused as I feel. Because I don't know why this is the voice I chose to listen to, but it feels right. It's what needs to be done. The universe is offering me a whole new world on a plate, and I no longer want to feel so empty, so starved.

'I'm very sorry for your loss. You were right, your girlfriend is unfortunately no longer with us.'

The room shudders. Darkness envelops us both. My eyes dart to the window, searching for light, but the sky outside is murderous. Rain begins to lash from the sky, pelting the glass like bricks. A flash of lightning, quickly followed by a crash of thunder causes me to flinch and instinctively I shield my eyes with my forearm for protection.

Finlay's hand grabbing mine makes my head twist to face him. As I lower my arm, my pupils widen, because I don't find comfort or safety in his. Because the eyes I'm looking into don't belong to him.

Before the storm, there were just two people in this room – and now, including the person standing behind his shoulder, there are three.

Fourteen

Blair

It wasn't too long a walk to my destination, but I'm kicking myself for not taking his car. If he's happy for me to drive it to his mum's, I don't see why I shouldn't be allowed to use it to go places I want. If *mi casa su casa*, then his car is also my car.

I decided to ditch the idea of grabbing a fresh coffee because the palpitations in my chest are pacy enough without the assistance of a caffeine hit. It's left me with ten minutes to spare and I just need some time to myself to get my shit back together after this morning. Finding a perch on a mossy brick wall, across the road from a row of sandstone bricked houses that have been converted into one-up, one-down style flats at some point throughout their lives, my mind begins to travel back in time.

George wasn't always so aggy, was he? I wouldn't have hooked up with him if he was, let alone agreed to move in with him so quickly. I still think it has something to do with whatever went on between him and Maria that day in her kitchen, but what I just don't know.

I bring my phone to eye level and allow it to recognise my face. I check the details on the YOU'VE

WON message and then go to the maps app. The blue dot confirms that this is exactly where I'm supposed to be.

Well, roughly. I'm looking for number twenty-two.

My eyes wander up a singular set of concrete steps, leading to the choice of two front doors: a brown one with what looks like a busted lock and a boarded-up window, and the other a weathered plum with slices of brown rust. The top flat looks quite eerie. There are no lights on and no sign of life thanks to thick, faded cream curtains that look stiff in position. In the bottom window, though, I can just about make out the shape of a headboard of a bed in the distance and no more.

That must be where I'm headed, I decide. There's no way it's the top one. You couldn't run a business from somewhere that looks like that.

The time on my phone's screen eventually changes to 10 a.m., so I hop up and swipe any dirt off my arse before I make my way across the road. With every step, I wonder if I'm doing the right thing. I don't know what good I think this is going to do and admittedly I don't have the highest of hopes, but what's the harm in giving it a whirl? It gets me out of the flat for a while – and it's a freebie. I wouldn't have booked myself in for something like this if it wasn't a competition.

I climb the handful of steps, form a solid fist, numb from the breeze, and knock loudly on the purple door. Now I'm here, I may as well just go with it and cash in my prize because it was either this or some sort of couple's therapy, I suppose. And I've never been big on the whole talking about my feelings thing – I doubt George would have been up for it either – so this seems the lesser of the two evils. Even if it is a bit bonkers.

Lighten up, I tell myself. It's just a bit of fun, at the very least. I might even receive some good old female to female advice and that might be refreshing. As lovely as my little love bubble with George is, and even if we don't need anyone else because we are a team, an outside perspective is definitely something I could use right about now. An ear would have been enough, though. I don't suppose I really needed something as extra as a crystal ball.

After a few minutes of waiting impatiently, I rattle on the wood again and then peek through the stained-glass window to the left-hand side where finally, I see a dark shadow approaching. The door is pulled open, revealing a pale, petite girl with scraped up auburn hair. I'm not sure if she's a natural redhead, or it's just a washed-out, shitty home dye, but physically she looks of a similar age to me. And yet, there's something behind her tightly held smile and old-soul eyes that look like she's lived a thousand more years.

For a brief moment, I hesitate, wondering if I've got the wrong address. Because she's not exactly what I was expecting. Dressed in a cropped salmon-pink sweatshirt and grey high-waisted leggings. Around her neck is black string, cradling a caged red rock and although she isn't quite the Mystic Meg I was expecting, I think that's the very reason I feel a lot more comfortable about doing this now. She feels more relatable to me, nothing at all like an old witch with a pet frog and a glass eye rocking back and forth on a chair.

She is naturally beautiful though and does have the potential to pull off the whole Nicole Kidman vibe in *Practical Magic* if she wanted to. I wonder if her outfit choice is a conscious decision to ease nervous clients, or it's just who she is. Either way, I'm not all that fussed because for some reason, just looking at her makes me feel warm and safe.

'Hey, thank you for coming.' She welcomes me inside and closes the door gently behind us before she steps in front and takes the lead. All the time holding that perfectly pinched smile. Like a mask that never slips because it's stapled to a face instead of tied. 'Please, follow me.'

As we enter the room on the right, the first thing I notice is the large table in the centre of the room. It could easily fit a family of ten around it at Christmas, but there are only two chairs positioned at each end of it, which seems a colossal waste of something so grand. I'd have have had that thing tossed in a skip and replaced it with something a bit funkier, but each to their own, I suppose. There's also an old fireplace, seemingly redundant though judging by the dust it's collecting, so I'm not sure why she's not done something about that either, but at least she has a fairly modern television hanging above it.

I squint at the screen and spot the YouTube logo. Some sort of zen tune is playing, and I hope for the love of God she at least pays for a subscription because I'm not here to listen to any ads.

The room really isn't what I expected, but then again, I'm not sure what I thought was waiting for me. Walls painted red with blood? Hieroglyphics or satanic symbols sprayed on the floor underneath us? The smell of tobacco and whisky clogging my nostrils as I followed a pathway lit up by candlelight? Nope, none of that in here. At worst, it's just a little outdated, but

I'm OK with that, relieved that it's nothing the stereotypical bullshit you see on the telly.

Perhaps this wasn't a waste of time after all.

She gestures for me to take a seat closest to the door, and I happily plonk my arse down where I'm told, dropping my phone down on the table with an accidental thud that makes her jump.

Sorry, I mouth, as I watch her shuffle towards the window.

Pulling out her own chair, I notice that she perches on the edge of it instead of settling in comfortably. She almost seems a bit scared to relax around me and I'm not sure why. Have we met somewhere before, and I've been rude to her? Maybe she caught me at the bar on an off night because of some prick I'd been dating.

I want to ask her, put her at ease, but before I get a chance, my phone starts to vibrate against the wood.

George.

His name continues to flash across the screen and even though I'm looking down, I can I feel her eyes on me. Not wanting to look rude, I quickly decline the call, swiping down the option for aeroplane mode so there's no way it will go off again.

'You can record this reading if you want. I don't mind,' she says as our eyes meet. Although, I get the feeling that she'd actually rather I didn't.

I decide that I will for a couple of reasons: I've never done this spooky shit before and my memory is terrible at the best of times, so I want to remember everything she says.

And I guess I'd also like to have something for George to listen back to if there's some worthwhile advice in there.

I tap the screen. ‘OK, I’m good to go. It’s recording now.’

‘Great. It’s lovely to meet you. Blair? I assume.’

I smile with confirmation, although it hardly takes special powers to figure that out.

I hope she doesn’t talk like Mary Poppins through all of this.

‘Before we continue, I have to let you know that the service I’m providing isn’t a replacement for any professional medical advice. I’m not a doctor nor a therapist. Nothing like that. OK?’

‘Yeah, that’s cool. Whatever,’ I agree, tapping my red nails, as chipped as the wood.

She picks up a deck of cards that are sitting in front of her and begins to shuffle, but her movements are messy, chaotic. Like she doesn’t really know what the fuck she’s doing. Performing a magic trick that she hopes she’ll nail one sweet day. I hope she’s joking, and it’s actually all part of the act.

Suddenly stopping from her hand jive, she lifts her chin, and our eyes are sealed together from across the table, firmer than a chain of bricks.

‘Oh my god, I’m sorry. I almost forgot. I’m Nova, by the way. But I’m sure you already knew that.’

FIFTEEN

CASSIE

My jaw falls to the floor, but no sound comes out. I return my focus to Finlay's handsome face, but he's strangely calm and composed. Did he not feel the room shake? Can he not sense an intruder?

Rubbing my eyes with the heels of my hand until I'm seeing orbs of colour, I fully expect the figure to have disappeared when I dare to reopen them. My left eye flicks open first and my stomach swirls.

She's still here.

But how do I know that this is even happening? Especially if I'm the only one who knows she's here. What if it's just all in my head?

I've never witnessed a spirit or a ghost before. And that's what she must be, because I most certainly did not invite her into my home via the front door.

Oblivious to anything else happening around him, visibly heartbroken, and turning pale with grief, Finlay blows out a long sigh. 'I knew it. I knew she was gone,' he says blankly. 'Can you tell me anything else?' he asks, trying to bring my attention back to him instead of the space behind him.

The figure steps closer, places a hand on his shoulder, but I'm the one who jumps at the touch.

Is she here for him? Is this unknown person his missing girlfriend?

'Oh. You mean, like…what happened?' I gulp too loudly. 'No. I only managed to connect with her for just for a moment. I really am so sorry.'

I don't know what lie I'm telling anymore. Perhaps not any at all, now that she's here. But I'm not sure how much of this strange experience I should share with him. I've already stunned him with the dreadful news. Telling him what I'm seeing might be taking things a bit too far. He believes me, and for the very first time, I'm starting to believe in myself, too.

My eyes keep darting to both faces. I'm trying to study her as subtly as possible to avoid looking like any more of a loony. Her mouth is sealed, and a reddish light is seeping out of her porcelain white skin, but I don't have a clue what that might be. Her energy? Her aura? It looks aggressive, violent. Like spilled blood.

Maybe I should sage the room. Or myself. Or her. I don't know what to do. And how do I get rid of her?

There must be something stuck in my brain from one of those stupid books I've read, but I don't recall ever reading anything about how to banish a ghost from your house. I should have studied for this type of thing, but I guess I didn't ever see it happening.

'I'm sorry, I know this is difficult, but can you just…bear with me a bit longer? Please,' I plead with him as I close my eyes.

I try to do the whole grounding thing and force myself to calm down long enough for me to come up with the best course of action. The place I go to has no corners or edges, no doors, or windows, just a never-ending void. The room could be circular or square, but you'd never know because it stretches for miles and miles, and I try to shut everything physically around me out, but I'm failing miserably at Psychic 1-0-1. My emotions are too strong and unbearably intense.

But let's just say that this is Finlay's girlfriend, and that she has passed on to the other side – however that might have happened, that's not my fault. My mission – no, my purpose – is still to help him, regardless. Because even after telling him that she's no longer alive, he's still looking around the room like a lost puppy searching for her, willing her to return home to him.

What I cannot do though, is tell him that she might have done just that, because it might not even be her at all. I have no solid proof.

She could be anyone.

He groans under his breath, and I wish I could do something to ease his pain. I want to open my arms and invite him into my personal space, filling the gap in my heart that has laid vacant for so long and hold him tight enough that he'd never want me to let go. I'd grip the back of his neck while soothing and assuring him that everything is going to be OK now – for the both of us.

However, I have to admit that his reaction is quite peculiar. Because I did expect more questions. A lot more, actually. And if the shoe were on the other foot, I'd be falling over myself, begging him to tell me why or how. I wouldn't take no for an answer. But now we're just sitting here, both staring into space, and the sound of rain coming to a halt is creating a silence more palpable than any we've found ourselves in before.

I don't know what to do next but before I can come up with a plan, he suddenly pushes back from his chair and rises to his feet, straightening his hoodie at the cuffs of his sleeves and then strokes his stubble beard, seemingly deep in thought.

Wait. No. No. No. I begin to panic, because I realise he's preparing to leave me, and I feel like I've been punched in the stomach.

This cannot be how it all ends. And so suddenly. Something was supposed to happen after I followed through with my gut instinct and told him that his girlfriend was no longer with us. OK, yes, it was technically a lie, but it was supposed to bring us both together, fated to unite.

And then she actually appeared.

Or at least someone did. Didn't they?

Oh my god, please no, we're not finished yet. We just can't be. Not after all we've been through. After everything I've put myself through this morning to pass the universe's test.

Thrusting my hips back and jumping to my feet, my chair clatters to the ground as I stand to attention.

'You're not…' My voice wobbles, my eyes filling to the brim. Without saying a word, he ignores my pitiful cry and exits the room. 'Wait! Just wait a wee minute. Are you leaving? We're not done yet.'

I'm quickly at his tail, following him down the hallway that really should have a red carpet rolled out for royalty like him.

It feels like someone has pressed fast forward. I'm desperate to latch onto him, wrap my arms and legs around his body like a koala, and never let go.

Please don't leave me. Please don't leave me. Please don't leave me.

He reaches for the handle of the front door.

'Finlay, wait. Maybe you could send me a text? Let me know how you're getting on after the shock sinks in? Or if there's anything else you want to ask me. Honestly, anything at all, just get in touch. I'll be here for you.'

No response, only excruciating silence.

'Finlay?' I try again, desperate for him to say something. Anything at all.

I almost lose my footing as he turns around abruptly, now standing just inches away from me. My face is almost planted into his chest, and it takes everything I have to tilt my chin upwards so I can see his face, but when I do it's staring down at me with such scorching intensity that I think I'm about to topple over.

My body begins to sway back and forth. It feels like he's about to kiss me. This is it. I think. Where it all changes for the better. I lick my lips in preparation for our special moment, but instead of pulling me into him, he reaches his arm behind his back and pulls his wallet from his pocket. Flipping it open, exposing a bundle of twenty-pound notes, he points it towards me.

'How much do I owe you?'

I stumble back, my cheeks burning crimson red as if he just slapped me across the jaw. I'm so ashamed of myself. I can't believe that I created such a ridiculous fantasy in my head. I was so sure. Despite everything that had happened, meeting Finlay felt like my fresh start. My one shot at real happiness.

'Oh, my god. It's fine. I don't want anything.' I yelp, completely mortified and ready to throw up on his trainers at the sight of the first purple slice being pulled from the bunch.

It wasn't supposed to end like this. It wasn't supposed to just be a business transaction. I was supposed to be more than that, but I feel cheap, dirty, and utterly disgusted with myself acting so pathetic.

I can feel it stirring, the familiar darkness swimming around the pit of my stomach. It feels like everything I've been working hard to fix has all been for nothing. I've clearly not learnt a single thing from any of those stupid self-help books.

This might be it for me now, the end. Where I finally lose my mind once and for all and call it quits. I'm a lost cause. I never deserved him, anyway.

Considering my words for a short but agonising moment or two, he chucks his wallet in the air and then snatches it back with his left hand, returning it to his jeans pocket. He turns and pulls the brass door handle and there it is – his freedom and his grand escape. Far, far away from the wreckage that is me, Cassie Torrance.

It's still pouring down, but he shows no hesitation, practically leaping onto the top step without giving me a second glance, because he evidently can't wait to get away from me. The sting of it lingers, like tiny ants crawling over my flesh as he jogs down the three concrete stairs that led him to me in the first place.

Still, I refuse to look away because as painful as it is to watch him pull up his hood at the end of the path and then rest a steady hand on the rusty black metal railing that keeps the wild unkempt bushes at bay. I feel compelled to savour every last moment of him.

A voice in my head is screaming at me to shut the door immediately, lock it tight, dash to my bedroom, and never dare show my face to the world again but his side profile – ever just as glorious as his front – comes into my vision as he turns to face me, forcing me to hold my breath.

'Oh, Cassie, I meant to say – you could never upset me. Look after yourself, OK?'

My hand clutches my chest as the wind howls and with a heart stopping wink that almost brings me to my knees, Finlay Munro is gone.

SIXTEEN

BLAIR

Now that Natters with Nova and I have been properly introduced, she seems ready to get this thing going.

'So, I'm going to get started by mixing the deck around a little,' she says, continuing to shuffle the Tarot cards. 'Then…um, I'm going to ask your guides, ancestors, or just anyone in spirit really who wants to come forward and offer help by giving some clarity through the power of the cards. OK?'

Clarity. I ponder over the word for a few moments. Guidance, yes. But clarity, no. That would suggest I already have an idea about what's going wrong and why and what I'm searching for today is a simple yes or no answer for back-up. But I don't know what the catalyst was in the change that's started brewing between us. I know that we were love's young dream one minute, and that nothing had ever felt better. But now I'm wondering if that's all it was, just a dream? Something I was allowed to enjoy for a short period of time before it escaped and became forever out of my reach.

'Sure, sounds good,' I reply regardless of any fresh doubts, pulling my sleeves over my wrists. It's baltic in here, and hard to tell if the corners are filled with cobwebs or icicles. Goosebumps have started to form a line down my shins.

'Then, I'll pass the cards over to you, and if you could give them a shuffle too, that would be great. Oh, and before I forget – I need you to know that I don't talk to ghosts or anything like that. I only work with the cards. Is that OK?'

'Eh, yeah…that's fine.' I laugh. Because didn't she just say that she was going to connect with dead relatives or whatever? Sounds a bit contradictory to me, but no ghosts popping up will suit me just fine. Although I'm a non-believer, I don't want to mess around with anything supernatural. It would be just my luck to call it a lot of shit and then spend the rest of my life being haunted by a creepy old man.

Her brow furrows, and she looks slightly offended that I'm finding her so humorous, so I try to pierce the tension by making things a bit more normal.

'To be honest, I'm just here for a bit of girly advice about my relationship. No ghosts are required to pay me a visit today, so this all sounds fine.'

She offers me a meek smile before collecting the cards together and then placing them into her left hand. With her right hand now pressed on top of the pile, I watch her lips move as she closes her eyes, but none of the words are audible. Must be some sort of witchy ritual.

Her grip on the cards is shaky, but she still seems confident enough in her ability. She's probably done this so many times with people from all different walks of life. I wonder how she even found herself doing this. Especially so young. I really did think anyone who did this sort of thing would be older. Stranger.

Rising to her feet, she stretches over the table to pass me the cards and so I stand and extend my hand to meet hers halfway.

'So just shuffle them like I did. Close your eyes if you want, and while you're doing that, I want you to think of why you're here today. Just like, ask what you want to know. That kind of thing.'

I hold the deck in my hand for a moment and brush the edges with my thumb. Then, closing my eyes like she instructed, I picture George's face: handsome, chiselled, eyes emerald pools of love, and teeth that look like expensive pearls. So, I ask myself: What is it that I actually want to know? I haven't come here because I want to leave him, so that's not my question. But something has gone awry, and I do want to fix that before a life with my perfect man goes up in smoke. Basically, I'm looking for a solution to whatever rocked him so much during his lunch with Maria that's caused some friction between us – not a getaway car and a new life. I just want to go back to the one I thought I was getting in the first place.

'OK, I'm ready,' I say, opening my eyes and blinking my focus back into the room.

'Can you split them into three piles now? Just on the table. And then whatever one you feel most drawn to, pick that one back up.'

I do as she asks and then take a few moments to decide which pile to grab. How do I know what's the right one? Eeny meeny miny mo? I guess I'll just go for the middle.

'Now what?'

She flutters through my instructions like she's sung the same song many times, and I can't help but admire her. She's so different from anyone I've ever met. This woo woo shit isn't for everyone and yet she doesn't care what anyone else thinks about her. I can relate to her in some way because I've always tried to be different, never wanting to live by anyone else's rules, but she gives off the impression that she was born with an alluring uniqueness to her. It's just something she's just always been, effortlessly. And choosing to do something like this at her age is a pretty ballsy move.

I spread my chosen pile out on the table in front of me and then slide out three with my index finger without giving it too much thought.

'Go ahead and flip over the first card, please, Blair.'

I slide it towards me, flick it up, and then place it back down for us both to see. I notice that it's upside down, so I reach to correct it.

'STOP,' she shouts, and I pull back my hand as if she's just slapped it with a stick and drop my arm by my side. 'Can you leave it as it is, please? It's supposed to be that way. You're not supposed to change its position.'

'Oh,' I reply, feeling foolish. And also, a little pissed off.

As she clears her throat, a subtle shade of pink begins to spread across her cheeks. 'This first card represents your past and as you can still see – even if it isn't directly facing you – it's the Fool card. It's upside down or in reverse, for a reason.'

'And what does that mean, then?' I ask, unable to stop myself from pouting.

'It means you're…' She hesitates. 'Well, it just wants us to be aware of recklessness.'

I lean back in my chair and try my best to swallow her explanation without spitting it back in her face. She's coming across a little bit rude. As if she thinks she knows me well enough to make that kind of judgement on my personality.

'Hmm,' I reply as I keep my gaze on the card, because I don't trust myself to not get into a catfight. But also, because I suppose she is right in some way. I'd say more impulsive rather than reckless, though. I act in the now, think later. I'll crack open that bottle of tequila after three bottles of wine and worry about the hangover later, I'll hook up with the handsome stranger with no name and assume that I won't get murdered and will make it back home perfectly fine the next morning. I might even do a runner without paying the bill in a restaurant, but all of it is just for fun. I couldn't bare if my life got stale.

I take a deep breath and try to simmer my temper.

'I mean, maybe there have been times where I've been impulsive. But you said this card is about my past, right? So that's fine. I'm cool with that.'

Fiddling with her fingers, she decides to move on. Maybe she feels the tension between us now, too.

'Yeah, of course. I'm sure you're right. Anyway, why don't we turn over your second card? This should tell us a bit about where you're currently at in life. The present.'

I flip over my second card and wait.

'So, you've pulled The Magician, and he's upside down – because, again, he's supposed to be. But when this card is reversed, it tells me that there's a trickster in your life. Someone pretending to be something other than what they say they are. Does that make sense to you?'

'No,' I reply firmly and without any hesitation. Because it doesn't. For the first time in my life, I've actually found a decent guy. She doesn't even know what she's talking about.

Maybe coming here *was* a huge mistake. A complete waste of my time when I could have spent the day at home with George, snuggled up on the couch. I could have just sat down with my boyfriend like any normal person would and discussed our problems amicably and then worked together. He would have understood and kissed me and made it all better.

She bites her bottom lip as she stares down at the man in the card, as if searching for something positive to tell me instead, but she can't seem to find it, so I decide to give her a helping hand. Hopefully, I can speed this along and be on my way.

'There is nobody in my life right now that I don't trust. If anything, I've never trusted anyone more in my life, so I'm sorry, but the card must be wrong.'

Her chocolate button eyes begin to melt, almost dripping down her face. I don't feel bad though. It's not my fault she's not winning today at whatever fortune-telling bingo game she's playing.

'Sometimes…' she stammers. 'Sometimes we can't see things that are right in front of us.'

My jaw drops and I pull the knot on top of my head tighter. Who the hell does she think she is?

Leaning forward, I place both palms flat on the table. 'Nova, are you calling me stupid?'

Her eyes pop in alarm. 'No. What? No. Absolutely not. I would never. I just meant—'

'Look, forget it.' I stop her, holding my hands in the air. 'It doesn't matter. Let's just move on and get this over with, shall we?'

I can't believe I thought this would help and now I'm itching to leave and forget I ever came here.

She sniffs back a tear, wipes her nose with the sleeve of her sweatshirt, and nods, but the two of us are locked in eye contact, both refusing to let go.

Calm down, Blair, I tell myself. Because I didn't mean to make her cry for fuck's sake.

'Fine. Go ahead. Turn over your last card, Blair.'

With tension bubbling like an invisible cauldron, I flip my final card and reveal the worst card I think could have appeared: The Devil.

'Is this supposed to be some sort of joke?' I sigh, more than frustrated now with this whole ridiculous charade.

Her face has turned porcelain. I can see she's nervous and both of us know that one wrong word might cause either of us to crack. But The Devil? Really? I mean, come on. What kind of message is that? I'll be expecting my fairy godmother to pop up next at this rate.

'Blair. I promise, the card is no joke. They all have specific messages and if you would let me explain, I'll tell you what this means for your future.'

'Sure, why not?' I fold my arms tightly across my chest and scoff. 'May as well. I'm here now.'

'Somewhere in your life, at work…or possibly at home. You did say that you came today for guidance on your relationship, right? Well, The Devil wants you to know that something isn't right. And if we look at all your cards together, I think the message today is pretty clear.'

I lean forwards again, but still refuse to uncross my arms. 'What do you mean by that?'

Her bottom lip wobbles and she bites down hard to calm herself. I've rattled her big time, I can tell. Maybe she's used to being the dominant one, the leader?

'So, your first card – The Fool – maybe you've not always made the best decisions in the past. Maybe one of those resulted in where you are now…in the present. What if that person in your life who might be up to something, someone to be careful with, is your boyfriend?'

I go to stop her, because I think I've finally heard enough, but she surprises me by raising a hand in the air, silently commanding that I let her finish.

'And maybe you don't want to hear that, even though the Devil card is warning you that someone is going to show you their true face in your near future. All those cards as a whole are pretty informative. But just in case you want any more hints from me or the universe, or whoever it is you believe in that you don't think is telling the truth, look at the Devil card again.'

I almost push my tongue through the inside of my cheek. I'm simmering with rage, but I can't lie. I'm curious about what she's talking about. What will I see if I keep looking at it? Will it change colour or something? This is ridiculous.

'Fine,' I say and lift the card into my hand, fully expecting another one of her freak-outs, but she doesn't move a muscle as a mischievous fourth card reveals itself, falling to the floor.

I push back, peel it off the floor, and turn it round to face her. 'Sorry, I didn't know there was one underneath. I did only mean to pick three, like you said.'

'No, Blair, it's not your fault. There shouldn't have been another card, but for some reason there is. And that's The Tower card. Which means there's something in your life you need to fix. Fast.'

Silence fills the space between us. I know there's something I need to fix, that's why I came here today. But you're not giving me anything helpful, I think to myself, and wait for her to carry on.

'Time is running out for you if you don't think smart. I'm sorry, but that's what the cards say. And I'm sorry you clearly aren't happy with my reading today, but you came here looking for answers on your boyfriend. If you don't like what you've heard, that's fine. But I'm warning you…'

She pushes all ten fingers through the front of her hair, taking her first breath in what I realise has been far too long. 'Be careful, OK? Just be careful.'

'Is that all, then?' I sigh, rolling my eyes. 'Am I good to go?'

I'm so over this and I spring to my feet and get ready to leave before she bursts into tears, and I feel guilty, and am forced to comfort the person who's offended me in the first place.

I make my way out the door and swiftly down the hall. 'Don't worry,' I shout sarcastically sweet behind me. 'I'll see myself out, Nova, yeah?'

She follows me but doesn't try to stop me. We both know this meeting is over.

I open the door and have the same urge to run as I did this morning, only this time, I want to run back home to George.

'Blair?' she says quietly before I take my first step outside.

I turn my head but keep my body facing forwards,

'Look, if you ever need a friend, you know where I live.'

Whatever, I think, and leave without another word, allowing the chilly wind to slam the door behind me.

I jog down the steps with my phone clutched in my right hand and press the stop button on the recording. I doubt I'll ever listen to that again. Or I'll maybe just play it for us both later for a laugh when I get home. Maybe that will even bring George and me closer together? He'll hear for himself the unwavering faith I have in our love despite whatever bullshit she tried to throw at me.

As I approach the bottom of the street, I see a black Volkswagen Scirocco, parked haphazardly, alloys scraping the kerb. One almost identical to ours.

Oh wait. Is that…But how did he know where I was? Again. I frown as I double check before I make a show of myself.

My head throbs. What is going on with him right now? I just wanted a morning to myself. It wasn't too much to ask.

As I approach the car, the window slides down, revealing what should be the best sight in the world: George smiling brightly at me.

Pouting, I cross my arms and tilt my hip forwards. 'George, what are you doing here? How did you know where I was?'

'Babe, I'm so sorry for this morning. I was just shattered and taking out my bad mood on you. I wasn't being fair. Fancy a lift back home?'

Taking a deep breath, I consider staying mad at him and telling him to fuck right off, but he's so convincing and knows all the right things to say. Plus, I really can't be arsed with the walk home.

'We can even go via the coffee shop that has your favourite mini croissants?' he teases with a wicked glint.

He's such a bastard. He knows I can't stay mad at his beautiful face for long. And bribing me with carbs and coffee is a no brainer. Deep down, he really is just so fucking adorable, and exactly what I need. I'm sure whatever is going on with him is just a phase and will pass soon.

Yanking the scrunchie from my head, allowing my newly highlighted hair to fall out that messy way he loves, head around to the passenger side and pull open the door and get in. 'Fine. Seeing as you've found the ability to drive for yourself again instead of acting like little Miss Daisy, take me home, please, Driver.'

After I click my seat belt in place, he lunges towards me and forms a fist in my hair as he presses his forehead against mine.

'My morning sucked anyway,' I whisper into his mouth after locking with his delicious lips. 'I won't be back here or anywhere like it ever again.'

Cupping my chin with his free hand a little too firmly, he grins, and I know that he thinks he's won. That he has me in the palm of his hand.

'Good,' he states. 'Because I won't let you leave me ever again.'

THE UNKNOWN

She starts and stops, over and over, but refuses to let fear take over. Writing things down is something that her weary body feels compelled to do. Her hand, gripping the plastic so tight it almost cracks, is desperate to purge the memories from her mind. Almost as if she were possessed.

Even though she knows the only person likely to ever read her words will be him, in this moment, she is completely in control of the narrative. Her story cannot be twisted by his manipulations if she's not around afterwards to hear the review.

Telling the truth – as she knows it – is the last thing she can do to bring herself peace before she finally escapes his bird cage. Her departure is approaching, one way or another, and she's more than ready to fly high. Out of sight, out of mind. However, writing to a blind audience is harder than she thought. Revealing her deepest, darkest thoughts and memories feels like a dagger being plunged into her heart with every full stop.

And yet, she's doing it, regardless. Her thoughts are bleeding out onto the page in a manic, but exhilarating fashion because today reminded her of one particular Christmas they spent together. There was no mistletoe, no pink fingers linked together in a shared pocket, as they had done many times before.

Sitting cross-legged on the couch, her attention briefly moves to the window. It's a gloomy afternoon, with a slice of moonlight already visible in the sky, and just like most winter months in Glasgow, the rain is lashing down from the heavens.

The weather today was her starting point, her catalyst in finally putting pen to paper. It felt like someone was throwing stones at the glass, appropriately fitting to the constant thud between her eyes. As if a light bulb had flickered above her, she realised that she didn't need to start at the beginning. All she had to do was write what felt painful, regardless of chronological order. And it was for the best, because going back to the start might have ended her life there and then. All that was once good in their relationship feels like a very cruel and warped fantasy, and she's not sure anymore if anything at all between them was ever real.

Thinking back to the time when she attempted to lose herself in the silhouettes of houses that blurred her vision as they passed by at lightning speed. The rain – awfully similar to today – was pounding heavily on the tracks with no sign of stopping as they inched one step closer from Edinburgh to Glasgow. She'd hoped that the two of them might have a romantic day. Like they used to. She hoped they would weave their way through the sparkling energy of the crowds, visit every single stall regardless of what it sold, and maybe even pick a ridiculous souvenir to hang on their tree. She wanted to devour a bratwurst topped with ketchup, mustard, and fried onions, and then drink hot chocolate from a disposable cup. She imagined savouring the feeling of warmth as it slid down her throat, mingling with the pure intoxication of being in love.

He had promised so much. A shot on the big wheel, perhaps even ice-skating. She couldn't contain her excitement, bursting at the seams with optimism as they donned their warmest jackets and matching bobble hats early that morning.

Today, all she could think of was his thunderous face when the train home shuddered back to life.

The signalling errors that day were a blessing and a curse. She was able to drift away from her painful reality and imagine the lives of other people, much happier than her own. Staring into amber lit windows, noticing the warm glow of various sized Christmas trees, she could see no faces, so she painted her own picture-perfect couple with her mind's eye. Perhaps they were snuggled up on the couch with a Saturday *Night Takeaway* – on the telly and on their plates. They might even have been sharing a drink together, finding themselves unable to keep their hands to themselves. Any scenario at all felt sweet to taste, but it also reminded her how bitter her own was.

At the Edinburgh market, after a tense wait in an hour-long queue, he handed over his card to a pretty bartender at the pop-up bar. He grinned at her as he accepted the two polystyrene cups of hot mulled wine and gifted her a charming wink, but when he turned back to face her, the edges of his mouth dropped. Handing her the cup, the one she never wanted in the first place because the taste reminds her of cough syrup, he erupted into a childlike tantrum about the price. As if she were able to do a single thing about it.

Starving after being rushed out of the flat before a chance to grab breakfast, she decided not to ask him for money to buy a bite to eat. He controls the finances, seeing as she no longer had a job, and it made her feel indebted to him.

Roughly fifteen minutes before they reached Glasgow, his sharp tongue confirmed his ever-growing spiky mood. Her final attempt to pull him out of his darkness was a total flop. Her voice too unbearable for him as he whipped out his earphones and blocked her jokes out. It was starting to seem like it was the easiest thing in the world, a magician forcing her to disappear as if she never existed at all, and as she finished up drawing a circle on the window with her finger, dotting it with two eyes and an upside-down smile, the train came to a halt. The pack of passengers scurried towards the door.

Spurred on by a crash of thunder, she prepares to delve much deeper into the moment, dig the bones back up, but just as she removes the end of the pen from her clenched teeth, her body turns to ice. The front door clicks and blows in a gust of wind that slams the living room door shut. Dropping the pen into the middle, she slams the purple book shut, leaps to her feet, and thrusts it under the base of the couch.

Slowing her breath purposefully, she prepares to exit the living room with one last thought: He, too, sped away from her, without a single glance behind, leaping out the door, and onto the platform. And with one last train to catch back to the Southside, not to the mention the final walk back to the flat, she wishes she'd made a run for it with the other passengers when she had the chance.

She could have disappeared into the crowd and never have to step foot through the front door to her suffocating cage ever again.

Still, even with all the awareness in the world that something felt very wrong, who could have predicted the night ending the way it did?

PART TWO

"Perhaps when we find ourselves wanting everything, it is because we are dangerously close to wanting nothing."

– Sylvia Plath

THE UNKNOWN

She feels the mattress beneath her shift as he slides out silently, creating more space between them. It should, she supposes, make her feel rejected that he'd left the room without planting a kiss on her forehead, something that was once as normal and as habitual as breathing. But now, it's only when he's gone that she's able to relax her shoulders, unclench her fists, and lower her guard.

She stays lying on her left side facing the window, knees tucked into the foetal position. She hasn't moved a muscle since last night's fight. Her tears were invisible to him as they rolled down her cheeks. The bed bobbing up and down to the beat of her sobs didn't even make him flinch. Not because she so expertly managed to disguise her feelings. She doesn't even try to anymore, because there's no point. He doesn't care. If anything, he gets a sickening kick out of it.

She'd had her reservations about moving in together. She had so much stuff, couldn't imagine it all fitting in the two-bedroom flat, especially since one was completely dedicated to his passion of health and fitness. But he'd promised that he'd convert it into a spare room once she was settled. Somewhere for her belongings and trinkets to exist freely. He gushed about how he couldn't wait for her to add her own touches to his new pad, transform it however she saw fit with a lick of paint here and a few framed photos there. She dreamed of bohemian coloured duvet sets and a brand-new bed frame. one of those really snazzy ones with the skyscraper headboards. He said it wasn't going to be just his home, but theirs, and the start of a very long and blissful life together.

She pictures the journal in her mind's eye. tucked away in a place she hopes he'll never find. The pen is still to touch paper because she can't quite figure out where her starting point should be. She might not have enough left time to write everything down from start to finish…whenever that is. But she knows the end is near. She can't carry on like this for much longer.

Perhaps she should structure her thoughts like a memoir? A new chapter for each new gruelling event, she thinks, tossing the idea around in her head like a ping-pong ball. It feels like a good plan, but she doesn't know what parts are the most important, what sentence might save her from disappearing into the abyss.

Today is a good day for her to start, because he won't want to have breakfast together as punishment for last night. Little does he know. she feels more rewarded by the snub than put out. She's relieved, grateful, and will stay under the white Egyptian cotton covers until she hears the door slam shut. Only when she is one-hundred and ten per cent sure that she is out of his reach will she dare start to tell her truth.

SEVENTEEN

CASSIE

It's been two excruciating weeks since Finlay Munro walked through my door, and like the Fresh Prince of Bel Air, he well, and truly flipped my word upside down – but in the most heart-wrenching way, ever.

Of course, I haven't heard a peep from him since. I mean, why would I have? The poor man probably ran for the hills after I closed my front door. And who can blame him?

I've really been struggling to find a real reason why I should bother carrying on. With everything I mean, not just readings but my sorry excuse for a life because once again, I'm completely alone. Even *she* – whoever *she* was – has gone, too, rendering me one-hundred per cent useless.

Although, I'm not sure why I'm even so surprised. It's hard to believe she was ever here in the first place because the only things I see now are my hopes and dreams, exploding across the galaxy of my mind. *Natters with Nova, hah. Nothing but nonsense,* I hear over my own, personal tannoy. More like a supernova. a poor star on its last legs, exploding, dying.

I really thought this gig would be the turning point for me. I've waited for enough rusty copper tips to last me a lifetime. No more bunny-hopping from one dead-end, corrupt, corporate disaster to another. My stomach flips: I still gag whenever I think about my stint in retail. Innocently being sent to check the fitting rooms for empty hangers – a telltale sign of shoplifting – only to discover that someone had felt the urge to take a gigantic shit in the booth. And then, for a reason I'll never understand, thought it was acceptable to wipe their arse with the swooshy curtain.

I couldn't handle life as it was any longer and I realised that it didn't matter what my role was because the tune of not belonging always played in the background. All I could do was cover my ears as I stumbled my way through each day. And just when I thought I made it, Sunday would always rear its ugly head, and the minute I dared open my eyes on the supposed day of rest, my guts would launch into a furious battle with my brain. Often, I'd projectile vomit like a creature from *The Exorcist*, but I always saw every hour as it edged closer to another painful Monday morning,

I baulk again, stopping myself from diving too deep into the soiled sanitary pads that wallpapered the dressing room mirrors.

The wooden door to my bedroom creaks open, and Luna pokes her nose through the gap. The tiny pink love-heart twitches as she nudges her head through, gauging the space until she spots my body under the covers and barges her way in, regardless. Without a shadow of timidness, she struts her way across the room, nails clip-clopping against the uncarpeted floorboards. It sounds as if she's wearing a pair of high heels. I imagine that they'd be skyscraper killer stilettos because she's got such a sassy personality, but her stumpy legs would undoubtedly see her with a few sprained ankles after a night on the prowl.

Still, she'd always get back up. Unlike me. I know it's crazy to be jealous of a cat, but the resilience she has reminds me of all the traits I lack.

As she gets closer, my mouth breaks into the tiniest of smiles, cracking the dry skin on my lips. A genuine moment of happiness feels so unnatural to me, but Luna always has this magical touch when it comes to lifting my spirits, even if just a little. Sometimes, after my own sobs have bulldozed me into a state of submission, I find myself struggling to feel anything at all.

Well, that's not entirely true. I know something is there, but it's almost as I become…I don't know, numb. My pathetic excuse for a body is nothing but a hollow shell taking up space on a beach that plenty of people would fight tooth and nail to live on. All those glistening grains of sand that look so beautiful under the sunlight don't feel so pretty to me, and the ocean in the distance is really where I long to be, swept up, and washed away.

However, Luna's unconditional love keeps attempting to thaw away at the coldness in my heart. Sometimes I do nothing but gaze at her while she's fast asleep, snoring, and can't hold back the tears. I really do love her so much. The feeling is genuine, raw, heart wrenching, and probably the only thing that's kept me here for this long. As close to a guardian angel as possible, if they even exist. Luna had been abandoned by her previous owner, completely discarded, as if she was nothing but an old toy and left to fend for herself. It made me feel sick.

I'd never had a pet before and didn't know if I was even capable of looking after another living thing because I could barely look after myself…but she had nobody, just like me.

Pouncing up onto the bed, trampling all over the purple-coloured elephants on my new duvet set, she climbs up my legs until reaching my chest. I'm grateful that the bohemian design arrived just in the nick of time, right before my morning reading with Finlay. It's almost like I knew I'd need the comfort beforehand.

Lifting one paw in front, she taps the back of my laptop, urging it to move out of her way. I was watching a documentary on YouTube about something called a *Spiritual Awakening*. A balding man with large circular retro glasses and a long beard was standing on a stage as he explained how to spot the signs that one was happening to you.

From what I've gathered so far, it's when your life feels as meaningless as an empty crisp packet. Sounds pretty accurate to me, because all I've done today is flick through all his uploads and ram each word down my throat with a large lump of cookie dough ice cream.

When I don't remove the obstacle between her and a cuddle, she lowers her head and rests her chin on the screen. I scratch her head as a token of consolation, and she snorts a puff of frustration right back, but nevertheless she decides to stay.

Now that's loyalty, and the only kind I need. I was stupid to wish for anything more. It's always going to be this way. Just me, the voices in my head, and Luna. No boyfriend, no friends – not even a friend with benefits.

I look around my bedroom, situated at the front of the flat, next to the door that has two robust locks. And a chain. Just to be extra safe.

Despite spending most of my time in it, I've never quite liked this room. Especially the fact that it's right at the front of a ground-floor flat. Even with the buffer of concrete steps, I feel like I'm practically in the middle of the road. I've tried my best to make it feel better and more like a sanctuary, but no matter how many crystals I display or how many smelly sticks I light, I can't escape the feeling that I'm completely exposed to prying eyes. Not to mention, an easy target for disgruntled customers. That I've managed to make a grand total of two of, now, for god's sake.

A single tear slides down my cheek, and I wipe it away with the back of my hand. Pulling the laptop over with a sniff, I chuck it onto the empty space beside me.

I can't grumble too much, though, because the rent for this place is cheap as chips, and the previous tenant left loads of their stuff behind: cupboards full of plates, pots, pans, and utensils. In fact, it was surprisingly easy to secure this place. I saw an ad online and exchanged a few messages with the owner. I didn't need to meet up with anyone or provide any references and a key was left for me under one of the plant pots along with a contract that although didn't look the most official, promised that the flat was mine if I signed on the dotted line and left it in an envelope on my doorstep for them to collect.

My fingertips find the side of the bed and start tapping on the wood, breaking the silence around me. I notice through a crack in the curtain that the street lights are now glowing amber. I'm not sure what time it is because lately the seconds have felt like minutes, and the hours have felt like days. I'm currently surrounded by empty brown McDonald's bags, unwanted Chinese food that's growing furry fungus, half-empty cans of Irn Bru.

Meowing and stopping me from spiralling, Luna pads her way up to my face, tilting her head, and rubbing it gently against mine. Her glossy black fur tickles my nose and I inhale her warmth and try to tune in to the radio waves of her soothing purr. She always knows when I'm struggling, and I think there might just be something witchy in that because aren't cats supposed to be spiritual companions? Like in *Hocus Pocus* or *Sabrina the Teenage Witch* – that kind of stuff.

And yet, as much as I'd like to believe that she has a sixth sense, and that we're divinely connected, I'm only holding on to that last bit of hope by a thread. She probably only keeps coming back to me because I feed her.

Desperate for another distraction, as I search for my phone, I catch a whiff of my incredibly ripe armpits. Should wash, won't wash, because…what's the point?

I fumble around beside me but it's not there, so I nudge Luna back a little and reach one arm down the side of the bed, where my fingers grab onto the charging cable, still connected to the handset that I must have attached at some point. It seems pointless having a phone at all when I don't have anyone to talk to.

Leaping like a gazelle from the bed, she parks her bum on my phone before I have a chance to snare it and proceeds to smother it with her tummy.

'What is it, baby? Why are you down there?' I ask her.

My voice is hoarse, almost unrecognisable after being switched off for so long and I wonder if she doesn't recognise it, and that's why she refuses to budge and continues to stare up at me with large piercing eyes, not moving an inch.

'Come on, beautiful girl. Let me have it.'

I slide my hand underneath her fur as gently as I can, but the intrusion still causes her to scarper, and I watch the tiny orbs of dust fall through the air in her wake.

I wonder if that's how spirits are actually visible to us. I've heard of them appearing in photos and people claiming they're signs of loved ones and to be honest, that's probably a lot more likely than the stupid fantasy I created in my head two weeks ago.

Claiming the device, I bring the screen closer to my eyes, but they're so dry and gritty that I can't really see. I rub my eyes, tossing my phone between my hands to do so, and as the haze clears, it leaves something incredible in its wake.

I have an unexpected notification. *One new message request*.

EIGHTEEN

CASSIE

My fingers are stiff and achy from the chill in the air. My phone feels much heavier than normal as I hold it in the palm of my quivering hand. There's no reason for me to receive a message from anyone because I cancelled any clients I had booked for the future. I even thought I'd successfully put a stop to any new enquiries by disabling my Facebook page entirely, removing *Natters from Nova* from the universe, as swiftly as Finlay Munro disappeared from mine.

I pull my bobbly dressing gown back over my shoulders and slip my arms through the sleeves. The temperature in the room has plummeted. I'm used to low heat from living in an older building. A one-up one-down, on a dull and never-ending street. As beautifully vintage as it might feel to live in one, the ridiculously high ceilings mean that it takes quite some time for the rooms to heat up, but there should be no chill right now. I'm sure I switched the thermostat back on this morning. It felt like a treat because shortly after Finlay Munro left that awful day. I flicked the switch to the boiler, turning it off. I knew where I was headed, was all too aware that I wouldn't be surfacing from my bed for some time.

Logically, I thought I'd save some money. I do have enough stashed away to keep me tide over for a bit yet, because it turns out that having no friends, boyfriend, or family to love you or invite you anywhere stacks up a decent amount. All I've done for such a long time is eat, sleep, work, pay bills, repeat. I've not had to buy birthday presents for anyone, I definitely don't go on dates, and apart from the odd spot of retail therapy when I feel in the mood – because I'm a believer that a delivery a day keeps the sadness away – I stay somehow stay afloat.

However, the awareness that I don't possess an everlasting magic pot of gold is permanently lodged in my stomach like a concrete brick.

I wanted so badly to make this work, but I failed. I deserved to be punished for it too, so although financially it made sense to cut the power to the luxury of warmth, I deserved to wear multiple layers instead of shorts and T-shirt, and watch my icy breath perform its merry dance in the air. After what I did. Lying to a customer like that. Because that's what it was, wasn't it? A stupid lie. A complete fabrication as a result of pure selfishness. And for what?

A thought occurs to me that I might just order a new blanket for my bed and keep it off forever. Maybe even one of those fancy weighted ones that makes you feel like you've been mummified, which honestly, sounds perfect to me right now.

My thumb automatically jumps, ready to search for the familiar Amazon app on my phone, but when I type in my passcode, I'm reminded again of the unopened message request.

How did I forget about that?

I seem to get lost in my head so often. I don't know how to stop myself drifting away or why I do it in the first place.

Maybe I *am* mad.

Refocusing, I quickly tap the icon once before I change my mind. The screen begins to load, bringing my attention to the brand-new message request from none other than THE Finlay Munro.

What. The. Hell.

My body propels itself upright and the phone flies from my grip as someone just yanked from my grip, but I quickly dive to retrieve it, praying the impact hasn't smashed the screen. 'It's fine,' I breathe. 'It's fine.'

I'm so bloody clumsy.

My left hand splayed out on the floor is holding the front of my body in the air, and my other is shaking so much that I'm scared I might drop it again if I don't sit back up properly, but I don't have the patience to wait for a second longer.

The device still unlocked, I hit *accept*, and begin to read.

Cassie, it's Finlay Munro. I'm not sure if you'll remember me, but I just wanted to thank you for the reading. It gave me a lot to think about, but I guess I got what I came for. Anyway, I hope you're good? I was a bit of an arsehole the last time we spoke. I've not been in the best head space, but it's no excuse, so I don't expect you to reply. I just want you to know that I appreciate it. Cheers, Fin.

My fingers have turned bone-white from gripping the gaps in the floorboards too tight. I wince as sit back up, shaking life back into my left arm and cradling the phone in my right hand like it's holding some sort of precious cargo. I suppose it is.

I read and read, over and over, and then notice the timestamp telling me that the message was sent an hour ago. I immediately start to panic. What if he thinks I'm ignoring him? What if I've missed another chance to speak to him?

My fingers begin darting over the keyboard like a game of whack-a-mole.

Hey Finlay. I'm sorr—

I stop typing immediately, dropping the phone into my lap in alarm because three little dots now pulsing across the screen.

The wait to read what else he has to say fills me with nausea and when a new box of text finally appears I baulk.

Sorry, I know it's not cool that I'm double messaging, but if it's not too weird...I'd really like to see you again. Do you fancy a drink sometime?

My heart has stopped beating, I'm sure of it. I've finally died and gone to heaven. A stupid cliché has never felt more real.

But how can it be? Two weeks ago, I crossed a line that nobody ever should. I've been beating myself up about it ever since because I knew, deep down, the minute I allowed Finlay to believe his girlfriend was dead, I'd be betraying not only him but myself. I didn't think it mattered if I gave things a little nudge. Not if it was always supposed to be. But the second he disappeared into the distance I realised how terrible a person I really was.

I can try to justify my behaviour until I'm blue in the face, but I know it was wrong and I well and truly overstepped the mark.

The shame I've had to live with has spread through me like an ugly virus with no cure on the horizon. The side effects of guilt and self-loathing have kept me from functioning the way a human is supposed to, and my mind has refused to even entertain the idea of taking a shower. I've been rolling around in my own dirt, revelling in the crumbs of my midnight feasts, ignoring the sloppy beige stains of tea spillages on my pyjamas.

I run the tip of my tongue over my two front teeth and am disgusted at how furry they feel.

Although…I truly did believe there were clear signs from a higher power that wanted me to grab onto him and never let go. And I did see somebody. So, now, as I stare down at the message, I wonder if I didn't make such a huge mistake after all.

Before I can change my mind, I start to reply.

Oh hello, Finlay.

No, that's weird. It sounds too posh to be something I would say, and he's heard me speak, so he'll think the same. that I'm trying too hard.

I highlight the text. press delete and try again.

Hey Finlay. Don't be daft. I thought you were lovely.

I stop again because it's still not right. Staring hopelessly at my thumbs wiggling over the keyboard, not knowing where to land next, an icy shiver caresses my spine. *What if this is too good to be true? What if he knows I lied, and it's a set-up?* My brain screams the word revenge over and over, getting louder with every loop, and a familiar invisible hand is starting to crush my lungs like an empty juice carton.

I mindfully release my bottom lip from the grip of my front teeth because a light stream of copper liquid is beginning to trickle onto my tongue. I don't know what I'm supposed to do.

Glancing over at the embarrassingly large stack of self-help books, I wonder if one of them might have the answer. Some are written by doctors and focus on the clinical mind, and others are a bit more out there.

Launching myself from the bed quicker than I have in the past two weeks, I yank the purple book from the middle and send the rest tumbling.

The colour matches my bedspread and has silver iridescent stars sprinkled across the front cover that change colour depending on which way you look at it. It even has cute little illustrations of crystals and some other things, surrounded by the outline of weird looking eyes. It's not a self-help book as such, but it does have little snippets of quotes or affirmations from various authors. Surely at least one of them will be able to help.

As I sit cross-legged on the cold floorboards, I hold the spine in my left hand and strum the pages until my fingers stick to one. I decide that whatever page I've landed on, whatever advice it has to offer, I'm going to go with that. I'm going to trust in the universe, one more time.

Opening the book wide, I look down at the page my thumb is holding in place and gasp.

'Run, my dear, from anything that may not strengthen your precious, budding wings.' – Hafiz.

I discard the book over my shoulder and dive back onto the bed, taking back possession of my phone.

I can do that. Of course, I can. I completely understand what it's telling me to do. I'll run from this life and never look back.

Deleting my previous text attempt immediately, I start again. *Hi Finlay. Sorry I haven't replied sooner. It's been a busy day. And don't be daft, I'm happy to hear from you. It would be fun to meet up –*

I pause.

What if he only wants to meet up for another reading? Because he hasn't actually said it's a date or anything. He might not want to come right out and ask for one because I've already told him I don't know anything else, but this would be a good way of getting around that. Chancing his arm like the charmer he is. And who could blame him?

I need to know for sure this time what I'm getting myself into. I can't go through this rejection again, so I carefully load the line with the appropriate bait.

– but I only carry out readings from home, and I don't think it would be worthwhile booking another one so soon after the first. Hope you understand?

'There,' I say aloud, pressing send with fear filled fingertips.

Now would be a wonderful time to launch it across the room, and out of my sight, but my message is read almost instantly. The dots begin to dance across the screen once again, stopping, and starting without any pattern. My stomach is fluttering, but I don't know if it's from cute little wings or an array of red flags. There's no way of knowing if I'm going to enjoy what comes after I reach the top because I've never been on this ride before.

The bolt of vibration as his reply landing in my hand makes me yelp.

LOL. At the risk of sounding like a dick, I didn't actually mean another reading. I know it's wild and really inappropriate considering the circumstances but…I just thought we could hang out?

'Yes.' I hiss, punching the air like I'm in a stupid rom-com.

The book was right. I must run from the life I already have, escape from this hell, and dance confidently into the light. And with who better than Finlay Munro?

I'm doing this. I'm actually bloody doing it. The universe has spoken. Hafiz – whoever that is – has spoken.

I think back to some of the guided meditations I've listened to in the past and remember how they close the deal. There's always a strange saying – "and so it is". I've never really understood it before, but I do now.

Cassie Torrance shall go to the ball with Finlay Munro.

And so it is.

NINETEEN

CASSIE

Sleep wouldn't come to me last night. My legs twitched and jerked me back to life every time I even came close to drifting off because my stupid, overactive brain just loves to torment me and remind me of things that I must do before I can claim my prize, my dream life.

After staring up at the old Artex, swirling around the ceiling like an ice cream from the Mr Whippy, wondering how I was ever going to be able to reach the finish line, the clock on my phone finally reached 6 a.m. It was still dark outside, but I desperately craved a coffee to kick start my day because everything around me looked so foreign to my sheltered eyes that never witness a thing before 10 a.m., anymore. Normally, I would groan at the sight of a time I still considered the middle of the night, but today I decided that this bird will catch her worm. I'd get ahead of the game and give myself more than enough time to get up and get things going. And let's be honest, I needed all the time in the world to prepare myself for the date of a lifetime.

I expertly manoeuvred my body out of the uncomfortable starfish position that Luna had forced me into by plonking herself in between my legs and creeped out of the room like it was Christmas morning. The only difference between this occasion and my childhood memories of the twenty-fifth of December is that I still had a while to wait before I could unwrap my gift. Finlay Munro wasn't waiting for me in another room with a ribbon around his waist.

As I padded my way into the kitchen, I found myself smiling at the fresh Barbie-pink toenails I decided to paint at half two in the morning. One less thing for me to worry about today. That was a good decision.

Although, I'm still not entirely convinced that any of this is real. I've been pinching my arms all day just to make sure and even though I've shamelessly reread our conversation about a million times. there's no denying it – it's still all there: The big plan of action for our very first date.

I can't stop saying it. *Date, date date, date…DATE.*

After finding a couple of pods stashed at the back of one of the cupboards in the kitchen, I pulled out the Tassimo machine I was obsessed with for a week before getting over it quickly and hadn't looked at since. I completely forgot I had it, could have been doing with that on display for my customers when it was here all along. God, half a brain, and I'd be dangerous. But I wasn't too bothered, nor did I get worked up about it, because today is a special occasion, and I enjoyed being able to treat myself to something better than the old granules that had grown so stiff they really needed a shovel rather than a spoon to scoop anything out of the tub. Carrying my caramel-flavoured latte back into my bedroom, I sat down on the second-hand blush sofa perched underneath the window and stretched out my stiff – and extremely hairy – legs. Something had to be done about them for sure. There was no way I could go on a date looking like Chewbacca, but I also didn't know if I was getting too far ahead of myself. It's not like he was going to see them. God forbid, touch them. But I wanted to anyway because I had this new enthusiasm to tackle everything today.

I even pulled open one of the curtains a little for the first time in God knows how long, and to my surprise, there actually was nothing scary outside. Not a single soul was watching or waiting to harm me, and I felt a bit silly for ever thinking there would be. I'm not sure where that fear even originated from. All I know is that being by myself always makes me feel so on edge. It's not even just outside that I worry bad things might happen because anything could go wrong, and nobody would know. I could slip in the shower and knock myself unconscious. I could have a headache and go to bed after taking a few painkillers and die in my sleep. Either way, inside or out, I'd just be left here, forgotten.

Although, it could be argued that I've already been lost for some time.

I think I sat for an hour or so, gazing out into the world that was bathed in complete silence. My mind whizzed with trepid anticipation because I couldn't for the life of me remember where to start when it came to prepping for a date, so I flicked through as many YouTube tutorials as possible, hoping that I'd be able to quickly pick up the latest make-up tricks and hairstyles, all the while asking myself what the hell the point was when it had been moons since I last dyed my hair. I used to maintain my foxy red mane expertly, never allowing it to fade in case people assumed there was something wrong. Now, it resembles dirty tomato ketchup dishwater, and it would have taken a miracle to transform that in such a short timeframe. Panic started to spike my anxiety instead of the caffeine, but I tried my best to stay calm. I could only work with the tools I have – even if they were rusty.

It's been a very long time since I've been on a date – if you could even call my past drunken encounters that – but I've never been more nervous than I am for this one. Still, somehow the adrenaline of seeing the absolute GOD that is Finlay Munro for a second time has kept me wanting to charge on full steam ahead.

Eventually, the silence began to crack as a couple of cars started revving their engines, attempting to defog their frosty windows before crawling down the road and heading to work. I actually enjoyed watching it happen, observing how normal, and happier people started their day while I'd still be asleep till noon. I started paying attention to loads of things I never would have before: crispy brown leaves racing down the path, bushes swaying back and forth in the wind. I became completely engrossed in the life of a little grey squirrel that scaled the length of the wall across the road and stunned myself by hearing my own giggle.

I knew I couldn't sit there all day and the cue for me to get up and at it again was when I attempted to take a sip of my coffee and almost choked on the cold, thin film that had spread across the top. Trying to scrape the taste from my mouth was when I realised how furry my teeth felt. It had definitely been a few days since me and the toothbrush had been acquainted. Hauling my backside off the couch and out of my bedroom, I made my way across the hallway and into the bathroom. Grabbing the electric toothbrush that I spent way too much money on considering the number of times I've actually remembered to use the thing. I scrubbed each grimy tooth vigorously until I was spitting blood. It didn't feel enough though, so I also tried out the weird coat hanger-shaped tongue scraper thing sitting in the plastic cup between the taps on the sink. I bought it after seeing it had a bestseller label and thought it was something I should get but it kept making me gag so I ditched that great idea too.

Finally, despite shivering my arse off, I peeled off my sweaty pyjamas that had practically moulded themselves onto my skin and tossed them into a heap in the corner for me to deal with washing at a later date. All that mattered in that moment was that I stepped into shower cubicle and before I knew it, I was tugging the chord to the shower, and it sprung to life. Warm steam quickly began to fill the boxy space, so I hopped inside, pulled the glass door closed, and emersed myself under the hot water.

It began to feel like I was performing a ritual or baptism of some kind. I allowed the water to cleanse me from head to toe and imagined it was washing away all my fears.

I shampooed my hair four times, massaging almost half a bottle into my scalp because every time I thought I was finished, I'd find another matted patch of bed head. I ended up with quite the headache, but when I smothered my brittle locks with conditioner, it gave me time to realise that it was my own fault. I shouldn't have left it that long. I shouldn't have been taking such poor care of myself, but now that I was making an effort to fix things I decided to indulge in this rare moment of self-care and I left it to work its magic for a further thirty minutes and simply took the time to just be present in the moment and really enjoy the sensation of the water as it pounded against my skin.

I did it. I shaved my legs and everything else. Two disposable razors later and I felt like the smoothest of dolphins. And the best thing about it was it all felt so…easy. I considered myself reborn after shedding my fuzz like a snake does its skin because things like washing or getting dressed are usually so tough for me to do. I'm not disabled or rendered immobile. Physically, at least, every part of me works – but most days basic hygiene is something that I couldn't care less about. It's painful enough just to open my eyes every morning and realise that I have no option but to face another dreary day.

But not this day.

Releasing the final strand of hair from the hair wand, I stare in the mirror at my pitiful attempt at creating the bouncy curls the vlogger seemed to nail first time. I run my fingers through them all in hope that it will loosen them up because right now I look more like orphan Annie with her tight ringlets.

'Urghhhh.' I groan, tipping my head upside down and return to the mirror looking more cave woman than seductive siren. I'll have to just pull it all back into a bun and hope for the best.

The biggest hurdle of all, though, is still lurking in the background – substantially more important than what I end up looking like – and I've kept pushing it aside for as long as I possibly could throughout the day. I don't even want to hazard a guess at how long it had been since I've left the flat, but I know the answer would be much longer than I'd like to admit.

Why am I so weird? I think to myself and sigh.

What is wrong with me?

I didn't plan on isolating myself from the outside world. It just sort of happened, and thanks to modern technology, there really wasn't any need for me to leave. Not when everything I need can be delivered straight to my front door instead. When I felt like playing chef, just the simple touch of a few buttons would see all the necessary ingredients – in perfectly measured quantities for dummies like me – appear in my kitchen like magic.

Zero human interaction and an alternative option to the much more stressful task of hauling a trolley around a jam-packed Lidl or Aldi has become much more my thing. I suppose it just escalated from there, because the convenience didn't just stop at food. When my fingers were itching and I just needed a little pick me up, I could visit loads of different stores from the comfort of my bed and take my pick without someone elbowing me in the ribs for the last size. It's even really useful for when I get a spontaneous idea that simply cannot wait because most places offer a next-day delivery option.

Tonight, though, the one thing I want more than anything in the whole world means that I have no choice but to physically throw myself out the front door. And not just down the steps or to the end of the street like I do on bin day, but to the other side of town.

After checking I've turned every switch off at the socket, the last thing for me to do now is feed Luna before I head out.

I peel open one of her sachets and gag at the rancid smell of something that claims to be beef, but I'd seriously beg to differ. I fill her bowl to the brim with biscuits too – just in case tonight goes really well and I don't make it back until late. Sometimes, I think she mooches off other people because even when she disappears for a night, she never returns hungry. Her tummy wobbling and hanging low as she potters around is a telltale sign that she's made friends elsewhere.

Now, standing in front of the front door, I all of a sudden feel very hot. Not in an *I'm feeling myself* type of way, more like *I think I might pass out at any moment,* and I don't even have my jacket on yet.

'You can do this. You can do this. You can do this,' I affirm.

I never used to live this way. I used to be able to go out without my heart feeling like it's been suffocated.

Taking a few steps forward, I unbolt all the locks on the door and undo the chain and grip the handle, but I jump back as the piercing screech fills my right ear.

'RUN,' a voice hollers. It's not Nova, but the same one from before, the one I've only started hearing recently.

All right. I get it. Jeez, I think as I cup my ear with my hand like you would with a shell to listen to the sea. I'm going. I'm doing it.

And without any more hesitation – or opportunity for my mind to start playing tricks on me – I yank open the door and finally leave my flat.

TWENTY

CASSIE

Biting my nails, I glance around, still not believing that I actually made it here.

Really, I have Finlay to thank for the successful jail break from my home. Without him, I would never. At least, not anytime soon. Or unless absolutely essential.

We agreed to meet at half eight in a quiet pub in the heart of Shawlands and right now it's only a quarter to, so I'm here with plenty of time to spare. I didn't phone a taxi or jump on a bus because I thought the walk would do me good and the fresh air would ease some of my nerves. I'm glad I'm here so early because I didn't want to screw up my chances of impressing him by arriving late, but now that I'm here I realise that I've given my nerves free rein to multiply with the spare time. The skin around the nail of my thumb is stingy and starting to bleed from gnawing down on it like a hungry rabbit.

Pulling another napkin from a bundle I collected from the bar, I dab my forehead to prevent my make-up spoiling from the sweat I feel building.

Finlay suggested that we meet up at Ashton Lane, closer to Glasgow city centre. It's like the yellow brick road of the West End – but duller, less magical, and way too busy for the likes of me. On either side of the cobbles, you'll find different kinds of bars, each one joined to the other and whatever you fancy is what you'll get. A pint of lager? No problem. A fruity cocktail? Easy peasy. I've actually been quite a few times, but it was years ago, with my then best mate from college, Louise. We planned to get top marks and leave with a HND in the dramatic arts, but most of the time we found ourselves at the lane and ended up dropping the course with nothing to show for it other than alcohol poisoning and a fair few fancy glasses that we'd smuggled into our bags in the toilets.

I didn't want to go back there. I couldn't. It holds way too many memories and only a handful of them are good ones. Mostly I remember Louise sighing and clicking her heels impatiently as she held my hair back while I threw up all the tequila shots I'd hammered on an empty stomach. Or waking up in a stranger's bed to find forty missed calls and umpteen panicked and furious voicemails after I'd decided to hit the road without letting her know.

The main reason I don't want to go back is because I'm not sure I'd be able to handle reliving our final night together. She grew tired of my bullshit and decided enough was enough and turned the tables upside down by reversing the roles and walking away, leaving me behind without a heads up. My calls went straight to voicemail, my texts were unable to be delivered, and she disappeared from my Blackberry Messenger. I drank myself into a tizzy for two weeks straight and found myself banging on her mum's front door at four in the morning only to be told that she'd moved out and wanted nothing more to do with me. Or her. Or anyone else for that matter. It was the strangest thing.

The end of our friendship completely shattered me because she was all I had, my only friend. It's been so many years. Who knows what she's up to now? I didn't stay in touch with anyone when I left school because I never felt like I fitted in with their clique anyway, so it took me a long, long time to accept that I'd lost her, too. The fact that she was still alive but just didn't want to know me anymore only made the grief worse. Sometimes losing a best friend can feel worse than being dumped by a boy, and even though I had plenty of experience of being given the brush of, Louise's felt like I'd been stabbed in the heart.

Obviously, it was far too soon for me to be offering Finlay some of my red flags on a plate and I knew he'd want to run away from me too. So, instead, I checked online for some alternative options: closer to home and with fewer…ghosts. There were a few old men's pubs that might have been OK and the number of restaurants available was overwhelming. Most offered the option of visiting just for drinks, but it felt weird looking at them when he hadn't asked me out for a meal. Which actually I'm glad of, because sitting across from him with spaghetti dripping down my chin didn't scream *attractive* to me.

Eventually, I decided on a little bar that I'd visited a couple of times in the past. It was never very busy back then and located way at the bottom of the high street, so people tended to forget it was even there and thankfully – and much to my relief – he agreed with no disgruntlement. Maybe it even looked like I was assertive or knew what I wanted in life – a bonus point to me, but that assumption couldn't be farther from the truth.

Yanked from my thoughts, I'm startled as the door of the bar swings open. It batters the wall the same way it has done several times since I arrived. The cold draught snakes under the table and tickles my ankles, threatening to pull me under, too.

Since my last visit, I realise that not much – if anything – has changed. The place definitely needs a little sprucing up, and my bum can feel the sharp ping of each spring underneath the green velour cushion that lines the bench of the booth I'm sat in, but all of it, including the tang of ale, fills my nose with a comforting nostalgia.

Actually, I think, eyes squinting to be sure. The good-looking guy standing behind the bar, pulling a pint for a steaming platinum blonde with legs up to her shoulders might just be the same one who served me one too many Jager bombs in my twenties. Through no fault of his own, though. Party Cassie was a different breed to everyone else and nothing and no one would stop her from downing another shot when she had her mind set on it. She was completely feral, like a cat –

although I'm embarrassed to admit that Luna has more class than she ever did.

However, in hindsight, sometimes I don't know if I was more Nova or Cassie back then. I had way more confidence that's for sure, and that's definitely a Nova quirk. My mistake might have been channelling her too often because facing up to who I really was – actually quite dull and boring and introverted – was too painful to face. I guess it caught up with me in the end.

Glancing above my head, I spot the same bronzed chandeliers that have always hovered far too low over each and every table. They have always and still do look ridiculous because despite being so obnoxiously large they produce barely any light and the majority of the place is for the most part, in darkness and the only things really illuminated are the dusty cobwebs tangled around the bulbs that have probably barely ever been changed. The spookiness of it all I suppose is a perfect companion for the matte black wallpaper that's pasted everywhere.

A couple of feet behind the booth I've chosen, floor-length windows are fogged with damp and dripping with condensation. A spiky-haired guy in a band T-shirt passes by me on the way to the toilet, confirming that the floor of the bar is still a safety hazard with all its sticky spillages as he screams out the words to the barman: "fuck, close one there, mate."

My stomach begins to flip as I wonder if I should have chosen somewhere else. Cleaner, at least.

I take a sip of the drink I ordered when I first arrived and try my best to earwig into the argument between the couple in the next booth to distract myself, but the music is too loud, and I can't really work out what the problem is. Maybe I should switch sides so I can hear better?

'Cassie?'

The shock to my system freezes my body like an ice sculpture. No. No. No, my brain repeats, because it can't be. It's not time yet. Then again, he was early for our session, too, wasn't he? Maybe that's just his thing, punctuality? It's not the worst trait in the world to have. Far from it. I should be admiring him for it, revelling in what a wonderful man he is and thanking my lucky stars for even be in his presence. Instead, I'm just annoyed at myself because I really should have prepared for it.

A firm but soft hand touches my shoulder, giving it a quick squeeze, leaving my bare skin aching as he pulls it away.

It's definitely Finlay.

How long was I lost in my own world for? I didn't hear the door slam since the last time and it's the only entrance – and exit – of the place. But it must have done if he's here now.

Panic rising in my chest, I somehow manage to whip out my arm and quickly tap the screen on my phone that's facing upward on the table, bringing it to life to check the time. I immediately regret the decision because I realise that I might have looked rude. Or that I'm self-absorbed. Or that I'm not even bothered about our date, which obviously couldn't be further from the truth.

Oh no, what if I've messed things up already?

He slides into the opposite side of the booth with ease, almost like he's done it a million times, and pulls off his black leather jacket.

Struggling to capture each thought, I'm in no way ready yet for our date to begin, and my body clearly agrees. Goosebumps have started to stack up and spread the length of my arms and I suddenly feel very self-conscious about the strappy black vest top I found at the bottom of a drawer and tucked into a pair of high-waisted jeans. The top has faded in the wash and the jeans are a little roomy around the waist because I lost a few pounds after the morning of his reading. Food was the last thing on my mind at that point, so I ate next to nothing for the first week and then eventually started to shovel down junk food towards the end of the second.

That beautiful, sparkling, and mischievous grin beams at me from across the table.

'All right Cassie. How are you?' he asks, but I can't find the words to reply. I'm still stuck in panic mode.

I'm questioning every decision I've made today. I pulled on my favourite heeled ankle boots and stared at myself in the mirror in my bedroom for ages, as Luna always decided to do some zoomies around my feet. Although I wasn't happy with my hair, it didn't matter because I barely recognised myself. In a good way. I was proud of what I'd achieved. It'd been so long since I made an effort and not even I could deny that it was a vast improvement in how I usually look.

Still, I knew that he deserved more. Someone more glam, with more sex appeal. He's always been too good for me. I knew it the minute I opened my front door that morning and I still know it now.

What am I even doing here?

'I'm…I'm fine. Thank you. Sorry, I was away in my own little world there. You startled me.'

I try to laugh it off, make light of the surprise, but intrusive thoughts about how I should never have agreed to the date in the first place are now crawling up and down my spine like tiny spiders.

On the other hand, the almighty universe clearly thinks otherwise, or else he wouldn't be here with me now, right? He wouldn't have even shown up. So why can't I pump the brakes on any of the racing cars in my mind, competing with each other to see who can do the most damage?

Do I look pretty enough to be seen with someone like him? What if people judge him for being out with me? He's undoubtedly dated far better-looking girls than me. Surely, I'm a massive downgrade?

He's wearing a crisp grey T-shirt that looks like it's been spray painted onto his perfectly sculpted body. And that smell…wow. Surprising myself, my eyes begin to steady as I inhale his scent with a fresh, optimistic perspective. It's the same one from the flat that day, so powerful it left me feeling woozy. And I do feel a little bit like I'm swooning right now, but I think that's because the alcohol is starting to kick in, too, so perhaps that's why I feel a tiny bit more confident. More hopeful that I might just get the chance to smell this every single day if I put on the performance of my life tonight and win the prize of a lifetime.

'Just fine?' He probes in a jovial manner. 'Maybe we can change that? What do you think?'

Yes please. I want to scream.

I want to jump up from my chair and celebrate him even being here. So, yes. I think that's a great idea. I want him to change everything. Anything. I want him to make my life extraordinarily better, so I'd probably agree to anything right now, regardless of what that involves or what he desires.

Still, all I can manage in return is an awkward smile as I twiddle my limp paper straw between my thumb and my forefinger and take a sip of my drink. It dawns on me that I might look strange already having a drink and not waiting for him. But it was for Dutch courage. I don't have a problem or anything.

God, I hope he doesn't think I have a problem.

He nods his head, gesturing at my glass that's just about empty. 'What are you drinking? I'll get a round in.'

It was a triple pink gin with lemonade.

'Eh, I'll just have a small glass of rosé wine, please.'

He stands up, edges his way out of the booth, and gives me a peculiar look. 'A wine?' He laughs. 'It doesn't look like you're drinking wine.'

I'm mortified. My cheeks heat up like red stop lights, but I was just trying to impress him. In actual fact, I hate wine. I hate rosé wine, red, sparkling – even prosecco. The bitter taste of it makes my eyes water, and the smell reminds me of the ammonia in Luna's pee back at home in her litter tray. Not to mention the debilitating headaches that come on the following day that bring with them an obscene amount of paranoia. I thought it sounded classier than what I already have, but I've just made a fool of myself. Again.

'Well, I was drinking pink gin. I've just had the one though, don't worry. I'm not a drunk or anything.'

He tilts his head back and laughs again. 'Cas, you can have whatever you like. You don't have to try hard to impress me.'

My feet do a tiny tap dance under the table. A nickname, already? You only give people a nickname when you like them, don't you? And the only people to have ever called me Cas are my parents and Louise. Actually, they don't really like me that much, do they? But this feels different. I want to press rewind and play it over and over again until it burns my ears.

This isn't going so bad. Why am I stressing out so much? It's fine, I tell myself over and over. It's all going to be just fine.

TWENTY-ONE

CASSIE

Finlay heads for the bar, pulling his wallet from his back pocket and I spot the head of every female swivelling so hard on their necks that their skull might just roll right off and smash on the floor.

And I don't blame them, let's be honest, who could? But all of them are much prettier than me, far more glamorous, and worthy of his attention. Any of them would probably be a better match for him than me.

I bet he goes for Scorpio women. Fiercely independent, brave, and magnetic. Or maybe even Leos, with their lioness confidence and alluring seductiveness that probably make men fall at their feet. I know one thing: it's not likely that he'd go for a Cancer like me.

Apparently, my zodiac sign is ruled by the moon – whatever that means – which means I'm too sensitive and over emotional. Totally agree, too, because not many of my traits are positive. In fact, maybe I should ask what he is when he comes back. Then I could wait until he needs to nip to the toilet and use Google to look up his full birth chart and check the exact details of our compatibility. If there is any.

Then again, they do say opposites attract, right?

Desperate to check myself for any indiscretions, I pick up my phone and study my face on the dark, reflective screen. A couple of previously curled strands have somehow managed to escape the low bun I attempted to secure the chaos tightly in, with not one, but three bobbles. But all in all, I don't look too bad. The multiple layers of concealer I plastered over puffy purple shadows have done a fairly decent job, and the blush stick that I'd dotted across my cheekbones is somehow managing to pull off the ruse of a healthy glow, which will be helpful when I need to disguise any embarrassment that's likely coming my way.

Strangely, despite not having much to worry about at the moment, I begin to feel a little choked up. Because acceptable as I may look, at the end of the day, it's still all a lie, isn't it? I might look half decent on the outside, but if he could pry open my skin with his bare hands, I know he'd run a mile. It's a dark world of chaos in there that nobody can seem to stomach.

Even my own mum and dad couldn't wait for me to move out and get my own place when I turned eighteen. Sick of the sight of me moping around and had given up all hope that they could shake me from a trance that none of us understood. God, I hated them for so long afterwards, resenting their perfectly wonderful lives. They were much happier and carefree without me weighing them down, and if I had to see one more Facebook post of another four-week cruise, it might have tipped me over the edge.

While I struggled to top-up the leccy and fill the fridge, the only entertainment I had was watching my own breath in the tiniest of ice cubes in Glasgow that felt more like the wild west. Boarded-up windows, kids wearing Celtic tops charging at a herd of Rangers fans who'd invaded their territory, creating a mosh pit of green and blue, not to mention spatters of red where blood still remained on the pavements. There was even a regular bonfire as cars went up in flames almost every weekend.

It was for the best that I cut them out of the picture entirely. At twenty-five, I'd had enough of being angry and bitter about not having the perfect family that everyone else seemed to have and decided to just let it all go. Five years since I hit *block and delete* on every contact option available, and my parents and I haven't exchanged a word since.

I guess though, if none of that had happened then I might not have met Finlay, so maybe my life was always supposed to go this way, and I had to go plough through all the weeds to be worthy of smelling the roses.

What is it one of my books back home says: Everything happens for a reason? OK, let's focus on that then.

'Everything happens for a reason. I'm exactly where I'm supposed to be.' I affirm quietly, allowing this unusual burst of confidence to straighten my spine.

Now he's heading back from the bar holding a black round tray, balancing an array of drinks. My phone falls from my grip at lightning speed. He gently places the alcoholic buffet onto the table. A pint of beer, a large glass of rosé wine, a tall pink gin, and four shot glasses filled to the brim with a clear but undoubtedly deadly potion.

'Um…thanks. What is all this?' I ask nervously, only having planned to stick to a couple. My self-destructive party days are well behind me and I'm more than capable of causing enough carnage to my life without a single drop of alcohol on my tongue.

'Well, you didn't really know what you wanted, did you? So, I thought I'd give you a few options. I'm a nice guy like that.'

He's being playful, but it doesn't matter because the embarrassment is still flushing my cheeks. He thinks I'm indecisive, and that's hardly at the top of a man's wish list.

I pick up both the glass of wine and the gin from the tray and sit them on the table. 'You're right, sorry. This is all great, thanks. And yes, definitely very kind of you. Thank you.'

Still smiling, he continues to empty the rest of the tray and then tosses it like a frisbee onto an empty table across from us. Picking up my glass of wine by the stem, he holds it above eye level for a couple of seconds and then whips a fresh paper beer mat from his back pocket. Slapping it onto the wood, he sits the glass back down – properly, I now realise – and then repeats the process with the rest.

Sliding back into his side of the booth, he picks up the tiny glass. 'Shot?'

Urgh, no. Please no. I can't do that, I've not eaten a thing all day and my stomach still hasn't forgiven me for this morning. I know better than to drink coffee on an empty stomach. The acidity of it gives me heartburn, but food was the last thing on my mind today.

But he looks so enthusiastic, so eager in his belief that he's going to have a great night – and with me of all people – so I also know I can't disappoint him.

'Sure,' I say with a meek smile, reluctantly joining him by picking up my own glass.

Necking it in one, the liquid I can now identify as Sambuca, slithers down the back of my throat like venom, scorching my insides, and creating a tornado of fire in my gut that immediately threatens to come back up. Clutching my stomach, my chest lurches forward involuntarily and my hand flies to my mouth to stop me from projectile vomiting all over him.

Thankfully, he doesn't seem to notice my discomfort – although I'm not sure how that's possible – and directs his focus on studying the scenery.

'This place is…interesting,' he says hesitatingly.

I'm not sure if he's being genuine or sarcastic. Probably just trying to be nice, I suppose.

'Do you think so? I used to come here quite a lot, actually.' I'm feeling a little braver now. Chattier. The shot has loosened my lips.

'Oh, did you, now? Who with, dare I ask?'

I'm stunned by his directness, but I guess there's still loads to learn about him, seeing as we've only just met. And it's not abnormal for him to want to know more about me, either.

He takes a sip of his beer and licks a bit of foam from his top lip, igniting what feels like a lifetime of suppressed lust between my legs. I know the feeling well from the past. It's the exact one that always used to get me into some sort of trouble with undesirable men who weren't very good for me. Very Nova, little to no Cassie.

'Awk, it was a long time ago. With an old friend of mine, but we don't talk anymore.' I brace myself for more questions that I don't really want to answer, pulling the stem of the wineglass until the bowl is pressed against my chest.

He takes another sip of his beer and sighs despite maintaining a smile. 'That's a shame. I'm sorry to hear that.'

'It's fine.' I hear myself screech. I don't want to admit that the rejection still haunts me and show how little resilience I have. 'Honestly, it's fine. It was a long time ago. I hardly go out at all anymore, so it doesn't really matter.'

As strained as my bond with Louise was, and despite the nights I lie awake triple guessing all the different ways I might have upset her, it was nice to still have someone. Who do I have now? It's embarrassing. There's not one single person I can text or call when I get home tonight for a girly gossip with.

Which is why it's even more important that tonight goes perfectly. Maybe there's been such a void in my heart because it's been waiting for him all along. He feels like the only person I'd ever need.

Thankfully, he isn't interested in probing further, but as I exhale a breath of relief, he changes the subject to something much worse.

'What about dates? Is this your usual haunt for a spot of the old romance?'

'Hah.' I snort, quickly followed by bulging eyes as I realise I've just displayed a massive ick. 'Sorry, I don't know why I did that – but to answer your question, absolutely not. No dates whatsoever.'

'Cassie, I'm touched,' he says, clutching his chest and feigning flattery. 'I must be the chosen one, eh?'

You're *the* one, I wish I could say, but I don't, and instead try my hand at flirting a little.

'You never know, you might just be.'

Smiling, he takes another sip of his beer, all the while maintaining some serious eye contact. Returning the gesture, matching his body language with a genuine smile stretched from ear to ear, I stare back at him so intensely that he starts to turn blurry.

This is how it's supposed to feel when you meet the one. I know it is.

As the night goes on, we continue to bounce off one another jovially, losing track of time because we're lost in playful conversation.

My gift from the universe. My star-fated soul mate. My one true love. He's going to be so good for me because it's him I've been waiting on all along. He's the one and only thing in this world that could ever cure me. That's why nothing else has worked, because I hadn't met him yet.

I'd do just about anything to hold on to this golden ticket promising a much happier life, so come at me, universe, I think as I stare at his ass while he walks to the toilet.

I'm now more than ready to go with your flow.

Twenty-two

Cassie

As the night draws to a much too soon close, I sway from side to side, basking in all things Finlay Munro.

God, I'll never get tired of saying that name: Finlay. Munro. Finlay. Munro. And judging by tonight, it might even become mine one day, who knows? Mrs Cassie Munro sounds perfect for me. Still, as excited as I am to finally become who I was always meant to be, I can't shake this horrible feeling of inadequacy lurking just outside my mind's door.

On the positive side, I've learnt so much about him tonight: aging like a fine wine at thirty-four, doesn't, or can't, drive, – I'm currently unable to remember which one because I'm a bit drunk – but it doesn't matter because even without a car, he managed to make his way to his reading with me two weeks ago. As it transpires, we've been living quite close to each other all this time. Of course, his flat will be better than mine, what with having a mortgage and behaving like a proper adult. He's closer to the heart of everything and I wasn't even surprised, because it would be where someone like him lived.

The nightlife in the Southside of Glasgow is as glittery and enticing as the city centre itself, whereas my rented flat rests on the outskirts, next to Hampden Football Stadium. The dead-end street I live on still falls under the bracket of prestige on Google Maps, but there's only ever any buzz when there's a gig or a match on and people start ramming their cars onto the pavement. Even the flat above me has been empty since I moved in. Nobody wants it.

Finlay lives about a thirty-minute walk in the opposite direction, and there's no way I could have afforded somewhere so sought after as Battlefield or Cathcart, where crowds of people scurry the streets at the crack of dawn, taking their pick from umpteen local businesses to get their morning caffeine hit. You can have anything you want from places like that: flat whites, soya milk lattes, a roll, and sausage or a freshly baked croissant that tastes like it was made in France.

And he's super motivated, too, working all the hours he can teaching classes.

Oh shoot. I've just realised that I totally forgot to ask him his star sign. He was so keen to hear about all things me that I just got lost in the whirlwind of unfamiliar attention.

I hope I haven't overshared. Sometimes when you don't speak to people for a long time you tend to spill the tea without caution, not knowing if the person listening is trustworthy or not. I couldn't stop myself opening up to him in a way I've never done with anyone before. Not with my parents, never with any glimmer of a potential relationship, and definitely not with any former friends.

Luckily, I just know Finlay is a good soul. He would never use anything I've done or said against me and actually, our date has gone better than I could ever have wished for.

I can't tell you the last time I've been given a compliment – or at least a genuine one and not just a line to get me into bed – but he more than made up for the lack tonight. His tongue was almost unstoppable, lavishing me in one after the other, far more than I really deserve. I'm basic at best, a six out of ten on a good day, but maybe that's what will work better for him in the long run. Ditching the sassy high maintenance ladies and settling down with someone like me. Someone who could make him incredibly happy.

Like he's making me feel tonight.

I don't think this confidence is shining out of me just from the heavy consumption of all things containing alcohol. I think this version of me is who I'm supposed to be. And even though, going by history, I should be sneaking off and inhaling a kebab as I hopped onto the wild ride that is the night bus, I have absolutely no desire to leave this bar. It's almost like we're high off each other, and as hard as it is to truly believe, it's definitely been a two-way street. We've guzzled one another's words, greedy and childlike, desperate to discover what we had in common, and to my surprise, everything I said I enjoyed, he said he loved too. The chemistry fizzing between us is palpable. His fingers found mine across the table at almost every opportunity, and at one point he even slid into my side of the booth and hung his arm around me.

It really does feel like two halves of one soul are finally uniting because I've never had someone put so much effort into understanding me. Not even Nova – the real me, just plain old Cassie.

The universe is a wee belter. I think, with the cheesiest of grins taking over my face as I rock back and forward on my heels.

Is this what it feels like? To be happy?

'You good to go?' he asks, placing his warm palm on the bottom of my back, returning from the Gent's.

He'd left me waiting at the door as I attempted to get some fresh air: a failed attempt to try to sober myself up enough that there might be a possibility of going somewhere else. Although, I'm not exactly sure where because we completely lost track of time and last orders were served a long time ago. This bar – and probably every other in Shawlands – is closing up, and there's just no way I could go to a club or anything like that. I suppose it would need to be…well, mine or his. I'm not sure which one is the most terrifying.

'Yup, I'm G to G,' I say, smiling up at him.

Guiding me out into the cold, we continue laughing at nothing and everything at the same time, but suddenly he removes his palm, each finger leaving behind a memory, and I want to grab his arm and put it back in that beautiful position because nothing has ever felt so good. So…right.

He lifts my hand from my side and wraps his fingers over my knuckles. In front of the entire world.

I sneak a glance at his face as he leads the way down the street and there's not one hint of embarrassment to be seen out in public and so intimately with me, or even a hint of concern that we might bump into someone he knows.

Or worse, I think, as the bitter knowledge I've kept squashed down pops out like a jack-in-the-box. Someone who might judge him for being out with another woman so soon after such a hugely traumatic heartbreak.

My stomach grumbles, churning at the other woman still very much present in his life despite being nowhere to be found. I wish I didn't have to tell a lie like the one I did, but I can't be ungrateful for what it's given me. Besides, he hasn't mentioned her once tonight. So why should I worry so much when he doesn't come across as crushed? I suppose it might see a little odd to some people, but who talks about exes on a first date? It's not exactly blossoming romance etiquette.

Even less so to talk about "dead" ones.

She's probably absolutely fine anyway and the only harm done is unto herself. She had her chance, she blew it, and her loss is definitely my gain.

Strolling hand in hand to the taxi rank, my legs practically skipping, I realise we must look like the perfect couple. Nobody is looking at me in disgust or questioning why he's with me. They're all too busy falling out of pubs, stumbling into taxis, or heading for a train into the still very much awake city centre. And now when I speak, it's as if someone has tilted my chin to the sky instead of always looking down at my toes.

Things are already starting to change, and it's only taken one night.

As we reach the corner of the main street, a few groups of people are waiting in line for one of the several black Hackneys. They're usually the ones you nab when you've absolutely no other choice than to sell your soul via the pound because they always charge considerably more. I would have quite happily floated my way home, but Finlay insisted that he see me off safely. Another adorable act of chivalry to add to his belt.

A few people down, nearer the front of the line, I spot a taxi driver refusing entry to an irate group of friends. Not that I blame him, or the many that did the same to me once upon a time, but I still can't help feeling a little worried for the girl who's definitely spewed Jägermeister all down the front of her pretty white dress. How else will she get home safely if she's abandoned?

Then again, who's to say she would be? At least she has other people with her. The raised voices of her friends are trying to convince the elderly man behind the wheel that she's fine, that it won't happen again, but he isn't buying what they're selling. He's far too old in the tooth for empty promises and has seen it all before and therefore has no desire to find himself in the middle of another clean-up job, not to mention the confrontation of issuing a fine.

Just as I think that this will probably give us some extra time together, Finlay's hand leaves mine and creeps up my spine before gripping the back of my neck and giving it a light squeeze. As he guides my head to the side, he whispers into my ear the answer to a question I haven't been brave enough to ask yet.

'Hey, why don't we just walk to mine, and you could hang out for a bit. When you need to get home, I'll get you a taxi from there. Or I could walk you home and then head back to mine by myself? But Cassie...' He pulls back and holds his hands up. 'I'll be completely honest with you...I don't want to end the night yet.'

My heartbeat kicks into some kind of romantic rave and he continues with his idea, nodding in the direction of the angry mob.

'You never know, it might be a sign that we're not supposed to say goodbye just yet,' he says, ending his idea with a heart stopping wink that seals the deal immediately.

I should at least try to play it cool, I think as I bite down on my bottom lip.

Smiling up at him, I can't help myself. I don't care how desperate I look because I want this more than anything. And I bloody knew I shaved my legs for a reason. Not that I'm going to do anything, though.

'Sure. Why not, right?'

'Exactly,' he agrees, taking my hand and yanking me out of the queue.

Dipping in and out of streets that all look the same, every tenement block is a clone of the other. He asks me more questions about my life. It's as if everything we've already discussed just isn't enough for him, and I'm so flattered by his lust for information that I tell him just about everything.

As we reach the top of a steep hill, after passing an old church that's been converted into a pub, I realise I've confessed my age, my career history, my lack of friends, and my relationship with my estranged parents.

It feels like our feet can't carry us to the bottom quickly enough, where just a few more streets away rests my most desired destination: his home.

I'm ashamed that this isn't the first time I've ditched my inhibitions and gone home with a guy on the first date, but this will be different. I'm definitely not planning on staying the night. I'll just join him inside for a little while to heat up a bit, have a quick cup of tea or coffee, and then I'll head home. It's perfectly safe. Nothing bad is going to happen to me.

'Just round the corner now. We'll be home in no time,' he confirms.

We.

Home.

Two words have never sounded so perfect when put together and as I look up at the night sky, I notice the stars are shining brightly, in all their glory to match the romantic mood. The moon is huge and kissed red, reminding me of my carnelian crystal that's hanging on a black rope around my neck. I bought it to help clear my undoubtably blocked chakras and boost my self-esteem, but according to my research, carnelian is also a love talisman, and apparently wearing it entices your soul mate – so what better night for it?

Finally, we turn another corner and leading me by the hand up the path to the front door of his block of flats, I feel the best I ever have in my entire life.

Breaking the link between us, he presses one hand against the red wine door and pushes his key into the lock, twisting expertly until he manages to release the latch with a loud click. I follow my shepherd as he steps inside and turn round to close the door before it slams in the wind and wakes his neighbours.

As I turn to catch-up, he lunges towards me, and I find my back pressed up against the door with my arms pinned above my head. His warm body is pressed firmly into mine. A subtle whiff of Carlsberg tickles my face, and I even think his heartbeat is pounding faster than my own. I lick my lips and tilt my head up because I'm more than ready for him to kiss me, but as soon as I get on my tiptoes, he snaps back like an elastic band, pinging away from me, leaving behind nothing but the sharp sting.

'Finlay. Oh my god, I'm so sorry.' I plunge my entire face into my hands. 'Honestly, please forget I did that. I'm so sorry. I got it all wrong. I thought…it doesn't matter. I'll go, OK? It's fine.'

Tears filling my eyes, ready to whip round, and pull open the door to the close and run for the hills. He begins to laugh, and I feel bamboozled. Stepping slowly towards me this time, he takes my chin in his hand, thumb firmly in the middle and directs my head back to his. It feels as if it's taking years for him to reach me, like he's enjoying teasing me, but in a split second he shocks me by lifting me into the air and wrapping my now jelly like legs around his waist. The back of my head thuds as it connects with the door, but I don't care. I'll worry about the consequences of that tomorrow because as he grabs the back of my neck and pushes his lips against mine, I can't focus on anything else.

After the most passionate, intense, and desire-fuelled kiss of my life, he pulls back, leaving my lips cold.

I realise we're in motion and as I wrap my arms tighter and smile into his neck. I thank the heavens that he's carrying me because I would have melted to the floor under the heat of his words.

'I've never felt this way before. You're perfect, Cassie. Just perfect.'

TWENTY-THREE

CASSIE

Turning off my alarm today feels exciting, but still extremely foreign. I've not had a reason to enjoy waking up for so long. But I do now. Especially today – our one-week anniversary. I can't believe I used to wish my mornings away, believing there was nothing good to come when actually all I had to do was get into a new routine. Like the one I have now, thanks to the incredibly organised Finlay. He's so efficient, always knows how to make things better and I trust what he says.

He suggested setting an alarm for six o'clock sharp, because that's when he gets up for work, and if we were both up together at the same time then I could start my day off productively, like I mean to go on. So that's exactly what I did and now I bounce out of bed like a spring chicken to make his morning coffee instead of wanting the mattress to open wide and swallow me whole.

I'm still here in his flat after seven days of what I guess you could call dating. We've not gone out anywhere else, no dinner dates, or cinema trips or anything like that, but that's suited me perfectly because I've loved having him all to myself and not having to worry about the outside world again.

Although I've slept here every single night since, I've been popping back and forth to my flat to check in on Luna and collect some of my belongings: clothes, clean pants, that kind of thing. I hate leaving her, but honestly, she seems fine, and not that phased by my absence. My cat has always been far more capable and independent than her owner. Perhaps she has a second owner somewhere else, and that's why she doesn't need me so much. I hope not. It would be sad if I needed her more than she needed me.

My feelings for Finlay have grown so intense and all-consuming and although I really can't believe my luck, it's terrifyingly that this one man has my heart in the palm of his hand and has the ability to destroy me for good at any given moment. I'm trying not to focus on the negatives or intrusive worries though, because how could things go wrong when everything suddenly makes so much sense? On the mornings I've woken up before him, I can't help but just lay there staring at him. Sometimes I even let my index finger loose on an adventure trail, gently exploring each crease of his face, the slight ridge in his nose, a tiny scar on his jaw that you'd only know was there if you were close enough to caress it. I wonder how he got it. He doesn't seem like a fighter to me.

I can't believe how fast my life has changed. The chaotic and messy person I was prior to meeting Finlay doesn't even feel like me anymore. Or Nova. It's like I'm someone new now. Someone better, and genuinely the only thing that's even bothering me too much is how much time we've wasted being apart. This life was always supposed to be mine and I wish I'd been able to claim it years ago.

Flipping round to face him, I panic to see that he's not beside me in bed, and I can't hear him moving around. He always gives me a kiss before he leaves for work. There's no way he would forget that. My stomach drops.

Have I done something to annoy him? Upset him in some way? Or worse, what if I was talking in my sleep and confessed to lying to him?

Only when I realise that his phone is still lying on the bedside table does my breath begin to consider returning to a normal pace.

I've never shared a bed with someone for longer than an hour. Or for any period of time after the nitty gritty was done. Those men didn't need to bother finding excuses about having to get up early or being presented with an emergency, because I was always just as eager for most of them to vanish into thin air so I could pretend like I hadn't dropped my morals as quick as my pants. I'd smile, pull my clothes back over skin that felt dirty and carry my heels to their front door. Both of us waving one another off with a sigh of mutual relief.

I reach out my arm, spread my hand wide, and feel for a patch of warmth still lingering on the mattress.

'Fin?' I call out with a croak.

My head is a little sore too, so I might be coming down with something – or it might just be from sleeping in this intense heat. He likes the thermostat turned up full notch at night, says the soaring ceilings mean it's always so baltic, and I couldn't argue with him because I completely understood with my flat being the same. When the moment's right, perhaps I'll mention to him that the thick air is making my head feel so horribly fuzzy in the morning.

Appearing at the bedroom doorway, wearing nothing but a pair of tight black boxers, with a buttery triangle of toast wedged between his lips, he's gripping a cup of coffee in each hand. Popping them both down on the bedside table, he hops back into bed beside me and pulls me into his milky white chiselled chest. Wrapping one arm around me, he uses the other to continue munching on his breakfast, but when he spots a couple of falling crumbs, he abandons everything – including me – to brush them off the bed.

I've noticed that he hates mess, so I've been trying my best to tidy up after myself, but I have to admit that his little frantic outbursts do make me giggle under my breath. Like when I've left a towel on the bathroom floor after taking a shower. I think it's cute. We all have our own strange little quirks and to me, his are adorable.

Sitting forward with a straight spine, he smooths down the white sheet, making sure it all looks pristine, and seems to be considering whatever he's about to say. As if he needs to build himself up to it. Find the courage.

Oh, my god. He's not going to dump me, is he?

Well, not dump me. I'm not even officially his girlfriend yet, but I could be. One day. Soon.

I'll do anything to stop this dream coming to a sudden end.

'Cas, I was thinking…'

I shoot up and gently place one of my trembling hands on his shoulder and with the other, I reach for my cup of coffee. I'm not at all thirsty, even though he's probably made it perfectly now that he's mastered how I take my caffeine hit: strong enough to get me going but sweet and creamy enough to disguise the bitterness. I love that he remembers the small details of things I've told him so this cannot be over, not before it's even truly begun.

I'm trying to act as cool and collected as possible, but I don't know if it's working, so I'm thinking of something to discuss with him to avoid this conversation taking place. Something that will make this problem go away.

'Cas, what if you moved in with me?' he suggests, catching me completely off-guard.

The mug instantly falls from my fingers and lands on the cream carpet, causing me to shriek in horror because I know the damage it'll cause. I stare down at the dark shadow soaking into the fibres that will probably cause a horrible stench of sour milk, knowing I should leap from the bed and into the kitchen to grab whatever cleaning products he owns. But I can't move. And I also can't believe my ears.

What if you moved in with me? What if you moved in with me? What if you moved in with me?

'Fuck's sake, Cas,' he yelps. There's a subtle flash of anger, but it disappears just as quickly as it arrived. I can't blame him. I'd be annoyed with myself too.

'Did you just ask me to move in with you?' I ask, desperate for solid confirmation.

He sighs and then breaks into a concerned smile. 'Too soon?'

He pushes a hand through my hair, snaking it around the back of my neck, and pulls my forehead against his. 'You said you were worried about money, right? And you said you feel the same as I do about our future, so it's pretty pointless having both flats when you've practically moved yourself in already, eh?'

What he's suggesting does make perfect sense, but his last statement has caused a scorpion like sting. *You've practically moved yourself in already.*

I didn't mean to impose. I thought he wanted me here. He pouted every time I even suggested spending the night in my own place, so I never did because I thought it was the right thing to do. But what if I've been actually misread the signals, smashing the lines of acceptable boundaries and looking like the world's biggest bunny boiler?

I might be reading into it too much. Perhaps I'm just being too sensitive – as always – because surely, he wouldn't ask me to move in with him at all if he didn't want it to happen too. Nobody's holding a gun to his head.

'It just seems like a good idea to me, a no brainer. We've got something amazing here, Cas. What do you think?'

Obviously, I think it's the best idea I've ever heard. I think it's absolutely perfect and that nothing would make me happier than setting up a home together with Finlay Munro. Maybe there really isn't anything to worry about anymore. Everything is falling into place the way the universe wanted it to. I swear I can feel it in my bones.

'But I'm not even…we're not even…' I gasp, struggling to get the words out because I'm terrified of sounding childish and spoiling such a precious moment.

He throws his head back and laughs up to the big man in the sky as if he's in on the joke, too. 'Boyfriend and girlfriend? Cas, we aren't teenagers. I thought you understood that there wasn't a need for a stupid chat about labels because me and you, we're different from everyone else.'

'No, of course not. You're right,' I confirm, agreeing like a nodding dog on the back shelf of a car.

We are soul mates. We don't need to live like anyone else or follow the rules of what society deems normal. We can create our own rules in our own little world. And we're much more than just a childhood romance, just like he said.

He caresses my cheek with his thumb. 'And you trust me, right?'

I nod again, because of course I do, but my teeth can't help finding my bottom lip because there's another problem that might stop us in our tracks.

'But I still have time left on my lease. I can't walk away from that because I signed with a minimum term clause, so we might need to wait a wee while.'

He rolls his eyes, clearly exasperated with all the excuses I'm making, despite wishing there were none. I wish I didn't worry so much about everything. Why is it so difficult for me to just say yes and accept something good? Why do I always have to find problems in the best kind of situations?

Maybe I've not grown as much as I thought I had.

'Then just keep it until the lease ends. I don't want a penny from you, so you won't have to find extra to pay for both. And even better, you won't even have to do your creepy witchy shit anymore. I'll take care of you now.'

'I mean, I guess that works. But I enjoy what I do. It keeps me busy, and I'll need something to do while you're out at work.'

'We'll figure it out, babe. Just say yes – that's the first step.'

'OK.' I blurt, thrusting my arms into the air like a cheerleader from Bring It On. 'Let's do it. I'll move in properly. When should we do it?'

'Well, what about today? No time like the present, eh? Besides, I'm off today, so I can help you.'

I look around the room that's about to become my permanent bedroom and then into the eyes of the man who's about to make all my dreams come true.

'Today it is, then,' I say, beaming widely.

He smacks his lips to my forehead in delight and I fall back onto the pillow, feeling drunk on love.

'Eh, don't get too comfortable. First things first – I think you've got a bit of a mess to clean up, don't you?' He reminds me by nodding towards the now dark brown stain on the carpet.

Oh, my god. I forgot. How mortifying and hardly the best start.

'Yes. Of course. I'm on it.' Bouncing out of bed, I dart straight into the kitchen and yank open the cupboard under the sink and pull out a cloth and some squooshy carpet cleaner.

The epic love story of Cassie Torrance and Finlay Munro starts now.

Twenty-Three

Cassie

Three Weeks Later

Sitting cross-legged on my multicoloured chakra rug, I place one hand on my heart, take a deep breath, and thank the universe for its blessings. Because who'd have thought it would deliver in a way I'd only ever be able to dream of? I have so many things to be thankful for surrounding me now: Finlay, Luna, and of course, this beautiful flat, that someone like me is beyond lucky to even be in.

The meditation-hype is something I've always wanted to master, but for some reason I've never been able to get the hang of. The YouTube videos I watch to guide me always make it sound so simple, yet every time I try to still my mind by dropping each pesky thought onto a lily pad, they refuse to float away into the abyss. And worse, more and more appear, relentlessly continuing to invade my mind's eye on jet-skis, leaving the pond more crowded than when I started. However, I refuse to give up. It's supposed to be good for you. I'm sure I'll get the hang of it, eventually.

At least that's what I've been trying to tell myself for last few days, sat in the centre of the box square hallway, facing the maroon wine front door of this immaculately kempt, south-side flat. Although I'd be lying if I said I was making any sort of progress, which is a little disheartening. Shouldn't I be able to do all the things I wasn't able to do before, now that I've passed such a grand, universal test?

Despite living in bliss, the walls, painted crisp white with not one hint of a dirty fingerprint, feel like they're closing in around me, shrinking me in size, forcing me into an Alice in Wonderland-like trance except there're no drinkable escape potions for me to chug down. And the *Chakra Meditation Rug* that cost me a whopping £29.99 – albeit very nice to look at with its alternatively coloured rainbow of purple, indigo, blue, green, yellow, orange, and red – feels more like a kite than anything else. Sometimes I still find myself wishing it would help me fly away from this world completely.

'This. Is. Good. For. You,' I tell myself out loud. I think it's best if you actually say the words for the universe to hear because how else would it be able to know what you're thinking?

In the final couple of hours before Fin is due back from classes, this is usually where I am: trying to calm my racing thoughts. I think his arrival is due quite soon, but I'm sure I have more than enough time to clear everything away, and make sure everything's as it was when he left this morning. It's not a big ask. He likes things kept very neat and tidy and that's the very least I can do to say thank you for how wonderful he's been to me.

I take a deep breath. Finlay Munro is maybe the nicest human ever created, and he really deserves so much more than someone as difficult as me. But I won't allow myself to be sucked into that pool of quicksand right now. I have to push those doubts to the back of my mind and so my brain sprints into a new task, out of harm's way. I must be the best me…for him.

I silently repeat my affirmations: *I am exactly where I am supposed to be. I am safe now. Everything is as it should be.* Once. Twice. Hell, I'll repeat it twenty times. As many as it takes until I start to really believe it. And I must make it crystal clear to whoever is listening: The strange ghost-lady, the universe, my ancestors, guardian angels, spiritual guides. Perhaps even the devil, I don't know? – I truly am super grateful for this this golden opportunity: a second chance to start living the life I was always destined to. With someone who loves me for who I am.

The cliché mantra of good vibes only sounds fab to me because I could really be doing with some of that positive energy. Although I don't regret my decision to move in with Fin so quickly, I'm struggling with the changes in my life more than I thought I would be. Actually, I didn't think I would find it difficult at all, and perhaps that was naïve of me because although I'd never admit it, I feel myself slipping when it comes to getting up at the crack of dawn. I no longer have the luxury of lounging about in my pyjamas all day because Finlay likes me to be showered and dressed every day, even if I am just mulling around the flat. I find myself agreeing to watch things on the telly that he loves but bores me stiff. I've been forcing down the supposedly healthy meals that he preps for me without checking in beforehand if I would even like it or not. But the guilt of what I did...that's what's really the most difficult thing to swallow.

The somewhat risqué path, shall we say – the road I ultimately took to get here – it was undoubtably the biggest I've ever dared to set foot on – I'm not completely crazy. It was obviously a terrible thing to lie about. I mean, who – even in all those fucked up Netflix thrillers – tells someone that their missing loved one was dead? Especially when they had no bloody idea where they were or why they disappeared. It was recklessly impulsive, and not something any normal person would ever do. But I guess that's always been one of my biggest problems: I've never considered myself to be normal. I've always felt complex and misunderstood – even by myself. Sometimes I can't tell wrong from right until I've leaped and before I know it, I'm being slaughtered by the consequences.

Anyway, I always try to remind myself that I did see someone. I know I did. I just don't know who exactly. It could well have been his ex-girlfriend, right? And if it was, then I have to believe that I did the right thing, and that I'm not the god awful, disgusting, and terrible excuse for a person I currently feel like I am. If it wasn't her...well, I don't even allow myself to go there, because what would that mean? I'm just insane?

Right now, my focus is solely on my relationship with Finlay. If I'm being completely honest, I can't ignore the fact that everything between us has been moving at lightning speed. I know that's how true love is supposed to go and all that jazz, all-consuming and passionate, but it's so new to me. The pace feels less of a romantic whirlwind and more like a tornado crashing around in my chest.

Recently, I've started worrying more that the roadblock isn't actually the lie I told, but who told it. There has to be something wrong with my DNA because the problem feels skin deep. The universe has given me everything I asked for, with a full set of instructions, but for some reason I'm still incapable of making all the pieces fit. I think I'm doing and saying all the right things to make him happy, but it doesn't feel enough.

I actually think I've been quite understanding, all things considering, because this flat – as beautiful as it is – has been giving me the creeps. The goosebumps that pimple my legs every time I step foot in the bathroom, or even the shadow that stalks me from room to room when I'm here alone in the flat, I've been batting them away as best I can. I struggle to ignore the sensation that I'm living with a ghost. Dead or alive, she's still everywhere.

Her clothes are still hanging on the rail inside the bedroom cupboard. Tubs of underwear and socks stashed underneath. Size five designer trainers and sexy leather boots are waiting for their owner to return. The bathroom cabinet remains full of feminine toiletries, intimately picked and used by someone else. The first day I met Finlay, I'm sure he said it had been a year since she vanished. It seems so bizarre to me that he's still holding onto enough memorabilia to potentially create a shrine of someone he's supposed to have moved on from.

I remind myself that he loves me now. Not her. I have to keep that at the forefront of all my thoughts.

I think back to a moment, stood outside my flat with rain pouring down from the heavens. We were moving some boxes of my stuff over to his and were waiting on the taxi when he pulled me out of the shelter of the door, down the steps, and onto the street. He pulled my arm high and twisted me into a pirouette fit for a pretty ballerina and laughed. 'Isn't this romantic? I don't think I've ever loved anyone as much as I do you, Cas.' He then pulled my body against his chest, kissed the top of my soaking wet head, and whispered in my ear, 'You're what I've always needed.'

So why am I still filled with the feeling that I'm never going to be good enough for him, no matter what I do? And even with me living here now instead, if he isn't ready to let go now, when will he be? What if the answer is never?

'No, no,' I say, catching my mind before it begins to wander somewhere dark, trying to conjure some helpful affirmations from my subconscious.

But again, am I the problem here? Am I just being ungrateful? Judgemental, even. I've never been in his position. I might have done the same if roles were reversed. And they're just things, right? They don't mean anything, and we can work on removing them over time. At a pace he's comfortable with because clearly my first attempt at starting over by offering to get rid of the lot didn't go down well. It's the first time I saw him angry. It scared me. It was like he morphed into a different person entirely. Someone who made my blood run cold. Even his beautiful, bright eyes became dark and dangerous.

I'm sure I was probably being too sensitive and reading into something that wasn't there, but it's for the best I don't bring the topic up again until I'm confident he'll be able to see where I'm coming from. And he will eventually – because who wouldn't be able to understand why being around another woman's belongings is making me struggle to feel at home?

But what if…My body jerks as an icy shiver trickles down my spine? What if it's me who's brought some seriously bad energy into this beautiful home, and it's nothing at all to do with clothes or perfumes still scattered around the flat?

Should I get sageing or would it be pointless? I just want all these bad vibes floating around to be gone so things can start to feel like they should.

'Good vibes only. Good vibes only. Good vibes only,' I mutter.

Sighing, I lean back on my arms and look up at the ceiling. I'm not even convincing myself. I clearly still have so much work to do, and the knot in my stomach isn't just getting tighter. It's breeding an army of mini nooses, threatening to hang me.

TWENTY-FOUR

CASSIE

Noticing the hallway feels a little darker, I wonder how long I've been sitting here hopping from worry to worry. Time has escaped me, and it's been ages since I've moved a muscle.

I allow my neck to crunch as I bend it from side to side and start to put the stones back in their small, black velvet drawstring pouch. Hoping to reap the benefits of their supposed energy, I held in the palm of my hands: a polished pink rose quartz to evoke the feeling of being loved, and a rugged purple amethyst – that looks more like a rock you'd find at the beach instead of something that's supposed to assist with relaxation – to just try to get the voices in my head to chill the hell out.

I have a little pocket-sized book in one of my boxes that are stacked in the spare room of my new home. It tells me what they all mean, so I know exactly what ones to use and when to charge them and what ones belong in sunlight versus water. I have all the information and I still don't bloody use them, which is beginning to feel like the story of my life because only

I could require a manual to be loved by the most perfect man in the world.

Most of the time I just grab whatever one I've recently bought or a colour I like the look of and hope that it works the way it's supposed to. Doesn't the universe program them for life or something? If so, I think I've bought some dodgy fakes.

I wonder what crystal would be good for liars. It seems I can't stop spinning tales even when completely unnecessary.

I knew this opportunity of happily ever after was too precious to jeopardise with any more exaggerations, but I was afraid that if I blinked, Finlay might change his mind and take back the offer of cohabiting altogether. That's the only reason I've lied to him again.

I haven't told him that I still have the keys to my old flat across the other side of town, number twenty-two. Indefinitely. It's not a lie that's harming anyone. Except maybe me because it's sitting empty, gathering dust from the remainder of my savings account. Fin thinks I'm honouring three months' notice on my tenancy agreement – which I did initially try to give my landlord. It's just I just couldn't get a hold of them – because we've never met, and I don't have an address or a telephone number. Just an email address that sometimes replies and sometimes doesn't. Of course, now I realise that I should have asked for all the vital information at the time, but it all seemed so easy. I just didn't think.

On this occasion, they did get back to me, but they offered to lower my rent to near enough buttons if I agreed to stay at the property until further notice. I don't know why I agreed, but I did. And now I'm just keeping secret after secret from the man I've gone through so much to be with.

I move position, shifting to my knees, and bringing my hands to the floor. Stretching my body forward, I press my forehead to the wood and try to relax my shoulders. Apparently, there's a spot in between your eyebrows that's supposed to stimulate something called your vagus nerve – not that I have any idea what that is – and it's supposed to activate some kind of peaceful response.

Although I can't explain why sometimes, when I'm trying to meditate, the voice that whispers that it was the right decision to lie to Finlay again, even makes me believe her. There's no reasoning to back it up or anything like that, because of course that would be too kind to me – so I'm assuming it's because when I scrunch my eyes tight and try hard to picture our future in my mind's eye, I see a huge red cross marking a piece of paper. I'm going to fail. I always do. And when that happens, at least I'll have somewhere to crawl back to.

Still having not moved from child's pose in the middle of the hallway, the front door smashes like a symbol against the crown of my head, and I yelp at the top of my lungs. A handful of tea lights take flight and I can feel little hot bites where the flames have quickly kissed my right arm. Mouth wide open, I gawk up at the familiar tall figure.

'What the fuck? You're off your nut. What is all this shite?' Finlay erupts, stepping further inside, and closing the door forcefully behind him.

But it's the unfamiliar rasp to his usually velvety soft voice that still makes the partially singed the hairs stand to attention.

It's my fault. I've made him angry.

'Hello. Hello. Sorry, you scared me,' I say, almost panting. 'God. I'm sorry, I didn't expect you home so soon. I'm just tidying up. it will take two secs and I'll be out of your hair. Well, the hallway at least.'

My joke falls short. There must be something else wrong. Something really, really bad because from the look on his face, you'd think he'd just witnessed me performing a séance or sacrificial ritual.

'I didn't know you still did all this…nonsense,' he says, glaring down at me with such peculiar disdain.

But it's the word that slaps me with disorientation and chokes me. Nonsense. My mind immediately takes me back in time to a much younger me, cowering alone in the corner of her bedroom. My heart thuds faster, aching. I see little Cas and how much she's hurting. I feel it. She's been told she's too weird, too much, that there's something wrong with her. She's too far out of my reach, though. I can't stop her tears and now I feel my own dripping down my cheeks.

Stop crying. Stop crying. Stop crying, I repeat in my head, aware of how weak and pathetic I must look.

But there's another voice battling mine: Nova's. She's wailing like a banshee, wrenching open metal bars, demanding to be let out. She wants to protect us – but from what? I'm safe here. I'm finally going to be happy now with Finlay and Luna, and I don't want to mess this up. I can't listen to her. I need to apologise.

'I'm sorry, um, this is just a bit of gentle meditation. Doctors even recommend it now,' I say, slowly getting to my feet. For some reason I feel the need to reassure him that no kind of black magic was being carried out in the flat. That there's nothing to be scared of, because he didn't want me continuing Natters with Nova after I agreed to move in.

His face continues to harden before my eyes, his jaw line sharper than the edge of a blade, as he blows out air, exasperation fizzing inside him.

'I didn't know you brought all this hippy shit here. I thought you'd have left all of that behind. Or even better, torched the lot.'

He drops his rucksack to his feet with a thud that makes me blink twice and then heads into the living room.

Clouds of confusion are doing roly-polies in my head. I didn't know he felt so strongly about it. It's not like my interest in spirituality or mediumship, or witchy things were a secret. He literally booked a session with me in the first place because of who he thought I was. His unrecognisable anger can't be just because I've brought some of my things into his flat.

I must have done something else wrong.

I feel my worst fears begin to crawl up my windpipe, acidic and piping hot. What if she's been found? The girlfriend. And is she dead, like I suggested? Or is she alive and kicking? What if he wants her back? What if she wants him back?

My head is heavy, chaotic, and I don't know how to fix the situation unless he tells me what I've done.

'For fuck's sake. What have you been doing all day?' His voice thunders from the other room. 'There are crumbs. Here, there…just about fucking everywhere to be honest. And the cushions – they're a riot. They better not have been on the floor. And what…THE FUCK is all this brown dust?'

I rush in, almost losing my footing as I trip over the skirting at the doorway but manage to keep myself upright by gripping the frame.

'I'm so sorry. It's just from the incense stick, but it's fine. Ignore it. I'll get the hoover. It won't stain. I'm sorry.'

Is he so angry because of the mess? Have I not been keeping things the way he likes while I've been here? If that's all it is then I'll hold my hands up because quite rightly so, because what is actually wrong with me? Why do I always have to make such a mess of everything? A house. A room. A carpet. A life. Literally everything.

God, Cassie, it's not hard, I want to scream at myself but don't because I know for sure he'll draw the line at talking to myself and he'll no doubt say I'm even more mental than he already thought.

I feel so ashamed because here's me, living rent free, with everything I could ever want and for the first time in my life it all makes sense and yet here I come. Chaotic Cassie, flying in on a wrecking ball named the only thing she never fails at: self-infliction.

I watch silently as he takes a seat on the couch and rests his elbows on his knees. His face falls into the palm of his hands.

My stomach lurches and I hold my breath. He can't even stand to look at me. I'm that much of a disappointment to him. And I don't know what to say, so I just stay exactly where I am, glued to the spot.

After what feels like the longest, most uncomfortable silence in the world he gets to his feet, stretches his arms to the sky and yawns loudly. Making his way towards the door, he begins to strip off: jacket, hoodie, T-shirt, all discarded in the hallway on top of my things.

Why won't he just talk to me? And am I really that awful to be around that he can't even wait until he's in the bathroom to peel off every scent of my inadequacy that might have attached itself to his body? He's so desperate to scrub away any residue. I'm like a virus.

Biting the nail of my thumb, I keep asking myself why I'm still just standing here. Doing nothing. But when I finally hear the heavy thrashes of water against the base of the bath, my chest expands with relief, and I no longer feel like the Tin Man.

I forget about the dust, and instead dart into the hallway and collect all our belongings, crystals and clothing, and rush into the bedroom to chuck it all in the cupboard. Now that's out of sight, I'll change into my pyjamas and just get into bed and close my eyes. When I wake up everything will feel OK again. This is just a blip.

One you've caused…again, a voice teases but I bat it away.

As I pull back the edge of the covers, my stomach churns as I realise I still have to brush my teeth.

I know it's gross, but before Finlay came along, I did often "forget" to scrub my gnashers twice a day. Sometimes I felt like I should have received an award for managing the once, but living with him is different. He never lets me drift off without reminding me, always catching me on the edge of sleep. But I guess that's what it's like when you live with a significant other. And I try my best not to let him catch a whiff of my morning breath even when I have gone to the double effort, so God forbid, I skip a night.

Slowly creeping towards the bathroom, unsure why I'm so scared to make noise, I take a deep breath and knock on the bathroom door.

'Come in, babe,' he practically sings.

Cautious of the change in his tone, I slowly nudge the door open and stick my head in the crack. 'I'm just going to brush my teeth, is that OK?'

'Of course, it is. Get in here, stop being ridiculous, Cas. Are you OK? What's wrong?'

I feel my cheeks blush with embarrassment. He's not even mad at all. He's fine. Everything is fine. It's me again, isn't it? I'm the problem. Once again, I've made a mountain out of a molehill.

Finally able to breathe, my lips break into a smile as I step inside and my face as I pick up my toothbrush and turn on the cold tap.

There's nothing to worry about. Everything is fine. Tomorrow is another day.

It's all in my head.

TWENTY-FIVE

CASSIE

Tonight is date night, and I have a surprise for Fin. One I hope will make him very happy, because ultimately that's what I'm here to do. It's my purpose, my true calling in life, and I'm surer now than ever before.

At least that's what I keep trying to tell myself. Because I hoped I'd be sleeping like a baby next to a man like him, but I guess I'm still having some teething problems. I can't seem to turn down all the noise. So many different thoughts, and I don't know what's true or not. Even when I do eventually manage to fall asleep, my nightmares are fuelled by worry. And it's stupid, because what do I really have to be so anxious about?

The fact you're crumbling quicker than a cookie in a fist, perhaps? a voice in my head suggests. *That you're a liar, and don't deserve any of this, the same one strikes again.*

The further I run from them the closer to danger I feel.

But not tonight, I tell myself as I fix a crease on my white linen dress. Everything will go perfectly tonight.

I run my fingers through the bouncy curls resting on my chest, gently freeing them from the stiffness of the

Elnett hairspray I found in the bathroom cabinet. The crispy thickness feels foreign yet oddly satisfying in my hands. I'm not sure if it was the smell of chemicals or just pure adrenaline that almost choked me to death, but I blasted loads, anyway.

Even though it wasn't mine to touch.

My top lip twitches, trying to encourage the bottom to play along and form a believable smile. Should it be this difficult to be happy?

I twist and turn, thinking the image will fade, but there's no doubt about it – the person in the mirror is definitely me. My eyelids are now lustrously smoky and long gone is my greasy washed-out bun that basically lived in a nest on top of my head.

I feel reborn. Finally ready to claim this new life.

'From here on in, I will do better,' I say to my reflection. But especially tonight, I think silently. He's going to love it. I know he will.

Yesterday morning, in preparation for tonight, I ordered a hair bleaching kit online with absolutely guaranteed next-day delivery. It was essential for it to arrive to make our date night that extra bit special and I was confident I could do it, because I vividly remember being fourteen, bouncing off the walls like a rubber wall when my mum finally agreed to let me get blonde highlights for the very first time.

All the popular girls were getting blonde highlights. Even the boys, too – on the tips of those spiky fringes that they gelled up in the air. And I wanted to be like them so badly, so I badgered her for weeks until she finally caved and got her hairdresser, Donna, round to the house one evening. Although not really being a professional, she sat me down in one of our dining chairs in the middle of our kitchen and almost suffocated me with some sort of jellyfish. Then, she tortured me for over an hour, stabbing at my scalp with a tiny sword, scooping strands of hair free from the cap, creating millions of long legs that she then smothered with blue paste. I was terrified then, but not now.

Back then, I didn't know better. I was completely convinced that she'd made a mistake, but I held back my tears in and kept my mouth shut, and in the end my hair didn't turn out anything like Marge Simpson's. Everyone was happy. Mum handed Donna a bunch of notes from her purse and then poured each of them a glass of what would be many bottles of white wine while I danced with glee in front of the mirror alone in my bedroom, swishing and swooshing around a head that felt like a hat made out of sunshine instead of orange peels.

Unfortunately, there aren't many memories that I have of feeling good or happy. I don't actually remember an awful lot of much to be honest and don't know if that's normal or what, but all my thoughts and feelings of the past are a blur to me. Most things I can claim to remember have likely been a picture painted by someone else's brush and I've just gone along with it.

I know I'll remember today, though, because I can't have messed this up. I've definitely made a good decision for a change.

Although can I take all the credit? It was technically Finlay's idea. He just doesn't know how seriously I've taken his likes and dislikes, and how quickly I'd move mountains to make him happy.

Which reminds me: I've still to make the finishing touches.

Heading out of the bathroom, for some strange reason, I find myself questioning why I always end up in there. Fixing my hair, checking my chin in the mirror for any stray hairs that need to be plucked, or even just perching on the edge of the bath while I try to steady my heart. Fin says I spend way too much time in there and I suppose he's right, but I guess out of the entire flat, the long chessboard floor tiles with walls narrower than cereal boxes feel the safest.

Now in the living room, I snatch the lighter from the table and ignite the wicks of three white pillar candles sitting on the window ledge. My eyes study the room. I've already laid our plates and cutlery out neatly on the coffee table and have even scattered some artificial rose petals that scream romance. Dinner arrived just five minutes ago and is still piping hot waiting in the kitchen.

I've never been much of a cook, so I cheated a little by ordering a Chinese instead. I can smell the salty curry sauce wafting through, causing my mouth to salivate because I've not eaten a thing all day.

My eyes glance over every detail once last time.

Everything is perfect. The flat is spotless. Dinner is here. Perfect.

Right on time, I hear the click of the key turning in the lock and can't help but dance excitedly on the spot, desperate to greet Finlay with open arms as soon as he walks in the room.

My heart skips a beat. There he is. Standing in the frame of the doorway is my incredibly good-looking man that I still can't believe I've bagged.

'You're home!' I exclaim. 'Surprise.'

He drops his rucksack to the floor and kicks it aside.

'Cassie,' he says curtly. 'What is all this?'

I drop my arms from the air immediately, but my fingers stay twitching.

'Well, it's Friday. So, I thought…date night. Surprise.' I try again, hoping this time I'll be able to ignite his enthusiasm.

He pushes his hands through his thick dark hair and flings his head back, scrunching his eyes like he has a bad migraine. 'Are you having a laugh? It's Thursday – not Friday – and I'm fucking shattered. You know I need to go to bed early on a Thursday night. I have a class at six tomorrow morning.'

My heart plunges into the pit of my stomach with a thud.

It can't be…can it? Thursday, really? There's just no way I would have messed up something as simple as the day of the week. And yet, I must have, because he clearly wasn't expecting anything but an early night. And rightfully so after – let's face it – a much harder day than mine.

I'm stupid. Incompetent. Or maybe I'm even a narcissist or a sociopath, like in all those true crime documentaries I've binged. Is that my problem?

I consider the best course of action, trying to bat away haunting memories of my past mistakes and decide that the best thing to do is to take full accountability for my error.

'I'm so sorry. I must have got my days mixed up. I'm sorry. You must be shattered, I understand. But listen, you still need to eat, so why don't I just plate us both a bit of dinner, anyway?'

He says nothing when he brings his face back down to glare at mine. Silence still deafening the room, I try again.

'We can just have dinner,' I say, darting around the room, blowing out all the candles. 'No fuss. Then we can go to straight to bed, yeah?'

'Fine.' He sighs, turning his back to me and disappearing across the small hallway and into the bedroom.

I don't waste any time knowing how tired he is, so I grab our plates from the table, scurry to the kitchen, and start ripping open the plastic bags, popping open the tinfoil on the tubs at the speed of light.

So, big deal that the night hasn't gone as planned, but it will be fine in the end, I tell myself as I start to pour the gloopy yellow chicken curry onto our plates, while inhaling a few prawn crackers on an empty stomach. I'm asking for indigestion from the grease, but I am starving. I forgot to eat breakfast again today, but I won't tell him that. The last time I told him I sometimes skip the first meal of the day he said he'd start making me dummy-proof meal plans. If you were blindfolded, you might have thought he was talking to a child, but I know he has my best interests at heart. He just wants to look after me.

But I can't shake the sting from my skin, still burning from his failure to notice my new hair. I'm about to bite into another cracker when my hand freezes in the air. Or, what if he did notice but was too angry with me to even care? I'm not sure which is worse and if it even matters, because the rejection will still scar the same.

'What's that?' he asks, startling me, and I jump.

Finlay reaches over my shoulder and pinches something from one of the plates.

'Last time I checked, it was an onion,' I joke, nudging him in the stomach with my elbow.

He backs up, grips the edge of the worktop across from me. 'I know that, babe. I'm not stupid. But I don't like onions.'

'Since when do you not like onions?' I laugh, assuming he's kidding. Because obviously he is. It's a joke. He devoured this exact meal last week, not one slither left behind. And so did I, despite the fact it's actually me who hates them, but I ate them anyway because chicken curry with onions was his favourite, and he says he doesn't like fussy eaters, so it seemed like a no brainer to just eat them rather than cause a fuss.

He pops like a champagne bottle, exploding into a furious rampage, unlike anything I've ever witnessed before. 'I don't know how many times I have to fucking repeat myself. I'm allergic, remember? I've told you this, but you don't listen. You never listen when you're supposed to. Your head is in the fucking clouds. I don't understand – do you want to hurt me? Is this a plan of yours? Running out of stupid spells and having to go back to basics? I've been so good to you. I cannot believe you've done this.'

I feel my throat tighten, and I'm choking on each of his words. I must have got this wrong, too. Of course, I don't want to hurt him, I never would.

'Finlay I'm…' I attempt to apologise, cautiously approaching him.

He puts his hands up in protest, and I stop instantly in my tracks. There's barely enough room for two people in the kitchen, and right now, it feels as if I'm being suffocated by a crowd of twenty.

'I've done a lot for you, Cassie. I took you out of that dark cave. I go out and work long fucking days. You don't need to worry about a thing, and I don't ask you for anything, do I? Tell me what I ask you for.' He probes at my collarbone with one finger. 'Go on, one thing.'

My lip wobbles and I catch it with my teeth. I don't know what to say. I know he shouldn't be laying his hands on me, but he's right, isn't he? I've been living here in this gorgeous flat rent-free. He hasn't asked me for a penny towards food or even to chip in for the money it costs to run my bubble baths that I've been soaking in every night. I've no doubt raised the roof on his utility bill. The very least he deserves is someone who is capable of remembering things that are actually quite important to him.

I wish more than ever that person was me, but I just seem to constantly let him down. And so early on in our relationship. What hope is there for a future together when I keep messing up?

'You're right,' I say, grabbing his hand the next time a finger bounces off my chest. 'I'm sorry, Finlay. Please, just let me pick them out for you. It won't take long, I promise you won't be able to taste them and if you don't like it – well then, I'll order something else, OK? I'm sorry I've upset you this much. It's never my intention.'

He pulls his hand away, pushes me aside, and heads out into the squared hallway, stopping bang in the centre, the same spot I used to meditate.

'Look,' he says, forming fists with both hands. 'I've had a rough day. And then I come home to find you like…'

'Like what?' I suddenly find the courage to ask.

Where did that come from?

'Well, this. For fuck's sake.' He throws out an arm in my direction before squeezing his temples.

'What do you mean?' I say, stepping towards him, wanting to get close enough to calm him down and let him know that I'm struggling to understand and I need his help.

'The hair, Cassie,' he spits. 'What the fuck is going on with your hair?'

TWENTY-SIX

CASSIE

I recoil instantly, as if a knife had just been plunged into my chest, instinctively clutching a handful of my hair in a bid to protect its feelings. I want to defend myself, but all that comes out is a whisper.

'I…I thought you would like it. You said I'd suit my hair lighter. That you preferred blondes.' Did I get this wrong too?

'I said lighter. *Ligh…Ter.* Not…whatever the fuck this is,' he says, gesturing at my head. 'You look ridiculous.'

My knees buckle, wounded by the shots he keeps firing. Tears are starting to drip down my cheeks, but I manage to stay standing, and I stay silent because I realise he's nowhere near finished. It feels smarter not to interrupt.

'This is exactly what she started doing. Not listening to me or paying attention. She only ever thought about herself. And now you're doing it to me, too,' he exclaims.

Please, no. I do not want to go down this path. I don't want to be compared to her. I'll always fall short. Perhaps this is my punishment. I'll never be able to get away from her. Or what I've told him. And how can I complain when I know I deserve all of it and more?

'It's like my life is repeating itself. It's fucking exhausting. I just want things to be normal. Like they used to. Did she tell you to do this? Have you been speaking to her?' he says, cracking his knuckles.

I can't hide my confusion. I feel my face twisting without permission. 'Finlay, I don't know what do you mean? Has who told me what?'

'Don't play daft, Cassie, or Nova, or whoever you are today. You know her, remember?'

'But I…I haven't seen anyone. I've stayed at home in the flat and spoke to nobody like you said. You said I didn't need anyone else, just us. I don't understand. Can you please just calm down and tell me what you mean?' I plead, bringing my hands into prayer at my chest.

And then it hits me, like a whopping big sledgehammer: he means the day of our reading.

I said I saw his ex's spirit. I think he believes that I've been speaking to the other side without his permission. But what I'm still struggling to grasp is why he thinks me and this other woman have been in some sort of spiritual cahoots. Gulping back down the bile that has risen to the back of my throat, I have no idea what to do, and the sharpness of his eyes still has me pinned to the spot.

Maybe I should fess up, come clean about every lie I've told him, and hope that he forgives me. Then we can start over with a blank canvas. Is that what I'm supposed to do?

The voices in my head erupt into a resounding yes, but my book of secrets stays locked. What if it ruins everything, causes the end of us? I'm not ready. I don't want to give it all up, I can't.

'Finlay, listen to me. Please. I don't know why you're so upset, but whatever it is, I'm sorry. We can fix this if you hate it,' I say, pulling my hair away from my face, securing it in a low bun at the nape of my neck with a bobble wrapped around my wrist. 'This is my fault, OK? Tonight is all my fault. You're exhausted, and I stupidly got the day wrong. I got confused with dinner, and I shocked you by changing my hair without telling you first. It was supposed to be a surprise, but it doesn't matter because it was all me, OK? I don't want to fight with you.'

The words are slipping off the tip of my tongue. I can't stop them, but I believe that I mean them.

'I…I love you, OK? Do you hear me? Finlay, I love you.'

To my complete disbelief, the pressure begins to evaporate like a burst balloon. It's almost as if someone injected him with a tranquiliser because I watch as his rigid stature softens and his furious face is finally melting back into its usual sparkling smile.

Finally, he reaches out, pulling me into his chest and kisses the top of my head. And despite the prominent stench of peroxide from my crappy bleach job, I feel like I can actually breathe again, too.

As he pulls away, I let him head for bed without trying to stop him and I quietly make my way around the flat, turning off the lamps, and tidying up the remnants of what should have been a romantic night.

'Cas?' he calls. Now he's made his way into the bathroom without me noticing. 'Have you had a shower today?'

Oh, my god. I feel the colour drain from my face – if there's any left. I haven't. How disgusting. I was too busy worrying about my hair that I forgot about the rest of me.

Completely mortified by my lack of hygiene, I have no fight left in me to lie to him. Not again. Definitely not tonight. 'Erm, no, not today, I didn't. I did yesterday, though I promise.'

Reluctantly, I nudge open the bathroom door. His eyes are closed as the water thrashes over him. He pushes his thick wet hair back with his hands, and his steel torso glistens as the soap trickles down his body. I feel star struck. He's still the most beautiful thing I've ever laid my eyes on.

'Well, why don't we fix that?' he says, opening his eyes and smiling wickedly.

He doesn't need to ask me twice. I'll do anything to make this night better and so I strip off my dress, yank off my underwear and kick the bundle backwards before leaping into the bath and pressing my body against his as he takes my gently mouth in his. In no time at all, his hands are all over me.

Our love making feels different. Rougher. Angrier. But before I know it it's all over and I feel satisfied I've done everything right, and now more than ever I can't wait to go to sleep and try to get some rest.

I dry myself with a white towel hanging from the prong on the back of the bathroom door and then follow him into the bedroom where I pull on the pyjamas I left on my pillow from the night before.

With one knee on the bed, ready to climb in and snuggle up like we usually do, he stops me.

'Listen, Cas. I think it might be best if you sleep on the couch tonight. I just need a bit of space to cool down.'

My jaw drops, but I don't say a word. I feel like I've just been given an electric shock. I thought everything was OK. I thought we were fine.

More than anything I want to beg him, to somehow persuade or convince him to let me get in our bed, but I feel like I've been sucker punched and can't find the words.

Instead, I cautiously lift my pillow and collect the blanket that's folded across the bottom of the bed, because I'll need something to keep me warm during the night I suppose.

'Wait,' he says, as I begin to take my final steps to the doorway.

I hold my breath, hoping that he's changed his mind. Just another glitch in our complex system, but no harm done. Nothing that can't be fixed.

'Your hair – it's the wrong colour, by the way. It looks too white. Cheap, actually. It's supposed to be warm, like honey. Why don't you try again, eh? See if you have better luck a second time.'

He pulls the duvet up to his neck and nestles his head on the pillow, not caring to wait for my response before he finally concludes tonight's events.

'Night, babe. Get a good sleep.'

TWENTY-SEVEN

CASSIE

My neck cracks like a glow stick as I sit up and peel the blanket off, disturbing Luna as I remove my feet from the warmth of her furry belly. The memories of last night, still loud and clear, kick-start the noise of too many voices competing in my head.

Trying to block them all out, I spin myself round and stretch out my legs, hearing the click of stiff knees unlocking, before allowing my bare feet to land on the wooden floor.

My eyes instantly find the door, fearing punishment for this too, because as a child, I was constantly told off for wondering around the house without any socks or slippers on. Most of the time, I submitted to avoid entering a battle I didn't understand. How could I possibly explain to my parents that it was the only thing that made me feel like I wasn't about to be swept away?

I rub my eyes with the heels of my hands, clearing the haze to try to get my bearings. Groggy is an understatement, and I'm not sure what time it is, but the room is wide awake with light. Which tells me that

Finlay has already left for work. Without waking me with a kiss on the forehead to say good morning.

My chest tightens as I try to keep a steady breath. I didn't think things could get any worse. I feel more drained than my iPhone battery, and as much as I'd like to crawl back under the blanket and play hide and seek with myself, I know that I can't. I feel urgently compelled to take a piping hot shower, desperate to try to scrub the rejection from my skin.

I watch as my fur baby jumps down and rubs her tail against my shins, and despite everything, I feel a sprinkling of joy because I'm so relieved that she's still with me.

Finlay wasn't keen on the idea: 'It's not even yours. You don't know where that thing has come from. The cat will be fine. It's nothing but a wild animal. A rodent. The thing hates me, anyway. It'd be happier somewhere else.'

I baulked every time he referred to her with such contempt, but there was no chance in hell that I would even consider such outlandish suggestions. Not even for him. Leaving her behind was inconceivable. She's the most reliable and consistent companion I've ever had, and right now I need her more than ever.

Although, it has been tough, I admit. Making sure the furniture shows minimal sign of her presence. That was the compromise. I hoover the furniture daily, scoop her shit out of the tray as soon as she goes to prevent a stench. He wasn't happy about its location either, being in the spare room. But he didn't want it in the living room, the kitchen, the hallway, the bedroom, or the bathroom. It was the only place for it, and every single day I meticulously study the floor for stray grey stones that have jumped from the lip of the tub.

My mind drifts back to earlier on in the week, to a moment that, for some reason till fills my eyes with tears. It was just an accident and I'm probably being too sensitive and overreacting. as always.

He tripped over her food bowl, stubbed his toe, and screamed bloody murder. I sat quietly, hands clasped together on my lap, listening to him bulldoze his way around the bedroom until I heard the slamming of the bathroom door. I waited a further five minutes until heading for bed, but when I finally found my feet, I saw that the door to our room was also closed tight. I instantly panicked, because I last saw Luna in there, and she might have needed to use her tray. The last thing I needed was to be scrubbing the carpet free of ammonia – or worse – but if she'd decided to relieve herself, then I had to get to it before he saw.

Despite being an outdoor lover back at number twenty-two, I hadn't let Luna out of this flat yet. I searched online for tips on how to help your cat adjust to moving and apparently. It was best to keep them indoors for a bit, let them leave their scent as much as possible. So, when I burst into the room and spotted the window wide open, blinds clashing together, I felt danger slap me across the face and I couldn't help but cry out for help.

Rushing in with a towel wrapped around his waist, I barely came up for air as I explained the severity of the situation. He swore, hand on his heart, he didn't know the window was open, that perhaps it had flown open itself. At the time, it didn't matter whether he did or didn't, because all I knew was I had to get my arse out into the rainy night and look for her.

I flung myself outside, without my usual fears, and wandered the streets of the Southside for over two hours, my body becoming numb with clingy wet clothes. Every block of flats looked the same in the dark: four, sometimes five stories high with red brick. My voice was becoming hoarse from calling her name. My white Converse trainers were caked in mud, and for the first time, I felt an uncomfortable dislike for Finlay. It would have been much easier if he'd agreed to help, and there were two of us out looking for her, but instead, he told me I was mad for going out to look and that she'd be fine. I couldn't wrap my head around how someone so gentle, loving, and considerate could lack such compassion.

Finally, I stumbled upon a threatening bridge which would eventually lead me into a creepy forest and was beginning to lose hope. I'm ashamed to say that I was too cowardly to carry on any further, but as I opened my mouth to call her name just one last time, a hand tapped me on the shoulder: Finlay.

'You've been gone ages, Cassie. I can't have you out here alone. What will people think of me?' he said.

I didn't have the energy to respond, so I let go of any anger and fell into his arms with relief and started to sob. I felt so grateful to finally have him by my side. That I wasn't alone.

And then there it was – that familiar meow. The best thing I've ever heard in my life. The heavens began to sing as I shouted on her repeatedly, pushed my way through jaggy bushes that pinched my legs even through the fabric of my leggings and found her cowering under a fallen tree. Shielding herself from the rain. I picked her up gently, and she pushed her soggy face into my neck.

Although Finlay was so far behind, I could still hear him shouting my name, so I hurried back out to him with my baby still cradled in my arms. With a single nod, he looked at me, looked at her, and then shook his head and said nothing.

We've never discussed it since.

Twenty-Eight

Cassie

Pouncing off the sofa, jumping to my feet before I have a chance to change my mind about taking a shower, I head to retrieve some of my things from the boxes in the spare room for afterwards. I said I was going to keep trying with the whole meditation thing and I meant it so, hopefully today I'll finally crack it and shift some of this honking energy once and for all.

The spare room isn't really fit for guests – not that we have any – because it's filled with nothing but robust fitness equipment and rubber mats. And without having anywhere for me to properly unpack and hang or display my things, I've just been constantly rifling through my boxes that are still stashed in here whenever I need something.

I'm still trying to find the right time to ask when I can add a few of my own touches to the flat so it feels more like home for me, too. We don't even need to discuss the sensitive topic of getting rid of his ex's stuff again. He could maybe just let me put out some of my crystals, add a few new cushions or candles. Nothing extravagant.

The time definitely isn't today, though. Not after last night. So, I'm happy to keep plodding along for a bit longer. Besides, we've spoken about moving away anyway and finding our forever home, so I'm sure things will be different when that happens. Maybe all we need is a fresh start, a place of our own without any history and we can make new memories, surrounded by things we've chosen together.

Am I just being incredibly ungrateful? Again. Like always. I know that I'm lucky to be where I am and if what he says is true, and it's only temporary, then I shouldn't feel so uncomfortable about it. It's not the end of the world, and actually I don't suppose it's fair of me to expect to change things when I don't contribute a thing to the mortgage.

He's so good to me. I really hope I haven't messed things up. Maybe I should text him and apologise for last night? Hopefully, I can squash the tension before it explodes to a point of no return and when he comes home, everything will be OK again.

Yes, I'll do that after my shower, too, I decide.

As soon as I enter the spare room, I realise that something looks wrong. I can't put my finger on it right away, but I soon realise the difference: there're only two of my boxes left.

Where is all my stuff?

I rush to the corner of the room, ripping open the cardboard lids and breathe a sigh of relief to see that they still contain my clothes, which at least means he isn't chucking me out after our fight last night. But where has the rest of it gone? I don't understand. Where is my chakra rug that I sit on? I can't find my bag of crystals and my only Tarot deck that I use for readings – not just for other people, but when practicing for myself too – it's all gone.

I claw at my hair. Is there a chance that I've been sleepwalking again and moved them somewhere else? Because he would have told me if he'd done something with them. I know he would've.

I'm sure they're in the flat somewhere, so I head for the cupboard in our bedroom. No boxes in here either.

Hands on my hips, I stare down at a pair of trainers that aren't mine. It's probably preposterous, and I'm going mad, but I just have this urge to head out into the garden at the back of the flat and search in our wheelie bin. Neither Finlay nor I would have intentionally binned them, but maybe there's been an accident and they were dumped with the rubbish.

I push my feet into another woman's shoes without further thought and then unlock the front door and flick the latch so that I can get back in easily. Taking a left, I jog outside and into the winter air.

The cold stings my arms and legs and I wish I'd at least shoved on one of the jackets hanging up on the rail too, but I wasn't thinking about anything else except finding my things.

It's probably about one degree, and I can see how fast my heart is racing by my panting breaths, visible in the air. The spiders' webs attached to the row of green and blue bins have transformed into a work of art, and the lids crack as I break the icy seal on each one and poke my head in.

As I reach the last one, I pray to the universe that it will be the luckiest, but I hear myself begin to cry when

I see it's no different from the others. Completely empty. *Of course, they are,* I think – it's bin day. So even if my stuff was there, it's long gone now, that's for sure.

Tail between my legs, I rub my pink arms and head back into the flat and stand in the middle of the hallway, wondering where to look next. Maybe there's somewhere else I haven't thought of, somewhere he decided to unpack the boxes for me as an apology of his own. But where could that be if not in the living room, the spare room, or even the cupboard?

Unless I just wasn't looking properly the first time I checked.

I dart across the hallway, through the two doors, and start tearing the hangers of clothes from the rail. If I can just clear everything out, I'm sure I'll find my stuff stashed in the back, simply hidden in plain sight, and everything will be fine.

Although completely shattered, I'm fuelled by some sort of supersonic strength as I yank at each item, chucking them over my shoulder, refusing to hold them in my hand for too long because just the material of someone else's belongings feels like I'm touching something poisonous. I can feel it seeping into my skin, someone else's story.

When I've finally pulled everything off the rail, I still see no sign of my belongings and begin to feel even more panicked. *It makes absolutely no sense,* I think as I get to my knees and begin to sob.

Suddenly, I hear one of the voices in my head, far louder than the others. It's telling me to search the bathroom, which seems ridiculous, but I practically fly there, anyway.

As I pull open the bathroom cabinet with bated breath, my last bit of hope finally leaves my body when I see that, of course, there's nothing there either.

My jelly legs give way and I melt to the floor, burying my face in my hands at the unavoidable realisation that all my stuff is gone. It's all gone. And if I didn't get rid of it, then it had to have been Finlay, but I just don't understand why.

Sitting on the white and black tiles, I lean back against the wooden panel on the side of the bathtub, but I feel something dislodging behind me. Great, now I've broken something too.

I spin round and get on my knees to investigate the damage, but as I push the slice of wood that looks a little disjointed from the others, it wiggles. I don't think I could have broken it so easily just by leaning on it. Forming a fist, I give it a gentle knock to see what I'm working with, and surprisingly it opens like a laundry chute. Holding the wood to stop it flapping, I peer inside, but I can't see a thing except pipes. Although, what am I really expecting to find? Why would my things be stashed under the bathtub?

Regardless, I push my hand inside – and oh my god. Yes. I can feel something. There's something in here. I twiddle my fingers until I feel a sharp edge slice my middle finger, giving me a paper cut. Could it be some of my books? Are they really inside? They can't be.

I continue to pinch and pull and tease something into my hand. It is a book. It's flimsy but I recognise the shape of a spine instantly.

Able to curve its shape, I coax it out of darkness and into the light.

Part Three

'Out of the ash I rise with my red hair, and I eat men like air.'
– Sylvia Plath

THE UNKNOWN

Sitting on her backside, the lack of fatty tissue makes it easy for the coldness of the tiles to chill her to the bone. With jittered teeth and without a single flinch, she applies pressure between her fingertips and yanks a strand of hair from her scalp. Placing it on the page in front of her, she decides to use it as motivation, tucking it inside the middle crease.

The topic of hair and what it looks like is completely irrelevant to her now, but once, she'd prided herself upon her golden crown. It was thick, long, and in excellent condition, being naturally fair-haired, and every tone painted blended beautifully like a warm embrace. Such a stark contrast to the jet-black, blunt bob now tucked behind small ears on a hollowing and pale face.

She's losing energy, weight is falling from her body and every time she looks in the mirror, she sees a skeleton staring back.

Trying hard to recall the reaction of his face twisting when he saw what she'd done, she starts a bullet list at the top of the page: *Dark. Defiant. Terrifyingly dangerous.*

It was definitely a bittersweet victory when she took the plunge, removing the last of her identity by taking the kitchen scissors to the side of her neck and started to chop. Erasing her halo felt like she'd gone straight to hell but destroying the one thing he loved most about her – if that hadn't already dissipated too – but for the first time in who knows how long, she felt the heat of a wild bonfire exploding in the pit of her stomach. The smoke was just as black as the dye that filled the bottle, and she knew it was her riskiest move yet.

She was right to give her hair a funeral, because the flames didn't last long, snuffed out completely the minute he grabbed the back of her head with a clenched fist.

This might be the hardest part to write out of everything she has managed so far, because she's certain now that her time is running out. It started with cruel words, escalated to threats of punishment, and now she's reached the point of purple bruises embroidered across her body.

The fact she has to admit she never saw any of it coming is why she believes him to be capable of absolutely anything now. Duping people he claimed to love fills him with a sick thrill, and for such a long time, she lay awake at night questioning if perhaps she was the problem. Not believing her own mind. Replaying disaster after disaster, searching for the *aha* moment that would make everything feel better.

Wiping her tears, she drags her brittle nails down her face. She wishes she could claw the whole thing off. Her wrist aches from the whipping of her pen as it took part in another tell-all. A voice in her head is encouraging her to keep going, tell the world exactly what he's said and done, but her arm feels paralysed, hovering at the bottom of the page.

Looking her dead in the eyes with one hand seizing her jaw, he rammed her body into the wall and placed a palm flat beside her ear. 'This was your last roll of the dice. Do you fucking hear me?' Unable to move her face enough to nod, he continued, confirming something she'd feared for a while. The threat was always waiting in the shadows, ready to pounce. 'Next time, you're going to force me to do something I really don't want to. Do you hear me?' Practically foaming at the mouth, he continues to spit words that land on her face. 'You'll be haunted with regret, mourning the consequences of your own actions while you're six feet under, buried in the dirt.'

TWENTY-NINE

CASSIE

I stare down at the purple suede rectangle waiting on my lap. Although stained with damp, I can still make out the image of a tree as my finger caresses the grooves on the front cover. But it isn't one of mine. It looks like a diary or a notebook.

I'm reluctant to invade someone's privacy without permission, but it feels odd that it was in there in the first place. Maybe I should have a peak.

As I go to open the cover, I freeze, realising that it must belong to Finlay and I'm winded by the realisation that by going to such an effort to keep it hidden, he doesn't trust me enough to leave it lying around. I feel like rather than finding a book, I've stumbled across a big red flag, confirming that he has no confidence in me. Or us. Or this relationship.

Perhaps there are tales of his life before me. A happier time for him, shared with the real love of his life.

If I have any chance left to fix things between us, wouldn't it be better if I read what really goes on in his mind? Then I'd be able to make him happy, seeing as I'm currently not doing a very good job at that.

My fingertips feel red hot as I turn the book over in my hand. I close my eyes and take a deep breath, consciously dropping my shoulders and releasing my tongue from the roof of my mouth.

I'll ask the universe for the answer.

Placing one hand over my heart, I say aloud, 'I know it's wrong, and I shouldn't do it, but please – if anyone is listening – just tell me what to do here. Let me know if I should open this book or leave it be.'

'Read it!' a voice hollers loudly in my ear making me flinch and my arms instinctively launch to cup my ears. So close, it feels as if someone is sitting right next to me. Louder than anything I've ever heard before.

My finger nudges the floppy cover open, exposing a page of red words that I can't bring myself to read. Because am I actually trusting a voice in my head? It might just be something my brain has created because it's what I want to hear. Just like Finlay had said when I told him that I ask a higher power for guidance. He looked at me like I was crazy and told me that none of what I believed made any sense. That perhaps I needed professional help. And I was so desperate to convince him otherwise in case he ended our relationship, but I just seemed to stumble over every sentence. I couldn't persuade him to look at things from a different perspective. No answer I provided was satisfactory to him. The only logical answer in his mind was that there was something wrong with mine.

I have so much still to learn or become aware of. Maybe if I'd done more research, paid proper attention instead of just skimming through the pages of the books I read, then I would feel more confident that it's more than just insanity. But I didn't. And what leg do I have to stand on if I'm constantly just guessing and getting so many things to do with the spiritual realm embarrassingly wrong?

I just want to do better. I want to be better. And although Finlay doesn't believe in the same things I do, I can't just ignore all the previous things that have happened in my life: things moving around in the middle of the night, voices calling me in the distance, making me so scared at a young age that all I could do was hide under my purple Groovy Chick duvet.

'Read it,' the voice booms again, almost bursting my eardrum.

Both hands find the edges of the book as I pick it up carefully, avoiding any more paper cuts. The first is still leaking blood that's accidentally stained the top of the page that now has my full attention because of the beautiful handwriting. I don't recognise it as his though. It seems too feminine with its curls and wisps, but there's something familiar about it. There's no date at the top, but after skimming the first few paragraphs of the first page, I conclude that the topic is of Christmas and so I read on, hoping it will all become clearer.

Reaching the end of the entries, I slam the book closed and cover my mouth with my hand to stop myself from throwing up. But the horror of it entices me back in and so I reread it again from the beginning, and that's when I haul my trembling body over the edge of the bath and let the bile erupt from my throat like a volcano.

I know who it sounds like it was written about, but it can't be. It just can't. There has to be an explanation. There's just no way Finlay would ever treat someone the way this book describes. I know him. I love him.

But even the writer sounds like someone I know.

Tears relentlessly drop onto my knuckles as I grip the white PVC to steady myself. The room is spinning, closing in around me as I frantically try to ignore all the similarities.

When I finally manage to stop retching, gripping my throat, I force myself to take long, deep breaths, and then slump back onto the cold floor. Just when I think I've calmed down enough to think rationally, the voice screams at me again – 'read it.'

'But it can't be,' I say as I pick the book back up, deciding to do as I'm told and go through it all again for a third time.

Although few and far between, I can't push past the fact that these stories feel a little bit too close to home. Could they really be about who I'm lying next to at night? Finlay? My beautiful gift from the universe, the one that was supposed to save me. It seems inconceivable that he could be capable of being so twisted and manipulative. And there's no real proof, I tell myself. His name isn't mentioned once.

But I can't calm myself down enough to believe my own reasoning. The voices in my head are kicking off and I want to scream at them all to shut the hell up so I can figure this out but it's no use, and now every muscle in my body is screaming at me to get out of this flat and run.

Maybe if I just get out of here and head back to my old flat, I'll be able to think clearer there. The air will do me good. I'll just take the book with me, read it again, and then I'm sure I'll realise that I've got this all horribly wrong.

As I shakily get to my feet, I hear the click of the lock and my heart plummets. He can't be home already. It's too early.

Tucking the journal behind my back and underneath my top, secured by the waistband of my pyjama shorts, I quickly spit some affirmations. *Everything is fine. You are safe. Nobody is going to hurt you.*

Forcing my mouth to stretch from ear to ear, I call out to let him know I'm here. 'Just coming. Be right there.'

I pull open the bathroom door and skid into the hallway at the exact same time the front door swings open, and my jaw falls to the floor.

THIRTY

BLAIR

As my first foot crosses the doorway, a familiar but alarmingly gaunt face stumbles out of the bathroom, skin painted pale with horror, panting. She stops immediately when she sees me. Stunned. Although I do detect a glimmer of relief, I don't understand why she'd be pleased to see me. Not after what she's done.

Without knowing all the ins and outs, I concluded that the only explanation as to how she managed to slither into my life without a hitch, successful in her mission of sabotage, was by somehow tracking down George after our reading. Still, I can't quite get my head around it all. I have so many questions: *How did she even find him? And more importantly, why did she go looking?*

However, putting aside the fact she has totally breached client confidentiality, a cat fight isn't top priority right now. There's another grave issue that's far more urgent, and it must be discussed before anything else. It doesn't matter that I don't like her very much. I knew I had to put my feelings aside. I had to do the right thing and warn her.

'No need for introductions, I assume,' I say, stepping back into the danger zone and closing the door firmly behind me.

When I saw them together, standing outside her flat, you could have knocked me down with a feather. I actually came back to apologise. Can you believe it? I felt guilty for being so abrupt and bratty with her during our session and wanted to tell her that she was right after all. That he had a darker side to him. But then there she was – and with him. Waltzing in the rain as if they were actors in a soppy romance film.

The change in her now is frightful, and what's even more horrifying, is how quickly it's happened. It seems he's wasted no time with his latest project, but I shouldn't be so surprised, because the same was happening to me. I just didn't realise how fast the train was going until I finally managed to jump off.

'You do remember me, don't you, Nova?' I ask cautiously. 'You gave me a reading not too long ago.'

The previously confident – not to mention naturally beautiful – psychic is long gone. The flame has fizzled out behind her eyes, and her previously thick and healthy hair has been frazzled by what I assume was a hefty amount of bleach. Her collar bone is sharp, and those curves that gave her the perfect hourglass figure without any help from surgery have melted away, leaving behind a fragile shell. The dark purple shadows under her puffy eyes scream exhaustion, and her knees are doing everything they can to avoid buckling.

My eyes scan her entire body until they land on her toes. Are those my trainers she's wearing, too? She's made herself very much at home, it seems.

Evidently overflowing with panic, she finally opens her mouth. 'I'm sorry I…Wait, wait, I remember. Blair? Um, what are you doing here? Why are you in my home? How did you even get in?'

'With my key,' I reply, waving it in the air like a magic wand.

'Your key? What are you talking about?'

She looks genuinely fogged with confusion. As if I'm the last person she ever expected to see, which strikes me as odd because, of course she knew this was my home.

'Why don't we sit down and have a chat? Coming?' I ask, making my way across the hallway, my block heeled boots clicking on the wood below.

'Wait. Come back. This really isn't a good time. You have to leave.'

I hear her cries, but I don't turn back. Instead, I cross the threshold of my former living room and start looking around, searching for…I don't even know what the fuck I'm searching for.

Everything is exactly as it was the night I fled. Not a single thing has changed, despite having a brand spanking new female resident. Hindsight has uncovered a lot of truths that were burrowed beneath the sand, so I wonder if that's because, like me, she wasn't given permission to.

Adrenaline infused with fear pounds against my chest as I perch my bum on the edge of the plump couch, cross my legs, clasp my hands on my lap and wait for her to join me.

'OK. Fine,' she shouts, stumbling through the door, palms held high in resignation before gripping her hips. 'Never mind how you managed to let yourself in. Why are you here, Blair?'

The Botox embedded in my forehead attempts to frown, because isn't it blatantly obvious why I'm here?

'Nova, you gave me quite the reading. One that changed the course of my life. You must understand my confusion as to why you're now shacked up with my bloody ex.'

'I think you've made a mistake, Blair. My boyfriend's name is Finlay, and he's never mentioned you.'

'Well, I'm not surprised, he's not exactly going to tell—' My tongue freezes. 'Did you just say Finlay?'

She paces back and forth, takes a peek around the door, and then finally comes to a halt and turns back to face me.

'Yes, I did. Look, I'm really sorry that your relationship didn't work out, but my boyfriend is called Finlay. Finlay Munro. And he's had this place for years. You've made a mistake.'

My body propels itself up off the couch, lunging toward her. I grip her bony shoulders with my hands, wanting to shake her.

And myself. For only just realising this isn't her fault at all.

Staring into her blurry eyes, desperately trying to fight off a downpour, my entire body crawling with tension, I wince as I open my mouth.

'Look at me, Nova. Look at me right now and listen to what I'm about to say, OK?'

She bites her bottom lip and reluctantly nods her head.

'You're not in a relationship with who you think. The man you think you know has been lying to you, and if you don't get out of here now, there's a strong chance that you won't ever be able to again.'

THIRTY-ONE

CASSIE

The echo of her words refuses to fade. The walls are closing in around me and I break free of her sharp nails and dive to the couch before I pass out.

'His name is George, Nova. Not fucking Finlay – that's his middle name. He's been lying to you. Do you get it now? Comprehend?'

I can't speak. I can't breathe. The room's spinning and all I see are giant letters bouncing off one another, spelling out the dreaded realisation that it really was too good to be true: George Finlay Munro.

So many new thoughts are batting around my head now, like tennis balls at Wimbledon. If Finlay is who she says he is, then that must mean…Oh. My. God. It's her. The ex. The author of the book digging into my spine.

'Blair?' I whisper unconsciously, watching as she crosses her arms with a somewhat frustrated eye roll.

Stretching both arms out, red sleeves of a rollneck dress poking out from the cuffs of her black leather jacket, she starts snapping fingers and thumbs in the air.

'Well, yes, obviously. We know who I am, for god's sake. But didn't you hear what I said? Nova, you have to leave. I'll explain everything, but you have to leave with me now.'

'But…you're alive?' I ask, in desperate need to hear confirmation from the horse's mouth that she's not a ghost.

'What the hell are you talking about? Of course, I'm alive. Do I look dead to you? He didn't actually say that, did he?'

'No…' I shake my head, feeling like a wet dog nobody wants to touch. I can't believe I'm about to say this. Admit something so awful. 'But I did.'

Her jaw drops, tongue threatening to push through the roof of her mouth before she releases the words.

'What the fuck, Nova? So, you did know we were together, then? And how did you even manage to pull that off? George knows fine well I'm not dead.'

'No. Well, yes, but it's not what you think. Look, it's really difficult to explain.'

I still don't understand how our worlds have collided in this way, but if what she's saying is true, then the journal makes perfect sense. The stories of moving in together, Christmas dates, and a huge arrow pointing at the colour of her hair darker than an eclipsed sky. And she must have written that bit quite some time ago because the ponytail she's secured to the crown of her head is long and thick.

Wanting to scream, I cover my mouth with my hand. I should have known. I should have asked more questions about his girlfriend, but the truth is, I really didn't want to hear it. Didn't think I'd be able to cope with a double-edged sword reminding me that I'd never compare to her, but also that I killed her off without permission. As if she were an annoying character in a book or a TV series.

'Look, it's fine, whatever. It doesn't matter right now. We. Have. To. Go. Come on. Shift,' she commands, clapping her hands together with every word.

I obey like a puppet without any hesitation, because it's all coming back to me – the reading, I mean. What I told her, that she was in danger in her relationship. I felt it. We both did, but I couldn't explain to her any better than the cards she pulled: The Magician, The Fool, The Tower, and then the extra card – the Devil.

I can't bring myself to think about my own relationship with Fin. Or George. Whatever his name is. I'm just relieved she's actually alive and well – the woman I now know to be Blair Cameron. She listened to me, after all. She left before it was too late, and finally, the guilt of my own wicked lie is starting to break free, too.

She grabs my arm tightly, creating future fingertip bruises, and ushers me into the hallway.

'Go. Go get a jacket and grab anything you need.'

'I…I don't have much to grab,' I admit, embarrassed, and unable to say why. 'But I can't leave without Luna, my cat. I have to take her with me.'

She sighs and taps her boot off the floor. 'OK. Whatever. Just do it quickly.'

I tug on the stiff handle to the cupboard in the hall, where Luna's carrier cage is stashed. Fortunately, she's right beside me, startled by the chaos but still wanting to be part of the scandal. With the little flap on the top open, I waste no time trying to coax her inside with treats and pounce, bundling her into my arms like a baby before pouring her inside and clicking it tight.

'I'll just shove clothes on and that's me, OK?'

I want her approval. She knows best. She's a far stronger woman that I could ever hope to be. God knows what else she must have gone through.

After she nods, I put one foot in front of the other, but only make it one step into the bedroom when I hear the click of the door once more. I let the handle of the carrier drop and Luna meows with horror as she clashes to the ground.

Forcing myself to turn around, the front door swings open and mine and Blair's heads both swivel to find each other, fear painted across our faces.

Thirty-Two

Blair

His pupils dart wildly from left to right, but his face remains like stone. He's completely unreadable, not just to me, but also to Nova. I can tell by her vacant stare. Perhaps she's trying to use magic powers to pin the bastard to the door so we can make our escape.

'Cassie,' he speaks directly to her, averting from my gaze. 'You didn't tell me you were having a friend round.'

First of all, I wonder, who the fuck is Cassie? But still, it doesn't matter what she calls herself because we all know I'm definitely not a friend of hers – or his. I'm much more than that.

'I, eh I…' She tries but can't grip the sentence with her trembling hands.

She steps back into the hallway, mimicking my shadow.

'George, you can stop with the act. She knows who you are. This isn't a game.'

His emerald eyes darken immediately, revealing the monster hidden within. The same sinfully ugly face I witnessed first-hand, the night after my reading with Nova when I played him the recording. It was both a terrible decision and yet it turns out, a lifesaving one. I thought he'd laugh, find it funny how I managed to get into a tiff with someone who promotes all that woo woo zen stuff. But, when he edged closer to the end of the sofa, elbows pressed hard into his thighs as he gripped my phone with such ferocious disdain, I knew in the pit of my stomach, before he even spat a single word, that things were about to change forever.

He launched like a rocket, urging me backwards against the wall without needing to lay a single hand on me. His anger was terrifying enough to make me back away. Then, with one palm pressed against the wall beside my left ear, the index finger of his right threatened to gauge my eyes out as he jabbed it in front of my face. I wanted to run, but I couldn't move. I wanted to shout, but I couldn't speak. I cowered under the weight of his words and the power of his intimidation alone.

He wasn't making any sense, accusing me wildly of things that never even happened, and how he didn't want to have to do this again – whatever *this* was – but I kept leaving him with no other choice.

And that's when I did it. It was my first thought, so I thrust my knee into his groin and watched him crumble to the floor. And then I ran. Slipping and sliding as my socks acted like ice skates, almost bringing me down with him. I fumbled furiously with the keys still hanging in the lock of the front door and when it finally clicked, I fled without a thing to my name.

Except the keys to his car.

'I'm sorry. I think there must be some mistake,' he lies to my face, straightening his back, and grinning from ear to ear. 'I don't think we've met before. I'm Finlay.'

I don't know whether to laugh at his Oscar-worthy performance or cry because with skills like that, and the state Nova is in already, there's a strong chance she might believe him. And then what? I'll have put myself back in the danger zone for nothing.

'No, you're not,' she whispers behind me. Although, still loud enough for everyone to hear. 'Your name is George. You…you lied to me. You're not who you say you are.'

The corners of his mouth drop to his chin in an instant and he pushes his hands through his hair while releasing a low guttural groan.

Both of us step back, edging closer to the bedroom door, not knowing what's coming next, but more than aware that it isn't looking good.

He turns his back to us, takes a couple of steps and turns the key, locking all of us inside.

With his hands in the air, he slowly twists around. 'OK, OK. You've got me. I'm sure you two have had plenty of time to catch-up and reminisce, sooooo let's go back to some basic introductions, shall we?'

His posture is rigid, his jaw clenched, and the picture-perfect mask he wears so well has been well and truly discarded. It's astonishing how quickly he can change. It really is like two people living in the same shell. You never know who you're going to get. Or when.

'Cassie, meet Blair – again. You remember her, right?' He claps his hands together, securing the answer for her. 'Of course, you do. You had a lot to say to her back then, and even more to say to me after, didn't you? And yet look, here she is. Isn't that amazing?'

I swear I can hear the rapid beat of her heart hammering like a drumroll from behind me.

'You look confused, babe. Wait. Wait. I'll try again,' he insists, lunging forward and grabbing my wrist, yanking me to his side. 'Cassie, this is Blair. My dearly departed – yet not so dead, after all – girlfriend. Alive, and for now, very much still kicking, it seems.'

I try to rip my hand from the burn of his fingers, but it only adds gas to the flame. He's so strong, he could crack the bones in my arm at any minute if he wanted to.

She needs to do something – Nova, Cassie, or whatever her name is. There's no way he's giving me any rope to flee again, and I don't know what's going to happen to me now that I've returned. I'm small but could probably put up a good fight, although it would be pointless because I know he'd overpower me. My back teeth grind as my jaw clenches with anger. Adrenaline is fizzing up my spine, urging me to lash out, but the awareness that he's capable of anything keeps me still.

It's her turn to step up for me now, and she must act fast.

Thirty-three

Cassie

That angelic smile, the softness of his hand clasped with mine, lips that kissed me tenderly, tasting sweet and kind. It all feels like a trippy dream. And now I'm spiralling down from the high at lightning speed.

I thought I'd experienced rock bottom before, but as I find myself trapped in the moment – one I wish so badly, I was actually capable of seeing coming – I realise that there was in fact much further for me to freefall. Now that I'm here, I recognise my final destination instantly. The thud in the middle of my forehead only confirms it. My brain feels like it's cracking open. Realisations I should have come to earlier oozing with embarrassing clarity.

I don't have a special gift, never have. I've known all along that it was way easier to pretend to be Nova than it was to live as weird, little me. Never understood by anyone. Not even myself. I've spent my years squeezing in and out of different women's personalities like they were body-con dresses and this one just burst at the seams, exposing my soul. Everything I've ever thought has always just been make believe.

I really didn't pay any attention to all those YouTube videos. I only really used them to fill the room with some virtual company. Their voices helped me ignore the ones whirling around in my head. And now I know they were never real. As for my Leaning Tower of Pisa of self-help books, I skimmed every one of them, leaping over the chapters that felt too painful to read because exploring those feelings would have meant admitting that I knew there was really a huge problem. That something is wrong with me.

Help was always something I've been too ashamed to ask for, and I need it now more than ever. But Blair needs it more urgently, and I don't know what to do. I still can't bring myself to even look at his face.

The temperature of the room is dropping by the minute, freezing me to the spot, but my palms are sweating profusely.

'Look, we can talk about this. All of us,' I plead. 'Let her go. You're hurting her. Please, Finlay.'

There are so many questions I want to ask, but the stranger standing in front of me, his answers hold no value anymore. He's been lying to me from the beginning and now I'm left hanging on to the edge of a cliff, with nobody coming to help.

'What is it you think I'm going to do to her, Cassie?' he sneers. 'She's my girlfriend. I wouldn't hurt her. She just needs to remember that.'

'I'm not your fucking girlfriend anymore!' Blair screeches up at him.

My jaw falls open the second the back of his hand skelps her across the face. I imagine the sting feels as painful as the punch in my stomach. I was just a pawn in whatever game he's been playing.

He never loved me. He never loved me. He never loved me.

The mask hasn't just slipped, it's exploded into smithereens, but I see him now. The real him. Nothing like the fantasy I had in my head, or who I thought might be the one to save me. But a veil over my own face has also been lifted, allowing me to see clearly for the very first time in years. He's a liar, just like me. Everyone is capable of pretending. Except you can't run from your authentic self forever. I'm realising now that and in the only person you can really trust is yourself.

'Let go of me, you mother-fucking piece of shit!' Blair screams as he forms a fist in her hair, dragging her into the kitchen. He pulls open the cutlery drawer, almost taking it off the hinges, and arms himself with the sharpest blade he owns.

I want to run at him, kick him, punch his revoltingly smug face but my feet won't allow it, so instead I focus on Blair's eyes. Filled with both fury and fear. She's trying her best not to show how much she's hurting, doesn't want to give him any more of herself to him without a fight.

'What is it you think I'm really capable of, eh? Is it this?' he probes, placing the side of the knife flat against her throat.

He can't harm her. Not after she got away from him the first time. She was so terrified in her journal, clinging to the solace of what she thought would be her own last words. And still, she came back to help me. Someone she doesn't even know, someone who doesn't even deserve it. I have to do something. This can't be how her story ends, and I owe her.

It's all down to me. *Time to be brave, Cassie.*

Now or never. Now or never. Now or never.

I still can't move. I need stronger affirmations than that to convince my legs to shift. I clench my fists and grit my teeth and roar. 'I am capable. I am brave. I am a good person.'

And then I throw myself towards them.

Thirty-four

Blair

'No. No. Nova, stop!' I yell.

One wrong move and he could quite easily slice my throat.

Her head is down, arms out in front, and she plunges into my stomach. My head whips back, knocking George's chin, and it sends him stumbling backwards.

Thankfully, the knife has broken free from my neck, but it's now pointed towards Nova like a poisonous arrow. She starts backing away, terror filling her eyes. It was such a stupid thing to do, but it has given me an opportunity.

Before he has a chance to grab me again, I dip to the side, yank the plug from the wall and pull the cord of the steel kettle towards me. Thrusting my right arm high, my elbow quivering from the weight of the metal, I swing like a cricketer playing for my life and it connects with the back of his skull with a crunch. Blood swiftly begins to trickle down his neck, causing him to drop the weapon as he instinctively clutches his open wound.

My eyes follow the knife as it lands on the kitchen floor and without hesitation, I kick it in Nova's direction before he has a chance to collect it again.

Snatching it from the floor immediately, wrapping her fingers tightly around the handle, she lifts it into the air like she's preparing to enter into battle. I don't know what she plans to do next, but I know she's acting on impulse, wanting to protect me. Protect both of us.

The shriek is animalistic as she once again dives towards us, only this time shoving me out of the way and plunging the knife into George's shoulder like it's an epi-pen. But it has the opposite effect and instead of bringing him back to life, it stuns him for enough time to leap out of the way and grab her.

'Come on. Run,' I beg, tugging at her arm, trying to pull her now rigid frame away from him. 'Leave him. We have to get out of here.'

Face pale as a ghost, she turns to face me and almost collapses into my arms, but I refuse to let her drop to the floor. She has to get out of here. We both do, so I lift her arm and wrap it around my neck and begin to pull her towards the bedroom.

'You fucking bitch,' he spits, trying to grab at us but we're out of his reach and he's stumbling, still dizzy from the whack to the head never mind the knife just plunged into his body so we've got the advantage of speed.

Slamming the bedroom door shut behind us, I grab the stupid cat box and launch it onto the bed before searching for something to stop him from getting in.

'Quick, help me move this,' I pant as I begin to push the chest of drawers towards the door.

Thankfully, she's now snapped back to life, realised that the danger we're in is much more important than the fact she's just attacked George, and helps by grabbing the other end and pulling it as hard as she can until we've manoeuvred it in front of the bedroom door. Next, she flies across the room, pulls up the handle of the window and thrusts it open with both hands.

'Grab Luna,' she instructs, darting into the cupboard.

I do as she says, grateful that she's taking a shot of being in charge and hitch myself onto the window ledge. I swing my legs round and dangle them outside. It's about a 5ft drop, but I can jump down safely enough and reach back up for the crate.

She quickly returns from the cupboard with a set of keys in her hand and I take that as my sign to leap and, looking back up at the window in panic, I wait for her to do the same.

Boom. Boom. Boom.

'I'm going to fucking kill you.' His fist continues to pound the other side of the door relentlessly as he yells. 'BOTH of you.'

'Come on!' I scream. *What the hell is she waiting for?* 'Don't look back, just jump, you'll be fine.'

Clambering onto the window ledge, she twists her own legs out and then closes her eyes and falls into my arms. She hits the ground at an awkward angle, twisting her ankle, but she pushes past it and quickly straightens up, taking back the crate containing Luna.

We both begin to run but I don't know where we're going. Anywhere, I suppose is better than where we were before, but we need somewhere to hide until we figure out what to do next.

Although the bastard deserved it, she did just stab him, and for all I know George might phone the police and say I tried to murder him with the kettle, too. Flashing lights will come looking for both of us because we're well and truly in this together now.

'I don't know what to call you,' I gasp as our feet pound the pavement, heading in the direction of the other side of town.

I can only assume we're running towards her old flat, but what use will that be? She doesn't live there anymore.

She turns to face me, cheeks as pink as her bare arms. 'Eh? What do you mean?'

Taking a swift right, we make it to the main street without being followed.

'Is it Nova or Cassie? We might go down for attempted murder and I don't know who you really are.'

With total disregard for the green man, she spots a gap in traffic and bulldozes on, crossing the road diagonally.

Finally, when we reach the railway bridge above us, she begins to slow down and then comes to a complete halt.

'My real name is Cassie. Cassie Torrance. Nova is…well, she doesn't exist, I suppose. Not really. Just in my head, I guess.'

I'm about to dig further, ask what she means or even just where we're going but her chest propels forward, and she starts to convulse and then she empties what little substance she has in her stomach.

As she brings her head back up, I notice the tears running down her face from bloodshot eyes.

Wiping her mouth with the back of her free hand, I notice that her bare arms are now blotched purple. She must be freezing and looks like she might snap in two if there was a gust of sudden wind.

Glancing over my shoulder, still checking for immediate danger, I shrug off my leather jacket and wrap it around her shoulders and link my arm with hers.

'Come on then, Cassie. I think I know where you're taking us.'

THIRTY-FIVE

CASSIE

With support from Blair, my gelatine legs somehow manage to take me home, and as I climb the final concrete step, I burst into a tsunami of tears.

We've made it back to number twenty-two, where all this madness began. But we're safe now. It's going to be OK. The keys, still tightly gripped in the opposite hand that I've been carrying Luna with, have caused my skin to sting. The spiky edges have almost punctured my palm, but we made it.

Alive.

I glance over my shoulder, wiping my face clean, and check that nobody has followed us. Blair's own cold hand touches my back, giving an encouraging rub and I offer her a smile as I pass her the cat crate and push the yale key into the door and twist. We both leap like a frog inside and I slam it behind us, loop the chain and make sure that double check that there's no chance of it being opened by anyone but us.

My legs suddenly begin to ache and finally give way as I crumble to the floor, pressing my forehead against the wood. Luna begins to hiss from the crate above me, which is so unlike her, but I need a few more moments to stay exactly where I am, so I'll check on her in a second. The poor girl, she's been through the mill tonight just as much as we have.

Eventually I'm able to lift my head and so I unclasp the gate on her carrier and Blair puts her down on the ground beside me. I don't want to upset her anymore, so I give her space to venture out into the flat on her own terms. But she refuses to leave and instead bares her sharp teeth, lowers her head, and continues to hiss into thin air.

'It's OK, baby. It's OK. We're home. We're safe now. You can come on out,' I say, trying to soothe her from whatever has upset her so badly. But she backs herself even further into the plastic box, adamant that she won't be going anywhere.

'What's wrong with her? Why is she snorting like that?' Blair asks, now standing over both of us with her hands on her hips.

She seems so calm. As if the events of this morning were just a dream when I know that the memories will give me nightmares for years to come.

'I don't know. I've never seen her like this before. Well, not since I first took her to Fin—'

I stop to correct myself.

'I mean, George's, flat.'

She rolls her pretty blue eyes, throwing her hands in the air then letting them flop back down by her side.

Suddenly, a low crackle makes both of our head's swivel. I recognise it instantly, the needle hitting the vinyl as it begins to play. Turning back to look to Blair for confirmation that she can hear it too, because I don't really know what to believe is real or not anymore, my stomach drops when I see that she can.

'Is that fucking Patsy Cline?' Blair mouths under the melody.

I put my index finger to my mouth immediately and stare up at her. The volume is increasing. Someone is turning the dial. The bass booms and we both throw our hands to our ears.

My throat is tightened by a hand clenching tighter and tighter. I can't breathe. Someone is inside the flat, but who? It can't be Finlay, because as far as he's concerned, I have nothing to do with this flat anymore. I moved in with him. There's no reason for him to think I would come back here or that it would even be an option.

I'm trying to catch my breath as I work out what to do next.

'Maybe it's a squatter?' Blair suggests.

I nod slowly, trying to convince myself of her explanation, but it just doesn't feel right. A squatter wouldn't be playing loud music. They're supposed to lie low, inconspicuous.

Rising, I slowly remove my – well, Blair's – trainers, pushing them off at the heel and begin to tiptoe down the hallway. I'm not really sure what my plan is, but I'm being pulled by a string, passed my bedroom, the bathroom, and the kitchen. Now stood in front of the door to my former Tarot reading room, I see the crack of light at my feet.

I feel Blair's hot breath on the back of my neck as I reach for the brass doorknob. The sweat from my palm smothering it like I'm wiping off a sticky sweetie.

'Cassie, maybe we should leave?'

No, the voice in my head retorts sharply.

And I don't want to listen to it. Because I can't trust myself with anything anymore, but for some reason, I still do.

I twist left and push the door open, stride inside, and Blair stumbles in behind me, attached to my back like a koala.

The curtains hanging either side of the window have been pulled over. The table is empty apart from one lit pillar candle, sitting next to the hefty chunk of raw rose quartz that cost me more than any crystal ever did. Dust dances in the air, but it's only visible around the middle.

My eyes don't know where to look. At the man sitting at the head of the table, the same way he had that first meeting, or the woman slowly approaching me from the same direction. Both are equally terrifying – because Blair is still behind me. The blonde-haired stranger is the same from before. The one I thought was Finlay's missing ex, Blair. But of course, I know now that can't be. I was wrong.

My blood runs cold as I watch each of the stitches that had sewn her lips together snap. Her mouth opens wide enough to swallow me up and mouths one very clear instruction. One I've heard before.

'RUN.'

Thirty-six

Blair

Rocking back and forth on his chair, clunking the legs off the floor with every swing, is George-Finlay-Mun-fucking-ro. Immune to kitchen utensils, this bastard is relentless.

I say nothing as he suddenly stops, stretches his arm out, casually flicks the stylus of the record player in the air and repositions it to play all over again. What is this? His fucking theme tune?

'Hello again, ladies. Nice of you to finally join me,' he says with a sickening smirk.

I look to Cassie for help with what to do, but for whatever reason, she's staring in the opposite direction, trapped in a trance. *Hello.* I want to scream at her. *Can't you see the big fucking problem in the room here?*

I think she must be in shock or something like that. Whatever goes on in that girl's mind is beyond me, but this might have just been the thing to finally tip her over the edge. And yet the fact remains that whatever she's playing at, I need her right now, and she has to snap out of this, for both our sake.

'I bet you're wondering how I'm here, right?' he commands my attention back.

Under his grey hooded zipper, he's wearing a white basketball tank top. I spot the PVC looking tape that people use for fitness injuries under the collar. He's managed to stop the bleeding from Cassie's stabbing, but now he's here, and twirling the exact same knife in his hand like a majorette.

'She should have aimed lower, you prick. Deflated a vital organ or something,' I spit.

'Shhhh. I'm talking now, Blair. OK? I'll deal with you soon enough.'

My temper flares as wide as my nostrils, but just this once I do as he says, because I need to think about what we're going to do here.

'So, as I was saying, that's an easy one. Ye see, Cassie – the clumsy cow that she is – didn't hide her flat keys very well. I found them stashed in a box inside the cupboard and well, you can imagine my surprise. How hurt I was that she was keeping a secret from me.'

I'm allowing him to talk, but only so I can buy some more time for Cassie to come back to life. Her body is here, but I have no idea where her head is. It's like someone pressed the pause button but found a way to leave me and George on play.

'But it wasn't just one secret though, was it? She's always been a liar, so I thought it was only fair that I was allowed to keep a few cards close to my own chest. Got a great two for one on key cutting if you're ever looking, by the way.'

He's so fucking pompous. I can't believe I ever found him attractive. Ugliness is ripping out of those beautiful features that he uses as tools to dupe women into falling for his sick little act.

'Oh, and before I forget.' He slaps his head obnoxiously, as if we're all just stood here in playful jest. 'Thanks for bringing back my car. It was good of you to return what's mine. It really helped me out today, you know? Much easier, not to mention quicker, when I'm driving. It's been a while.'

'Oh, for fuck's sake, George,' I scream at him. 'Are you being serious?'

'Deadly,' he states flatly. 'You won't believe the night I've had, babe. Some crazy bitch broke into my flat and tried to murder me and my girlfriend. Can you believe it?'

What the hell is he talking about? And why isn't Cassie doing anything? I'm way out of my depth here.

'Unfortunately,' he pouts and tilts his head to the side, 'she succeeded. And after the horror of seeing your beautiful, limp body lying on the floor, she ran at me, too. I had no choice but to act in self-defence. Losing you…well that would be agonising. That pain could drive a man to do…well just about anything, don't ye think?'

He menacingly thrusts the point of the knife into the table, raising it above his head and then hammering it home. Again and again.

I notice a flicker of movement out of the corner of my eye.

Finally. Cassie is back in the room, but what the hell is she doing? It looks like she's starting to take small but subtle steps towards George. She needs to stay back. Is she crazy?

Thankfully, he's too wrapped up in his own ego, bragging like a deranged psychopath to notice, but if I try to stop her, it might alert him, and I don't know what he's capable of.

'We were so good together, Blair. We could have lived the dream life. The good life. Just the two of us. And Mum, of course. But you fucked it all up. And now look what you're making me do.'

'Look,' I say, holding my hands in the air, reluctantly indulging in his madness. I need to keep his attention on me and not on Cassie. I don't know what the fuck she's doing. I want to call out and grab her, pull her back to me, and then both of us can leg it out of here. 'This has just gotten a bit out of hand. Why don't you just put the knife down and then you and I, we can get out of here. We can sort this. You do want to fix this don't you? Fix us?'

He scoffs like a pig. 'Well, aye, of course. That's all I've ever wanted. Well, at least in the beginning. I wanted to find you and bring you home, where you belonged. What are the chances that it was Cassie Torrance of all people who told you to leave me? As if she wasn't enough of a thorn in my side already.'

What the fuck is he talking about? He's literally insane. Making absolutely no sense. None of this was her fault at all. If anything, it's mine for going to see her. If it wasn't for our reading, she'd have been absolutely fine.

'And then what?' I rebuff. 'You thought she'd know where I was? That she'd fall for your bullshit and tell you. That's insane, George. You know that, right? We weren't even friends. Why would I tell her where I was going?'

Cackling, he throws his head back and speaks directly to the ceiling instead of me.

'Cassie. Or Nova. Whatever. She doesn't have any friends. She only wanted to make me happy. I could smell the desperation off her. It was stronger than any of your cheap perfumes.'

It's not entirely appropriate – given the severity of the situation we're in – but I'm still offended. I feel like he's just slapped me again. nothing I own, or wear, is cheap. *Like hello? Ever heard of Chanel?*

'Why waste time looking for a selfish, ungrateful cow like you when she practically begged to crawl into the mousetrap? She was the better fit. You were too chaotic to ever compare.'

I'm barely listening to what he's saying because I realise Cassie has stopped her shuffling and has somehow made it to the middle of the table without George glancing in her direction even once. Her left arm creeps towards the wood below George's eyeline, but I still don't know what she's planning to do if she makes it any closer.

One of her fingers hitches itself onto the lip of the table. Then another, and another, until she's formed a tight grip around the edge and now, I'm really starting to panic that he's going to pounce on her, so I slowly take my own steps forward.

'Let's just go, babe. Just you and me. We can go home.'

I'm saying everything I can to convince him that there's still a chance for us. I'll even beg. I'll say I was an awful girlfriend, but that I can be better if he just listens and gives me another chance.

Somehow, I've managed to pique his interest, he's allowed me to get close to him without lashing out and seems too engrossed in every lie that's falling from my tongue to even notice that both Cassie and I are now just inches away from him.

A low growl at my ankles makes me glance down, causing me to break my eye contact with George for just a split second. But it's long enough for him to spot Luna, too. Creeping low, spine poker straight, fur flared, and ears pointed to the heavens, she looks feral.

Ignoring her, hoping he'll do the same, I take another step closer.

'George. Babe. Let's go back to our flat and be together. Just the two of us.'

His arm whips out, his strong hand grabs at my wrist and twists, causing me to yelp in pain. And that's when Luna leaps into the air, sharp claws pointed. She bounds onto his chest and starts to slash at his face, and he thrusts back in his chair, tipping over, and crashing to the floor. The knife flies high before landing on the table and I frantically dart to grab hold of it.

With it in my hand, I step back and raise my arm, ready to plunge it down into his chest, but before I can, Cassie surges, just like her cat did.

My eyes couldn't possibly open any wider as I watch in what feels like slow motion.

Shrieking like a wild banshee, barely holding onto the biggest pink rock I've ever seen in my life, she throws her arms to the floor with supernatural strength, plunges it into George's head, cracking it open like a red velvet Easter egg.

The record player finally finishes with a crackle, plunging the room into silence.

THIRTY-SEVEN

CASSIE

Trembling, the hand on my shoulder attempts to soothe me, but I'm otherwise frozen in shock. I don't think that's quite how you're supposed to use crystals, but it definitely sorted out a huge problem.

My empty hands are hovering above his bloody head as if I'm casting some sort of spell. I can hear Blair calling my name over and over, but she sounds so far away and out of reach to cling to.

Oh, *my God. Realisation sinks in. What have I just done?*

The girl with golden hair and freckles that scatter her nose and cheeks like a starry night sky is still standing beside me. I know she's not really here, that I'm imagining her, but the warmth of her touch feels realer than any physical interaction I've ever had.

I didn't run.

She told me to, but I didn't listen to her because that's all I've ever done. sprinted far away from the things I don't want to confront. It was time for me to stop. I wanted him to go away. Wanted her to go away. I had to do something to end my cycle of poor decisions – and not just that, but save Blair from them, too – so when I glanced down at the solid chunk of pink stone, every puzzle piece just fell into place. For the first time in my entire life, I knew exactly what I had to do. And I didn't think twice. Have I always had such violence in me? Is that something else I have to worry about?

Later though, because what I don't know right now is what to do with a man's corpse lying on the floor next to my feet, his once beautiful face now smashed like a pumpkin after Halloween.

Blair is kneeling over what's left of his face, ear hovering over his wide-open mouth.

'OK. It's fine.' She breathes. 'I mean, he is dead – but that's OK. We're OK, Cassie.'

I totally got the wrong impression of her, judged her too harshly on the first day we met. The way she just adapts to any situation is inspiring. She's a beautiful chameleon of a woman. If it wasn't for her, I might have been the one to die today. And I can't believe I'm even thinking this, considering how many times I really wished that I just would already. I've never been so relieved to still feel my heart beating.

Blair stands up and wipes her hands on her legs. Despite not being the one to deliver the blow, she's still swiping away the trace of murder. She tucks her hair behind her ears and then turns to face me, gripping both my shoulders, and twisting me to look at her.

'Cassie, listen to me. Don't panic. It's going to be fine. I promise.'

Letting go of me, I watch as she bolts to the door, grabbing her leather jacket that fell to the floor from my shoulders when I burst into the room. She pushes her hand into one of the pockets and then tries the other.

Walking back to me, she stops, and drops the jacket over Finlay's face, covering the horror, and then starts fumbling with her phone.

'What are you doing?' I ask.

'What? Nothing. Nothing. I'm just going to google it.'

I snatch the phone out of her hand. 'Google what, Blair? How to get rid of a dead body? You can't search for that.'

She cocks a hip and puckers her lips, considering my words. 'Yeah…I suppose you're right.' Placing the phone down on the table, she stands back and assesses the situation again. 'Fine, we'll have to think of something ourselves, then. You got any suggestions?'

'No. Why would I have? I've never killed anyone before, have you?!' I shriek back at her, the realisation of what I've done now seeping into my skin and making me itch.

'All right, all right. Just calm the fuck down. Don't get your little witchy hat in a twist.'

Slowly, I crouch down and attempt to lift the chunk of rose quartz, but it feels much heavier than it did before. Staining my hands red with Finlay's blood, I manage to cradle it in my arms like a baby and look up at Blair for help.

'I have to go and wash this. It needs to be cleaned. It needs to be cleansed.'

'Put that back down,' she commands.

I ignore her and clutch it to my stomach as I shuffle my way out of the room and into the kitchen. I roll it up my torso and shove, dumping it in the sink and twist on both taps. I let the water crash like thunder over the stone and wonder if I'm doing the right thing. Because you're not supposed to get certain crystals wet. Right now, I can't remember if this is one of them, but I can't let the stone absorb his blood. That's definitely negative energy. Or worse, some kind of black magic. His spirit might possess it the same way one might with a child's doll.

I feel Blair's chest pressed against my back. 'That's it,' she says in my ear. 'Isn't there some sort of ritual you can do?'

'Blair. I know you don't know much about crystals, but I don't think they can bring someone back to life,' I explain as calmly as I can, although my voice is shaky.

'What? No, why would we want that? I meant can't you make him disappear somehow?'

I don't know if it's the stupid question or the stress that's making me lose my patience with her, but I snap regardless. 'He's not a letter, Blair. You can't just set fire to him under a full moon and hope the problem goes away.'

She backs away from me, pulls out one of the kitchen chairs, and sits down. Her mouth breaks into a cheesy grin: entirely inappropriate given the current situation, and I actually begin to wonder if she might just be as mad as I am.

'No…' she starts. 'But we could actually burn his body. We can do it tonight. His car will be parked outside somewhere if he used it to get here, right? All we have to do is get him inside, drive him somewhere in the sticks and light that scirocco up like one of your fat joints.'

'What? I don't even...' She means the sage, I realise. I gulp loudly, pushing aside her mistake. That isn't important right now.

Is she really suggesting we don't tell anyone about this? That the two of us pretend it never happened after we've disposed of a dead body? How would we live with ourselves? How could we?

Seeing that I'm going to need a lot more convincing, she gets to her feet and comes to take my hand in hers. 'Cassie, calm down. Deep breath in. Big breath out. You just have to relax.'

I'm exhausted, drained, and still reeling from the fact I'm not just hearing voices now but seeing people, too. That I'm insane, after all. And yet, with her tight grip, she manages to somehow soften me. This woman is like my real-life guardian angel. God, how I've always wanted one of those.

'OK,' I sigh, willing to hear her out further. But before I agree I have so many questions. 'Do you think we could get away with it? What about his mum? Wouldn't she report him missing? They'd search his flat...we would have to go back, make sure everything looked in place. We can't go back there. I don't think I can go back there, Blair. And what if it's not as easy as just setting a car on fire? What about the smell? The body? Oh my god, I can't breathe.'

My chest feels like it's about to combust.

'Woah, woah woah. Easy tiger, OK? So, maybe we don't burn it, then. We could just bury him somewhere, right? Between the two of us, we'll be able to roll him up in something and stuff him in the boot of the car. Then we'll figure it out from there.'

I can't find any more words. I've exhausted my vocabulary and I feel like I'm about to drop dead myself.

'Cassie, if this is going to be too much for you, I'll deal with it myself, all right? You can stay here. I've got this. It's going to be fine.'

My lib wobbles, eyes threatening to melt like a waterfall as I nod. I don't know what other choice there is. She's right: if we're not going to the police, then we have to get rid of him somehow, and if she's more capable than I am, perhaps I should just let her do as she says.

Letting go of my hand, she starts pacing back and forth, concocting a plan as she natters away to herself. 'Then I'll go back to the flat with the car and dump it there. I'll clean up everything and bring any stuff you left behind back here.'

She pauses, looks to the sky as if unsure of the next part.

'Oh, and probably mine too, actually. I'll have to bring my stuff here too until I figure out where I'm going afterwards. There can't be any sign of me there if I'm ever asked about him. It needs to look like a clean and amicable breakup. Whatever he did or wherever he ended up next has to look like it has nothing to do with me. I was already long gone.'

'But – but what about friends? Family? People he works with?'

'Well, I never met any of his friends, did you?' she asks, and I shake my head, realising he'd never even mentioned a single name to me, let alone introduce me to anyone. Why didn't I think that was odd?

I guess because I didn't have any friends. I thought we were similar in that way. That all we needed was each other.

'And his work…well, they'll probably just think he quit or something. He's arrogant enough, I'm sure they'd expect such disregard for a formal notice letter,' she replies, answering me before I even get the chance to ask another question.

I still have one more, though. A huge one.

'What about his mum, Blair? I mean, I've not met her, or anything, but she does call every day. He said he was waiting to tell her about me because he wanted it just to be us two. He said she'd only interfere this early on.'

I don't suppose that was true either, though. The red flags that I chose to stay colour blind to are now waving in front of my face and I feel like a total idiot.

'No, that's good. That's perfect. I'll send her a message from his phone. I'll say that he decided to go travelling to find himself, or something like that. I could even say that he's met some new girl after me and they're away together – just to really piss her off.'

It's not appropriate to laugh, but I can't help it with her. She's so deadpan, straight talking. Usually, people with her nature make me nervous, but for some reason she doesn't make me anxious at all. It's actually refreshing to know exactly what she's thinking instead of second guessing and coming up with my own conclusions.

'Then what?' I ask, seeing as she's clearly the brains of this operation. What does that make me? The brawns? As if.

'Then I'll ditch the phone somewhere…like in the River Clyde. That's where everything gets dumped in Glasgow isn't it? What's one more iPhone? I'm sure there's far worse down there, don't you? And the monster-in-law can do what she wants after that. She won't be looking for us because she'll be too busy packing a bag, chasing her precious boy across the world like Liam Neeson.'

I don't argue with her, because I have nothing left to say. Because what can you say to a beautiful whirlwind like Blair Cameron? She's unlike anyone I've ever met before. Ride or die 'til the end. Quite literally, in our case.

I don't know if it's some twisted turn of fate that on the day I committed the biggest sin, I'm filled to the brim with gratitude, and I genuinely believe that everything is going to be OK. Just like she says it is.

Did the universe bring us together, or was it by accident? I don't suppose I'll ever know, but what I do know is that she's my real blessing. It seems all I really needed in my life was a friend. A true friend.

She about turns and makes her way to exit the kitchen, fumbling with her phone, and searching for God knows what.

'Blair…' I stop her by calling out her name, surprising both of us.

'Yep?' She smooths down her jet-black hair and twists her head to look at me with a smile.

'Let's do it. But you're not doing it by yourself. I'm coming with you. We will finish this together.'

THIRTY-EIGHT

CASSIE

TWO MONTHS LATER

'Cas. Are you ready for your surprise?'

Despite my nerves, I can't help but laugh at her hallway hollering. There's no such thing as an indoor voice when it comes to my new best friend. Surprisingly, it didn't take too long for me to get my head around sharing my space with another female. It's something I never experienced in my twenties because all my friendships had been so…complex, and difficult to maintain.

I wonder when I first started showing signs? How old I was, or if I was born into a different generation, would it have been more apparent? Perhaps if I'd known more about mental wellbeing when I was younger, I would've made lots of friends. But that doesn't matter now that I have Blair. She's exactly the ray of positivity I needed to fill all the lonely gaps. So many empty voids, dry and thirsty for a drop of companionship. Asking her to move in with me permanently made sense. We needed each other, and in a horribly morbid way, I suppose we're sort of blood sisters now. Bonded for life by ending someone else's.

It doesn't even seem to matter to me that we are polar opposites in every way and were likely destined to clash, because in the end, we were both fooled by the same man. We have that singular thread in common. And thanks to George Finlay Munro, we've used our shared trauma and fused it together, creating a magnificently crafted yin and yang, superglued in the middle, never discussing the dark secret harbouring in between. None of us are willing to share the screens of our minds, despite being totally aware we're replaying the exact same scene.

'Don't make me come in there and drag you – because you know I will.'

I do want to make the move, because we're adults, we need our own space, and as much as I've loved sleeping beside Blair, I knew that the day would come when I'd have to stand on my own two feet again. I doubt either of us would deny that it's been a huge comfort just having someone else there. That one and only person who completely understands what the other is going through. Because something as huge as murder doesn't just go away. We're not psychopaths. Of course, we're still processing what we've done in our individual ways. Although I admit that I might be struggling the most. Blair makes it look like a breeze. I'm only just managing to tread the water of my own grief and guilt.

So, even though I knew this day had to happen, it's just...well, I'm absolutely crapping myself, to be honest. For once, not because of a sudden change in routine, but because I really can't think of anything worse than trying to fall asleep in the same room that I actually killed a man. Yes, he was a bloody awful one, but he was still a human being, and I took his life. I've been guilty of making some pretty wild decisions, ones that I never knew I was capable of, and that morning, when I thrust that rose quartz into his face, I acted on a whole different galaxy of impulsivity.

Giving myself a shake, I tell my brain not to go there. Not today. Today is supposed to be a happy and exciting one. A fresh start.

Blair's overexaggerated sigh of impatience echoing down the hallway doesn't go unnoticed, but still, I stay frozen, seated and quiet, trying to focus on the positives. I suppose all this is probably a really good way of testing out my newly learnt skills. I've been focusing on something called distress tolerance, and even though the rice paper booklets containing hints, tips, tools and techniques have become more like coffee mats than anything else while I wait patiently to be seen by a doctor or some sort of mental health team – I have actually read them. All of them. And quite a few times, actually, so I must have picked up at least some stuff that I can use today to make the change easier.

Fidgeting with my fingers, I search my brain. OK, I'll start with accepting a situation. That's what I need to do here because this is happening and that's that. I have no control over it, I can't change it…and although it doesn't say it in any of the leaflets, I suppose it's only fair that the murderer takes the room where she committed the crime.

I've accepted and know now that I need help from a professional. The voices…they weren't real. Just my head playing tricks on me because I worry too much. I like the way Blair words her advice on the matter: "Just give less fucks. Be the wonderful weirdo that you are and stuff anyone else." She read the booklets alongside me when I first got them, holding my hand, and forcing it towards the paper, aiming a Bic pen at the tasks and not leaving my side until she was satisfied I'd completed my homework. Not once did she judge me. I'm more grateful to her than she will ever know because I think I only ever thought of soul mates as something romantic. She made me see that you don't necessarily need a man to complete you, because our friendship feels like the most magical thing in the world. Almost as if we've known each other in many lifetimes before.

And I tell her that often.

Another thing I'm learning is that all my feelings don't need to be wrapped in a bow, never allowing anyone close enough to pull in case my soul unravelled and died on the floor with sheer embarrassment. Blair has been fully supportive of my decision to finally speak to someone for help, but also isn't fazed by my reluctance to give up my whacky ways either. She was so nonchalant and effortlessly cool lying beside me on the bed one night as I confessed that although the new meds I've been put on have stopped the voices, I still truly believed I might have some sort of special ability.

She laughed at me. Yeah, but she still told me to go for it, encouraged me to start at the very beginning, learn the basics, and then crack on.

As for the blonde woman, I only see her in my dreams at night. At least I think I'm dreaming, but how do you actually know where the line is, between being clinically insane and being blessed with a supernatural gift? The thing is, she still feels so real to me – even taking this medication – and I can still taste her contempt for Finlay, the bitter venom on my tongue.

Crashing into the room, yanking me by the arm, nails pinching my flabby bingo wings, Blair's commands boom in my ear. 'Right, that's it. Get up now. I'm done playing nice. It's now or never, and guess what? I say now. OK?'

Pulled to my feet, saying a silent farewell to my former bedroom with a melancholic glance over my shoulder. I can't help but agree with her.

Now or never. Now or never. Now or never.

Thirty-Nine

Blair

Tapping my foot like Bugs Fucking Bunny, I stare at the back of her head as she nudges the door open with her big toe, whimping out of touching the handle as if it might burn her.

With thick, freshly dyed flaming red hair, secured in a scrunchie at the nape of her neck, paired with her peely-wally skin and chocolatey eyes, Cassie Torrance has gone from a close ten to a solid fifteen. She looks better than ever, which is strange considering she's the worrier of us two and I can only imagine the turmoil in that little head of hers.

Still, nobody would ever be able to tell she, not so long ago, pummelled a huge rock into someone's skull. But hey, I'm not judging.

Growing even more impatient, I nudge her in the back. 'Go on then. I didn't break all my new stiletto nails just for you to hang around outside like a peeping Tom.'

Of course, I'm beyond grateful that she asked me to stay. Although how we were flung together wasn't the most conventional, I needed a place to stay, and it actually works. Yes, we're obviously bonded by one hell of a secret, but even without that, I don't know…I think I'd have liked her anyway if we'd met another way.

She's become the calm to my storm, teaching me about empathy, and getting me to open about things I'd really rather not, such as my overbearing mother – who by the way has no idea any of this has even happened or where I'm currently living. As much as I hate to admit it, it's been good for me to feel like I can tell someone how I truly feel, and I think it's been good for her, too. I'm trying to teach her how to just grab the bull by the balls instead of shying away from it, so in my opinion, everyone's a winner here.

Everyone except George Finlay Munro, of course. And guess what? I'm fucking glad that the bastard is gone. Not that we mention him. That's the one topic we don't touch with a barge pole and I'm not about to about to poke the bear today.

Up until now, we've been sharing her bedroom at the front of the flat, and as much as I've enjoyed playing sleepovers with my new bestie, she doesn't half flop around in the middle of the night. And I do not pay this much for my face to have it skelped by a sweaty arm.

She has to just rip the plaster off and it will be fine. A couple of days and she'll be laughing. Gripping both of her shoulders and pushing, I give in, and finally take charge. 'Get. In. Now. And for the love of GOD. Open your eyes.'

I do understand why she's freaking out, but it was her idea to take the room at the back of the flat and make it her bedroom. Yes, I admit that I didn't put up too much of a fight to be honest – I'd quite happily give that crime scene a miss – but at the end of the day, it's just a memory. He's not actually in there anymore. We made sure of that. However, to compromise, I happily volunteered to give it a complete makeover. And I've been so excited to show her how different it looks.

Her old Tarot reading room is now a far cry from something more fitting for a creepy old granny, rocking back and forth on a chair clutching a crystal ball. She was given strict instructions not to peek, but in hindsight, they were pointless because she practically runs past it whenever she needs to go to the kitchen.

As essential for my sanity as this revamp was, it was actually the second thing on my to-do list. The first being that I would convince Cassie to talk to a doctor about how she feels about herself.

We've opened up to each other a lot, and sometimes she'd tell me stories from her past and I'd think– what the actual fuck? What is wrong with some people? Some of the pictures she'd paint me burnt my bloody retinas, and by the sounds of it she's been treated pretty shitty by just about everyone in her life. The sad thing is, that girl doesn't know just how strong she is – or how much I admire her for her superhuman resilience and unwavering kindness.

It felt like the right thing to do, encouraging her to seek professional help. It's not that I don't think she's bullshitting about all the other stuff, but I think the two can be mutually exclusive. I think you can light your smelly sticks and meditate, and I also think you can accept help and medicate. Because…well why the hell not? My only concern was that she obviously couldn't spill her guts to the GP about everything.

Hi Doctor, I murdered a man, and now I can't sleep. Can you help? A huge nope.

I asked her to just start at the beginning for now and explain how she felt before any of that day had ever happened. So off we popped to the GP surgery after an initial telephone consultation, and I barged my way into her appointment with the hot doctor with sandy hair and prickly beard. He was everyone bit as lovely as he looked, and I did consider for a moment if it would be appropriate to ask out your best mate's doctor but, in the end, I decided against it and thought it was best I registered with the practice myself and visit him with some needs of my own.

Big words like anxiety, depression, mood disorders – all sounding like Greek gods or goddesses – were thrown around the room. I have no idea what she goes through on a daily basis, constantly battling with her own mind, but he offered up some medications for her to try. She even managed to bag a referral to the NHS Psychology Department because Dishy Doc could only do so much for her, but thought it would be a good idea to speak to someone professional on a regular basis. However, he did say that it might take quite a while for her to receive an appointment due to lengthy waiting lists, but in the meantime, he strongly recommended she try a prescription to calm her racing thoughts at least.

I saw how reluctant she was to accept, so I did it for her, grabbing the pink slip, and then her hand. As we emerged from the side door of the surgery and back onto the street, suddenly she began to cry. 'I don't want to take any pills, Blair. What will that make me look like? People will think I'm crazy. It might even change who I am.'

Thankfully, I managed to convince her that she was missing the point: she wasn't going to become someone else, she was being offered the chance to finally feel like herself again. 'Who gives a fuck what other people think, Cas? You can take medication and do all your holistic woo woo shit, too. I won't love you any less,' I told her and as far as I'm aware she's been popping her pills every morning like Smarties.

Finally, Cassie steps forward of her own accord, entering the room. Her head swivels, taking in every inch of the transformation. The avocado green walls that reminded me of my dead aunt's bedroom are no more, and in their place, dusky pink has given the room a warm hug. I even painted the coving, bringing it back to life with brilliant white and almost broke my back sanding down the old brown, DNA riddled, floorboards until they shined like a white sandy beach.

As for the humongous and hideous table that's unfortunately still staring us in the face, I lost the battle with that one. Boy oh boy, did she beg me not to get rid of the bloody thing and in the end, I gave up trying to change her mind because I didn't have the energy to argue any more. It is her room, after all. She can keep whatever she wants – even if it is, in my opinion, completely useless, so I shoved it to the bottom of the room and into the left-hand corner. I even displayed all her newly purchased coloured rocks and cards and books on it like a shrine. I drew the line with keeping the chairs, though. Instead, I decided lining the gap between her new bed and the table I'd accessorised so perfectly, with an old-fashioned pink, grey, and white rug that I spotted in the Barra's market in the Gallowgate. I thought it looked right up her street. Gothic-chic.

One day I'll take her there because I know she'd love it, with the smell of her favourite wee herby witch sticks floating around the air. Although I have to admit, I do quite enjoy them myself. The only thing that bugs me about them is how much dust they shed. Almost all my white socks look like I've stepped in shit.

Dying for her to say something, I point towards the window. 'Do you like your seat?'

I managed to find a lower to the floor styled bed frame, with a headboard that only just tickled the window ledge, making it a perfect match for the snug I created above her head. She'd mentioned before she used to enjoy sitting on the ledge and so I padded it out with some sort of dog bed cushion and moulded it to shape.

'I – I don't know what to say,' she gawks.

'Well, at least say you like it. Between doing this, working in the new bar at night, and finding time to write this bloody book – I'm afraid it's tough titty if you don't, babe.'

Her squeal zaps my head, as she pounds onto the bed and climbs up onto the ledge and leans back, feet pressed flat against the other side, and cups an imaginary novel.

'No. Blair, I absolutely love it. It's perfect…just, perfect. Thank you so, so much. I can't believe you actually made me a proper window seat.'

Carefully, I broach the subject, trying not to put a pin in her excitement.

'Listen, I know you're still a wee bit nervous about sleeping in here, so if you do struggle then just come back in with me. It's fine, OK? I'll understand.'

Wiping a tear trickling down her cheek, she taps the wooden headboard underneath her.

'Thank you, Blair. Not just for all this, but for everything. Encouraging me to see a doctor, for supporting my crazy ideas – even if you do roll your eyes when I'm speaking,' she says then pauses. Lips smirking at me because I know I'm doing it right now.

I fold my arms, unable to stop myself from smiling back at her.

'Most importantly, for letting me be myself, and sticking by me after what I did,' she says with a much quieter voice. I'm losing her. I need to keep her hyped up or she'll never sleep in here.

'Yeah, yeah, OK. Enough with the dramatics. You're very sweet, but if you keep talking, I'll end up taking the piss out of you in one of my future best-selling novels.'

Suddenly, Cassie swivels round and places her feet on the pillow underneath her. She wastes no time on jumping on an opportunity to interrogate me. 'You still haven't told me what you're writing about – harsh, by the way – but while we're on the subject of beautiful writing, there's something I've been meaning to ask you about. Well, more like confess to, I suppose.'

What is she going on about now? Honestly, sometimes I can't keep up. I love her more than I've loved any friend, because in some strange way I feel like I truly trust her, that she betters my life, but it's a million miles an hour in that head of hers. I often have to slow her down just to get a grasp of sense.

'Go on,' I say, tongue pushed against my cheek.

'OK, um, well the thing is, I don't even really know how to explain,' she laughs nervously, clasping her hands in prayer. 'I read it – your journal, I mean. Back at the flat. And the thing is, I still have it. Please don't ask why I grabbed it that night cleaning the flat. I just felt like it was something I should do. And yes, I've had it all this time, living together, and keeping it from you.'

What the hell is she waffling about? I've never had a diary in my life up until I moved in here. I thought maybe if I started jotting down ideas in a little book when the moment takes me might help speed up the process. And the only reason I haven't told her what's happening in my book is because I don't even know what the fuck's going on. There're only two words in it too: TITLE UNKNOWN.

Still rambling, she shows no sign of taking a breath.

'I think maybe I just didn't know how to approach you about it, which is silly because we tell each other everything, but I guess I was scared you'd be angry that I read it in the first place. It was when I was wondering what your book would be about and I wanted to wake you up and suggest that you write from personal experiences, use them as character inspo or something, I don't know.'

'Cassie, calm the fuck down, and breathe, OK? Just breathe.' I watch her chest rise and fall, the panic attempted to simmer. 'Start again. What fucking journal are you talking about?'

FORTY

CASSIE

My eyes bulge, no doubt bursting vessels, as I can't seem to make her understand.

'Your journal, Blair…I found it. I read it all. The one where you poured your heart out because you were so scared. The one you hid from him. And even though I think we're pretty close, you kept those experiences close to your chest, but I completely understand that they're your stories to tell. When you're ready. And so, you should have them back in your possession.'

'Will you just stop? You're cursing me with a migraine from hell,' Blair shouts, pinching between her eyes. 'Cassie, I really need you to listen to me, OK?'

I zip my mouth, nod, and let her speak, but the pressure in my chest feels like my heart is about to burst out of my top.

'I literally have no idea what you're talking about.'

Unable to hold myself back, I pounce off the window ledge the same way Luna would and fly across the room to my familiar bookcase that's now proudly positioned in the corner of the room, highlighted by the glint of sun through the top windowpane. It looks much better there. Dropping to my knees, I frantically pull spine after spine from the shelf.

It has to be in here.

Blair would never dream of purposely going anywhere near any of my spirituality for beginners, A-Z of crystals, or self-love for dummies guidebooks. And with a chunk of my books no longer towering lazily by my bedside in the other room, whatever two I squished her journal between should now be staring me in the face.

My heart begins to beat even faster as soon as I spot the plum purple that matches the shade of my front door and tug it out of the row. Spinning round on my bum, I hug Blair's journal to my chest and, with watery eyes, stare up at her, searching for recognition. For her to finally click.

'Oh, just give it here, Cassie. For fuck's sake.' She sighs as she steps towards me and pries it out of my clawing fingers. Tutting loudly, she carries it to the edge of the bed and takes a seat. She clears her throat, opens the cover with the tip of her fingers, as if she wished she were wearing rubber gloves.

There it is. She gets it now. I see it in her eyes. She understands.

Despite a good layer of Nars foundation, the colour completely drains from her face, seemingly shocked by her own words. I continue to glare at her while she reads it from start to finish, wondering why she keeps looking up at me with such incredulous eyes.

Why is she so stunned? Afraid almost. It was she who wrote it, and the danger is gone now.

Maybe she's just really angry at me? Crap. I don't want to lose her. This friendship means everything to me.

'I'm sorry, Blair,' I say, watching her frown, knowing she'll be raging about that later, too. 'I didn't know what to do with it, but listen, we don't have to talk about it right now, OK? I'll wait til you're ready. Even if that's never. It's fine. Pretend I never said a word.'

'Where did you get this?' she demands.

'I found it in Finl…no, I mean George's flat. Sorry, bad habit. It was under the sink in the bathroom, behind a dodgy wooden panel. I don't know if that's where you last left it but it's where I found it.'

'But it's not yours…'

She is definitely mad at me. I knew it.

However, all the while I'm panicking about getting a severe tongue lashing, I'm still confused as hell, trying to figure out why she said her last sentence more like a question rather than a fact.

'Well, no, I know it's not mine.'

She's looking at me as if I'm a green little alien, spouting words of a different language.

'Cassie, you know who this is about don't you? The guy, you realise what this is?'

'Um…yeah. It's kind of obvious, is it not?'

It screams George's name, I knew it the first time I read it, but I don't know where she's heading with this.

I can't find her train of thought to hop on it. She's being super weird.

Jumping to her feet, she starts to pace the width of the room and I brace my wrists to get up and join her, but as soon I get to my knees and stretch one leg forward, I feel the energy shift, almost knocking me over.

I feel awful. I almost don't want to look at her, afraid I might burn alive from the heat of her rage.

Reluctantly, I twist my head to the left, but my mouth falls open. It can't be. I'm not dreaming now.

'And it's definitely not yours?' Blair chimes in again, bursting through the whistle in my right ear. 'You didn't write any of this?'

I shake my head vigorously, but I can't meet her eyes. My attention is locked on something else.

Someone else.

The girl with the golden blonde hair who's staring me straight in the face as she walks towards Blair. Even firmly stood by her side, she refuses to let the chain between our eyes break.

She's real. I knew it. I always knew it. I'm not crazy. I'm not insane. Blair was right. You can have problems, and still be gifted.

I am gifted. I see spirit…like for real.

Blair turns her back to me, and out of the corner of my eye, I notice that she's gripping the edge of the table, drumming her thoughts into the wood.

But…why is the spirit that was with me in the room the day I murdered George not finished with me yet? Blair obviously can't see a thing, but I see her clearer than ever now, looking like a combination of all three of us. Her youth is the only thing that really differentiates us: as if her life were frozen in time.

I gulp, coming to the horrid conclusion that George was somehow responsible for this. He must have been. That's why she's here. The journal was hers.

Spinning round on the balls of her feet, a light bulb suddenly appears above Blair's head.

Getting to my feet, I meet her mid lunge, both of us trying to speak at the same time. Our hands gripping each other tight. Fresh fear running through our veins.

'You go first,' I suggest, urging her to confirm what I'm thinking.

I'm desperate for us to be on the same wavelength. She needs to have the same thought as I do, the same realisation. I know she can't see her, but it's obvious now anyway, isn't it?

'I know this is going to sound mental, but I didn't write this.'

Yes. Yes. Yes.

I nod in agreement, strangely excited for her to say it.

'I think…now don't freak out on me, OK? What if there was someone else? Someone before us, Cas. Just like us, except what happened to them could have been way worse. Because I swear to you, it's not mine. I've never seen that book before in my life.'

'I know. Blair, I know. That's what I'm trying to tell you.' She doesn't need to convince me anymore.

My eyes begin to flit between both women's faces, and I wonder if Blair notices that she doesn't have my full attention. Or even wonders why.

'I think that bastard tried to ruin someone else's life. Not just ours.'

FORTY-ONE

CASSIE

My nose scrunches as I take a deep breath. My chest feels like it's about to explode.

'Um…Blair,' I whisper. 'What makes you so sure that he didn't succeed?'

She pulls back from me, leaving pink blotches on my arms from her gripped fingertips. 'What do you mean by that? Look, we might be able to find her on the internet somewhere. We could track her down and ask her. Make sure she's OK or something, I dunno.' She stops. Rethinks. 'Actually, no. We can't do that. That would draw too much attention to us. Especially after what we did to the bastard. So, maybe we just snoop a little? But keep it between us. What's one more secret between friends, right?'

I shake my head. I'm going to sound crazy, but she believes in me, doesn't she? She won't laugh. Or worse, I shudder. She won't leave me. 'No, Blair. Listen to me. What if…' I exhale and close my eyes before I carry on. 'What if she wasn't as lucky as us?'

'You call what we've gone through lucky?' she snaps back.

I want to shake her. She's still not getting my point.

'No, obviously not. I just think—'

'Stop talking in riddles,' she interrupts. 'Just say what you mean. You don't...' She snorts briefly. 'Cassie. Come on. You don't think she's dead or something, do you?'

'No, Blair. I don't *think* she's dead, OK?' I practically shriek. I can't hold it in any longer. 'I *know* she is.'

'What the fuck?!' she screams, noticing my gaze lingering over her shoulder. Thrusting her hand out in front of her, she wipes the air, left to right. 'Oh, my GODDDDDD,' she moans, throwing her head back, covering her face with her hands. 'I can't believe I'm going to ask this – but is someone...like is there someone in here, Cassie? Can you see her?'

I bite my lip, fearing that words might be too much to hear. That it might be the one thing that sends her running for the hills.

'Cassie, is there a fucking ghost in this room? Tell me right now.'

I shrug and look down at the floor. Placing my toe one step closer to her, I nod.

Hands flit to her hips as she too edges towards me. 'And I'm guessing you want to do something about that, am I right?' She grabs both of my shoulders before I have a chance to answer. 'Never mind. Of course, I'm right. Obviously, that's something you would want to do. But how exactly? Are you going to take a training course on exorcisms now? What would you even do? Find a way to set her free or some spooky shit like that?'

Even in the most horrendous situations, she never fails to make me smile. But I'm still concerned about our guest, and who she is. What happened to her.

'Excuse me,' Blair hollers behind her, noticing my eyes wander to the unknown entity in the room with us. Someone she can't see but still believes is real.

I knew she was a believer.

'Can you give us a moment? Thanks, babe.'

Trying to keep a straight face, and failing massively, I try to be the one to soothe her for a change. 'Blair. It's OK. We can figure this out between us. With evidence from both this world and the other side. The two of us have proven that we can do absolutely anything if we work together, right? I think she might have some unfinished business. She obviously needs us to help her.'

I watch her resistance crumble as her mouth opens wide and barks a hearty laugh. She's nervous, scared, but still not running. She's sticking by my side.

'And anyway,' I begin to tease her, taking her hand in mine. 'What is it you always say to me? Just go for it and what? Give fewer what, Blair?'

'All right,' she yells throwing her hands in the air. 'I get it. I get it, give fewer fucks. You've made your point.'

Even though I'm itching to uncover this woman's identity, deep down, I'm just as scared as Blair. Still, I try to mirror her face and match her grin. She's always been so strong for me, now it's time to return the favour.

Blair's clammy fingers find mine as she takes my hands and then sighs. 'You're completely bonkers, Cassie Torrance. But do you know what? I fucking love you for it. Never change for anyone.'

The Unknown

Under the glistening stars, she remains seated on the damp wall across the street from where Cassie Torrance and Blair Cameron now reside together. Scooting as far back as she can go, becoming one with the bushes, the more thrilled she feels at having such a private viewing of the grand finale – even wishing she'd brought a bucket of popcorn.

Dressed in a black beanie, full-length coat, camouflaging with the night, she remains invisible to the naked eye. As she has done so successfully for some time now. Witnessing it all.

It has taken such a long time to get here.

When George and Blair's twisted love story began, she'd wondered if she'd be the one to find her book stashed in the bathroom. She hoped it would be. From what she knows, Blair is feisty, opinionated, and light years out of his league. She knew that he'd never be able to cope with someone like her long term, but that's why she was perfect. She had a gut instinct that Blair would be able to look after herself and that she'd handle him herself. Blair would be the one to stop him from causing harm to anyone else.

Then she would finally be free.

She knew staying so close to home was a risk, but wasn't it expected of a runaway to flee the country? The last place he'd come looking for her would be here.

And she had to be able to keep an eye on things if anything went wrong.

Which, she supposes, it did. Cassie was never part of this plan, and it killed her not being able to come forward and tell her all that had happened, but she had no choice. All she could do was lurk in the shadows, patiently waiting for the moment George would get his comeuppance.

She knew he was evil, but the extent of his cruelty almost blinded her as he knocked on number twenty-two that day. Even before her eyes landed on him, she felt his presence like a ghost, choking on the familiar, dark energy closing in on her. At first, she panicked, assuming he'd found her, and started to collate ways that she could climb out of the window and shimmy down the water pipe without much harm done. But she'd heard Cassie crying late at night and had noticed that she barely left the flat anymore. From their shared experiences, she knew that Cassie wasn't weak by any means, but without her, she could see that her best friend had lost almost all of who she used to be and didn't know how she'd handle someone as ghastly as him. She felt guilty. She blamed herself for Cassie being there in the first place. All she'd wanted was to help Cassie, giving her an obscenely discounted rental, not plant her in his sights. There was no way she was going to abandon her for a man again. The same man who made her ditch all her friends and family before.

Ready to risk it all by storming down the stairway and pounding her first on the door, she took one last look out of the gap in the boarded-up window and to her surprise, George was leaving without fuss. Cassie was still safe. But for how long? And what about herself? She wondered if she'd ever be able to emerge out of the shadows of the upper flat.

Yet despite worrying, nothing happened. Everything carried on as normal.

Or so she thought.

Tonight, just like she'd done before, she felt him arrive at number twenty-two. Although she couldn't understand why. Cassie had barely been back to the flat she bought for her. She thought she was out of harm's way, had finally found a stable boyfriend to take care of her. Like she deserved.

The rolled-up rug being carried to the boot of George's car confirmed that she had in fact had met someone – but to her horror, it was the worst person imaginable. The one man she should have protected her from.

She's still playing it over and over in her mind. Ever so cliché, but if she were in their shoes, perhaps she'd have done the same. She should have done the same well before Cassie became collateral for her shortcomings. It was such a relief to see Blair and Cassie working together tonight, even if she couldn't work out how that even came to be. Admittedly a little jealous at the friendship that was rapidly blossoming between them, she knew it was for the best she remained put. After all, she'd abandoned Cassie before, and the two of them together looked like a powerhouse. She didn't want to disrupt that.

Not yet.

Although she isn't privy to all the gory details, she has no urgent desire to find out either. All she knows for sure is that her body feels lighter, free-er, and that she can breathe normally again. It feels to her like a cycle has finally been broken, regardless of how or why or who was unnecessarily involved, and right now that's all that really matters.

It's finally the end of George Finlay Munro's story, which means she can now begin to rewrite hers.

Crossing the road as quickly as possible, she fumbles in her pocket for the key to her hideaway, the flat above Cassie's. Reaching the top step, she bypasses twenty-two, and inserts the Yale into the lock on the green door and twists to the right. Not having to look over her shoulder for the first time in so many years.

Phoenix quickly joins her side, rubbing her body against her and wrapping her black tail around her shin. She isn't sure what she responds to anymore and wonders if her cat might actually prefer the name that Cassie, believing she was a stray, had given her.

'Hello, Luna', she whispers.

The two of them creep up the stairs and into her sanctuary. Clicking on each low-level light with her foot, she smiles, proud that she has managed to conceal any existence of habitation for so long. The only thing she regrets is putting her best friend in danger, but figures everything has worked out exactly the way it was supposed to.

There's a funny saying that she's never quite understood, especially after her close call with George: *everything happens for a reason*. But perhaps there's some truth in it after all. She never predicted it all panning out the way it did, or that Cassie and Blair would surprise her with such determination. She supposes that's life, though. As skilled as you may be, nobody knows who anyone truly is. Everyone is hiding, wearing a mask of some kind to protect themselves.

It's time to rid herself of her own disguise now and introduce herself properly. To Blair at least – because Cassie already knows her very well. They could even become the next *Three Musketeers* or *Charlie's Angels*, Louise, Cassie, and Blair. ready to avenge all the women who weren't as fortunate as they were to survive George Finlay Munro. Because she's sure there are more. She refuses to accept that she was his first victim.

She smiles from ear to ear at the thought of getting reacquainted with herself again. She made it. She is here, she's alive, and when she comes clean, she will no longer be unknown.

THE END

ACKNOWLEDGEMENTS

There are so many people who played such a pivotal role in ensuring that *All in Her Head* was brought to life. The journey has been such a rocky one, and sometimes I doubted that this book would ever see the light of day, but something inside of me refused to let this story go and alas, here we are.

First, I'd like to thank my former agent, Jade Kavanagh. You believed in me before the book was even fully written, championed me at every corner, and gave me the copious amount of validation that I so desperately required. Truly, there is nobody more perfect to represent me than you, and I hope we find a way to unite forces again in the future.

A huge thank you to my editor, Emma Mitchell. I loved that you loved this book just as much as I do.

To my early readers: Shannon Wing, Robynne Williams, Megan Palmer, Shauna Barcoe, Sam Mouat – thank you for giving me your unbiased and in-depth opinions. I can't explain what it means to know that you all enjoyed my second novel just as much as my debut. You all played a massive role in helping me find me the confidence to take a chance on myself once again. Christina Kerr and Kirstie Buchanan, (founders of *The Book Club Glasgow*) I was terrified for your reviews to come in as I so desperately want to be a part of the club again. Is it safe to say that I've made it and will see you soon?

Of course, my dearest friends are always required to get in on the action. They say never show your work to your loved ones because they're less likely to give you their true opinion, but I can always count on you for brutal honesty. Gemma Andrews, Toni Sherriff, Ashleigh Downs, Helen Tsiolis, Kim Mckenna, Sam Smith, Jen McLarnon: I value your input more than you'll ever know.

Thanks to Simon and Gail for listening to me explaining the plot over and over again until it finally made sense.

To the boys at Train MBS, Craig and Johnathan, thank you for letting me use the office space and cover the floor in Post-it Notes.

How incredible is it to have writer friends? It still baffles me that such great authors take the time out of their own busy, creative schedules to offer me support, love, and advice. Holly Craig – my first agency sister – you always have my back and I'll always have yours. Liv Matthews, you pick my chin up off the ground more times than I can count. Philippa East, you've been my biggest fan from the very beginning, and you'll never know what that means to me. Also, special thanks to Sara Bragg, Emily Freud, and Danielle Owens for just being so bloody lovely.

Thank you to my family for pushing me at every hurdle. To my mum for reading the early manuscript – the one before an entire restructure – and then the second version. Dad, for getting just as excited about every milestone as much as I do. Gran, for always believing that her "little princess" can do anything she puts her mind to. Aunt Annie, for all your love and encouragement.

The last and probably most important thank you I want to give is to my late grandad, George. While restructuring this novel, my best friend was suddenly diagnosed with terminal cancer. Even in his last few months, his faith in me never wavered, and he still found great joy in constantly nagging me to crack on with things and get the job done. I'll never forget bawling my eyes out, questioning how I would ever manage such a humongous task, and him shrugging his shoulders and telling me "It'll be a doddle to you, dear". The promise I made to him about bringing this book to life is the entire reason that it currently exists and was ultimately the driving force during one of the hardest periods of my life. I hope I've done you proud, Grandad.

ABOUT THE AUTHOR

Paula Johnston is a psychological indie writer in her early thirties from Scotland, who lives on the outskirts of Glasgow with her fat cat, Rio. Having always worked around people, Paula Johnston has a fierce and keen ability to not only read those stood before her but cut to the core of their true intentions. Her fascination with the human psyche crossed over into her debut novel, *The Lies She Told*, which was self-published in August 2020 via Amazon, entering the doors of Waterstones shortly after. The unputdownable, twisted thriller soared to the top of the Amazon bestseller charts and received fantastic recognition from: Scottish Book Trust, The Scottish Herald Newspaper, readers, and authors alike.

An empath with a passion for creativity, Paula is also a qualified Reiki Practitioner and assists local businesses with branding and promotion in the form of feature writing and logo designs. In her spare time, she enjoys reading, hoarding different coloured rocks, making really bad jokes, and sageing her home endlessly.

Stay in touch:
All In Her Head #allinherhead
X – Facebook – paulajohnstonauthor

Books by Paula Johnston

There are three sides to every story.

His.

Hers.

The truth.

The Lies She Told

The Twisted Psychological Thriller That Proves There's a Price to Pay for Infatuation…
'Twisty, clever, pacy and fun!' - Best-Selling Author of *Little White Lies*, Philippa East

Karly Winters has waited ten long years to have the man of her dreams, the handsome but duplicitous Jacob Cruthers.

From her home in Glasgow she pines for the Londoner who casually keeps her dangling, never with a thought of giving her what she wants and never with any intention of leaving his wife.

For her part, Karly has no intentions of being second best any longer and she hatches an artful plan of devious intent that she is certain will work in her favour.

Now, embarking on her dangerous game of high stakes, she is all too aware that someone is likely to get hurt. But for the winner, the prize will be incalculable.

But Karly hasn't reckoned for new and equally underhanded forces that are at work.

Lurking in the shadows are others, with their own agendas to follow and equally ruthless in their objectives. With various factions hurtling towards a confrontation that none of them saw coming, someone is going to pay the price.

But who?

Printed in Great Britain
by Amazon